'You saved my life.'

'Did I?' He laughed somewhat oddly. 'Then certainly I must claim my reward before it is too late.'

Lucy was obscurely disappointed. 'I have promised that you will be well paid for your services, Rashid.'

He gave another odd laugh. 'Perhaps. But tonight I do not speak of money. Tonight I find myself in need of other rewards.' He brushed his thumbs across her eyelids, and she felt his lips cover hers in a gentle kiss.

Dear Reader

This month we offer you EMPIRE OF THE HEART from Jasmine Cresswell, where Lucy forcibly spends two years in Afghanistan before being rescued by 'Rashid', but on her return to London she finds that a certain Lord Ridgeholm bears a striking resemblance to the trader! This book offers a marvellous insight into the Victorian Empire, as well as a crackling romance. In THE PRICE OF HONOUR, Mary Nichols gives us Olivia, who foolishly defied her father to marry her sweetheart, and so found herself at the centre of heartstopping adventures in the Peninsular War! Two fast-paced and moving romances for you to enjoy.

The Editor

Jasmine Cresswell is English, and originally worked for the foreign office. They assigned her to the British embassy in Rio de Janeiro where she met her future husband. The day after the wedding they flew to America on a 'temporary' assignment that has remained permanent. After her husband was transferred for the third time by his company, Jasmine started writing, as it was the only career that could be taken anywhere without undue inconvenience!

Recent titles by the same author:

THE DEVIL'S ENVOY

EMPIRE OF THE HEART

Jasmine Cresswell

First published in Great Britain 1993 by Mills & Boon Limited

© Jasmine Cresswell 1993

Australian copyright 1993 Philippine copyright 1993 This edition 1993

ISBN 0 263 78056 2

Masquerade is a trademark published by Mills & Boon Limited, Eton House, 18–24 Paradise Road, Richmond, Surrey, TW9 1SR.

Set in 10 on 10 pt Linotron Times 04-9307-85587

Typeset in Great Britain by Centracet, Cambridge Made and printed in Great Britain

PROLOGUE

Afghanistan, June, 1875

ABOUT twenty miles out of Kabul, Miss Lucinda Larkin decided that she despised camels. Their smell was disgusting, their temper evil, and their swaying gait seemed calculated to induce nausea in the sturdiest British stomach. At the caravan's present speed, she estimated it would take two more days to reach the ancient city of Jalalabad.

Lucy wasn't sure how she would bear another forty-eight hours in intimate partnership with her camel. So far, she and Belzebub had ridden less than five hours together, and her throat was already rasped raw with grit and dust, while her posterior had long since passed into a state of advanced rebellion.

No wonder there had been a gleam of malicious humour in the Amir's eyes as he'd offered to replace the weary horses of the British trade delegation with fresh and sprightly camels from his own stable. Amir Sher Ali might owe his precarious hold on the throne of Afghanistan to the goodwill of the English government, but Lucy doubted if he felt any obligation to deal honestly with his allies. She was willing to bet large, unladylike sums of money that his camels would all prove spavined long before the trade delegation reached British territory in India.

Unlike her dear papa, who would undoubtedly find good in the devil himself, Lucy knew that she viewed the world with a deplorable streak of cynicism. Lady Margaret, her stepmother, often cited this unbecoming characteristic in the lengthy list of reasons why Lucy had attained the advanced age of one-and-twenty without receiving an offer of marriage.

Lucy wondered if it was only her cynical view of the

5

world that had made her so suspicious of Amir Sher
Ali's lavish hospitality. Her father's advisers, men of
considerable experience in Eastern affairs, had all been
delighted with the Amir's willingness to sign a trade
agreement. They had seen nothing questionable in his
desire to put on a good show for the visiting English.
Only Lucy had suspected treachery behind every
bowing servant, and intrigue behind every smiling dig-
nitary. What was more, her feeling of unease continued
to grow even though the delegation had left Kabul in a
shower of rose petals and good wishes. The crafty old
Amir was up to something, she was sure of it. She
wished she could believe the substitution of mangy
camels for spirited horses was the full extent of his
planned mischief.

Sweating and exhausted, Lucy wondered why in the
world she didn't stay at home and embroider sofa
cushions like any other self-respecting English lady. She
knew the answer, of course, and it could be expressed
in two words. Her father.

As if summoned by her thoughts, Sir Peter Larkin,
head of Britain's official trade delegation to
Afghanistan, jostled his camel into position alongside
Lucy's.

'Hello, dearest, time for our luncheon,' he called,
smiling cheerfully.

'Thank God for small mercies!'

Sir Peter's eyes twinkled. 'Can it be that my own
intrepid Lucy has finally found a mount she cannot
master?'

'A camel is not a mount,' she retorted grimly. 'It is a
fiendish instrument of torture, devised by the Eastern
mind to persecute naïve Westerners.'

Sir Peter laughed. 'Ah, Lucy, sweetheart, forget
about your camel for a moment. Breathe in the fresh-
ness of the air! Look at the mountains and see how the
snow sparkles on the peaks! Listen to the sound of the
river singing as it makes its way down the hillside! Who
can worry about a little physical discomfort when such
grandeur is all around us?'

'Dearest Papa, somehow I find it amazingly easy!'

He chuckled, but didn't reply, except to cup his hands around his mouth and bellow out the command to halt in execrable Pashto.

The warmth of her father's personality seemed to have worked its usual magic, for the camel drivers, often reputed to be as surly and uncooperative as the animals in their charge, immediately set about the difficult task of persuading the camels to stop and kneel so that their passengers could dismount.

Lucy gazed affectionately at the rotund, bouncing figure of her father as he climbed down from his camel. She swallowed over a sudden lump in her throat as she watched him hurry about, offering help and encouragement.

He is so kind, she thought, so *good*. Plenty of successful businessmen talked loudly about their service to the community, but Sir Peter didn't waste time boasting about his generosity. Four years ago, he had simply sold his profitable business and set sail for India. Since then, he had spent half his fortune building schools and hospitals in the remote frontier regions of the Indian Empire. Lucy admired him almost as much for his energy and efficiency as she loved him for his kindness.

Servants were arranging provisions for a picnic luncheon beneath two hastily erected awnings. Ignoring a malevolent, cross-eyed gaze from her camel, Sir Peter extended his hands and helped Lucy slide stiff-legged to the ground.

He gave an absent-minded pat to the camel's hump and somehow managed to avoid getting his hand bitten off. 'I think I want to wash the dust from my face more than I want to eat,' he said. 'How about you?'

'Mmm. Much more.' Lucy shaded her eyes against the sun. 'Where do you suppose all the camel drivers are running off to?'

'Their luncheon. They're probably afraid we'll ask them to do something if they stay too close at hand. Look, Mahmud's waiting by the stream with soap and towels. As always, he seems to have anticipated our needs perfectly.'

They strolled down to the water in companionable silence and, by the time she'd removed all the travel-dust from her face and hands, Lucy felt almost human again.

She returned the towel to the servant and smiled teasingly at her father. 'Now that we're thirty yards away from Belzebub, I'm prepared to admit that the view of the mountains is spectacular. I shall miss seeing them when we're back in the Punjab.'

'Will you? Then you've enjoyed this trip to Kabul?'

'Of course! Papa, surely you have not been taking my grumbles seriously? I wouldn't have missed this experience for anything.'

'My conscience has troubled me somewhat. Your stepmama warned me repeatedly that this was not a suitable journey for a young lady. Certainly, the Afghanis seem to have little respect for women, either their own or other people's.'

'Mama does not enjoy travel,' Lucy said neutrally.

Sir Peter hesitated for a moment before speaking. 'You are quite right. Your stepmama, in fact, feels that her health is suffering in this part of the world. She wishes to return to England, and so does your stepsister.'

Lucy bit back an inelegant snort. Lady Margaret, the daughter of an earl, had never concealed her dissatisfaction with the limitations of life in colonial India, so Lucy wasn't surprised by her father's announcement.

'But what about the school you are building in Guirat?' she asked, choosing her words carefully. 'And the new medical office in Lahore?'

'Your mama has rightly pointed out that I am not irreplaceable. There are many others who could over-see those projects. Besides, Penelope will soon be eighteen, and she is entitled to experience the pleasures of mingling with a more cultured society than Lahore can provide.'

In other words, her stepmother and stepsister were

bored, which wasn't surprising since their interests lay exclusively in the latest ladies' fashions and gossip about the London social scene. Lucy suppressed a useless little spurt of anger. She was a realist, and knew that if her stepmother had decided it was time to leave India then the rest of the family might as well start packing their trunks. Sir Peter's generosity would never withstand the onslaught of his wife's ruthless determination to move.

Lucy turned sharply away, not wanting to betray the bitterness of her thoughts to her father. He didn't need to have her sulks added to all his other problems. His wife and stepdaughter were quite enough of a burden for one man to bear.

The rat-tat-tat-tat of sound exploding out of the mountainside was totally unexpected. Lucy covered her ears, whirling around just in time to see her father fall to his knees. His hands were clasped around his waist as if he suffered from an acute belly-ache, and brilliant red liquid seeped horribly between his fingers.

'Papa, what is it?' She threw herself onto the sand beside him, calling for Mahmud, scarcely noticing the cacophony of shouts and cries echoing throughout the camp. Tears gushed down her cheeks, although her conscious mind hadn't yet permitted her to acknowledge why she wept.

'Papa, what's wrong?' she whispered urgently, cradling his limp body against her breast.

'Keep. . .your. . .head. . .down. Shot.'

'Shot? Shot?' she repeated wildly. 'No, you can't be shot. You mustn't be shot. It's only thunder. It *must* be thunder.'

Sir Peter closed his eyes.

'Mahmud!' she yelled over the ricocheting noise. She pulled feverishly at the buttons of her father's tunic. 'Bring the medical kit to the sahib!'

Her father opened his eyes. With a visible effort, he raised his bloody fingers to caress her face. 'God bless you, Lucy. I. . .love. . .you. . .'

'No!' Her voice rose into a scream of mingled terror and disbelief. 'No, Papa, you mustn't die!'

His body slumped backwards and she fell across him, feverishly patting his cheeks and chafing his hands.

'Oh, God, where are the servants? Why does nobody come to help me?'

The screams that were her only answer gradually faded away, and the barrage of rifle fire ceased. The agonised cries of dying humans were replaced by the jangle of harness as terrified camels and pack mules struggled against their tethers.

Slowly, Lucy raised her head and looked around. Bodies. Everywhere bodies. And blood. The camel drivers were coming back, she noted with a strange sense of detachment, crawling out from behind the rocks and boulders where they had hidden themselves in anticipation of the attack. The Amir had planned this treachery all along. She had been right to suspect him.

Realisation of what she had lost changed her apathy into a momentary burst of fury. She scarcely noticed when a small troop of Afghani tribesmen rode into the camp and began looting the bodies of Great Britain's official trade delegation. With the enamel bowl Mahmud had used to hold their washing water, she scrabbled in the soft sand of the riverbank, digging with maniacal energy until she had scooped out a shallow pit.

She paid no attention at all when half a dozen of the tribesmen gathered around her, hotly debating her fate. With the last of her strength she rolled her father's body face down in the grave — that way the vultures would not find his eyes so easily — and covered his blood-stained back with sand.

When every inch of his scarlet diplomatic uniform was covered, her anger drained away, like the last scoop of sand trickling through her fingers. Her body hollow and her mind blank, she sat beside the mound she had made, hands crossed in her lap, waiting.

An English lady never makes a spectacle of herself.

Stepmama would be proud of her for remembering the rules.

The tribesmen closed in upon her with threatening gestures. Lucy adjusted her skirt, so that the buckles of her riding boots were no longer visible.

An English lady never displays her ankles. She frowned. Why mustn't ladies show their ankles? She couldn't remember.

She didn't resist when one of the men pulled her roughly to her feet and tossed her over his shoulder. He stank of sweat, and garlic and murder, but she wouldn't give him the satisfaction of screaming, or begging for mercy.

An English lady doesn't converse with the natives, even when she is about to meet a fate worse than death.

Had Stepmama really said that? What an odd thing to say, even for Stepmama.

The tribesman carried her to his horse, and slung her carelessly across his saddle.

Miss Lucinda Larkin blinked. She was staring at the heaving, foam-flecked withers of the bay gelding which last week had belonged to her father.

Nausea swelled ominously within her, and she felt herself begin the spiralling descent into full-fledged hysterics. Closing her eyes, she took refuge in the ultimate sanctuary of every well-brought-up young English lady.

She fainted.

CHAPTER ONE

Kuwar village, Afghanistan, May, 1877.

LUCY wrung the icy water out of a black headshawl, then placed it in the basket alongside her newly washed *kamis* and faded red pantaloons. Six bitterly cold winter months had passed since she'd last been able to do laundry in the mountain stream, and she eyed her fresh-smelling clothes with satisfaction. Sometimes she thought that being constantly dirty was the worst thing about life as one of Hashim Khan's slaves.

She wiped her hands on the tattered edge of her *kamis*, scarcely noticing the twinge of pain as a coarse thread of wool caught in the open chilblain on her finger. Pain, she had learned during the past two years, was always relative and could often be ignored.

The sun felt good on her shoulders, warm but not yet burning with the fierceness of high summer. She sat down on the bank of the stream and dipped her feet into the water, gasping as the melted snow swirled around her ankles. When her feet tingled with cleanliness, she stood up and stretched, easing the cramped muscles of her thighs. Her English body still rebelled against the endless hours spent squatting or kneeling. She tugged her baggy trousers back into place, trying to remember what it had felt like to sit in a proper chair, but she had forgotten how to summon up any memory of softness or comfort.

Lucy shrugged, a touch impatient with herself. Nowadays she rarely wasted time in remembering. Checking to make sure her *chadri* was pulled low on her forehead as modesty demanded, she looped the free end across the lower half of her face and held it firmly in place with her teeth. She swung the heavy basket of laundry up on to her head, balancing the load with the ease of two years' constant practice. If only her stepmother could see her now, she thought wryly. Lady Margaret's lectures on the need for a lady to keep her head up and her shoulders straight would take on a whole new meaning.

Tiny clouds of dust puffed up between Lucy's toes as she walked down the rock-strewn path to the village. The ground, in fact, seemed unusually dry for this early in the year. If the summer ended in drought, Lucy had no doubt she would be blamed for the lack of water, just as she had been blamed for the blizzards and bitter cold of the long winter. Keeping her head attached to her shoulders was becoming more and more of a challenge as the days passed.

She had learned to be sensitive to every nuance of mood among her captors and, as soon as she reached the outskirts of the village, she realised something momentous had happened during the hours she had been away. Lucy walked on, her gaze fixed on the ground straight ahead. She knew she ought to be able to laugh at the ridiculousness of it all, but today she couldn't summon a smile. Being an evil *jinn* was a lonely business. Her vision suddenly blurred, and she rubbed her eyes, then stared at her fingers in astonishment. Why were they wet? She touched her eyes again, feeling more wetness trickle down on to her cheeks. Good lord, she thought, I'm crying.

She dashed the tears away, angry at her display of weakness, quickening her pace as she approached the whitewashed, mud-brick walls of Hashim Khan's palace. Miryam would be furious that she had taken so long over her washing, and she couldn't afford to offend the old woman. Not only was Miryam mistress of the Khan's female slaves, she was also one of the few people who had no fear of Lucy's magic powers.

Most of the villagers were convinced Lucy was a *jinn*, a paramour of the Great Satan himself. How else had she killed three fine men, brothers of the Great Khan, without leaving so much as a scratch on their bodies? Why else had the past two winters been so cold that double the usual number of sheep had perished, leaving the tribe hungry and isolated in their small valley?

Miryam poured scorn on these suggestions. In her opinion, Lucy was simply a slow-witted foreigner, with a feeble body, ugly face, and a nose so small it appeared deformed. Besides, everybody knew that *jinns* never assumed the inferior form of a woman. Why would they, when they had the choice of living as a man?

The argument between the two opposing factions flared up now and again, depending on how much other activity there was to distract the villagers. Lucy did everything in her power to ensure the debate never got resolved. She knew that if the villagers ever agreed unanimously that she was a *jinn* who should be sealed in a cave high in the mountains, Hashim Khan would make no attempt to save her. The Khan was willing to exploit her usefulness to him as long as it didn't bring him into direct conflict with the village elders, but he wouldn't raise a finger to save her life if she became an inconvenience. He had ambushed and killed all thirty members of the British trade delegation for the sake of a few horses and some gold trinkets from Amir Sher Ali. She didn't like to consider what value he placed on the life of a mere woman.

Lucy put her troublesome thoughts aside as she hurried through the gate set in the dilapidated palace wall. One minor blessing of her life as a slave was that she had little time for worrying. She skirted the ramshackle west side of the building and entered the enclosure behind the female slaves' quarters.

Her heart sank when she saw Miryam sitting beneath the shade of a shabby tent awning, drinking her favourite beverage of tea, flavoured with hard, salty balls of milk curd. Lucy quickly put down her laundry basket, and bowed deeply.

'Peace upon thee, Most Honoured Servant of the Great Khan,' she murmured in Pashto.

Miryam took several noisy slurps of tea before speaking. 'So, you have finally condescended to come back to us.'

'I am yours to command, Great One. What is your wish for me?'

'Huh! My wish is that you should go away from here and return to the eaters of pig's lard who are your family. You aren't worth the cost of keeping you in *pilau*.'

Miryam hurled the insult with all her usual vigour, but Lucy sensed the tiniest hesitation behind the servant's words. She wished that she dared raise her eyes to examine Miryam's expression, but such a breach of etiquette would have been punished by an immediate whipping. Lucy bowed even lower. Two years of captivity had taught her that pride was a luxury only free women could afford.

'May Allah show me how to give greater satisfaction, Most Honoured Servant of the —'

'Yes, well, enough of that,' Miryam interrupted. She reached inside the sleeve of her *kamis* and extracted a precious lump of mutton-fat soap. 'Here,' she said. 'Take this and go inside to give yourself a bath. Karima has heated water for you.'

Lucy's stomach lurched with terror. She had been allowed to bathe in soap and hot water only twice before, and both occasions had culminated in death and disaster. 'A b-bath, Most Excellent Daughter of Afghanistan? With soap? W-why am I to take a bath?'

'The Khan, blessed be his head and eyes, has commanded that you be brought to him. And that is all you need to know. Go, and in a few minutes I will bring you clothes to wear.' Miryam directed a half-hearted clout towards Lucy's ear. 'Stop talking and hurry up,' she ordered. 'Karima's waiting.'

Karima had not only provided three copper jugs full of heated water, but she had also laid out a coarse mat for Lucy to stand on, a clean cotton towel, and a small vial of scented oil for rubbing into her body. Lucy viewed all these incredible luxuries with anxiety verging on despair.

'If you give me the soap, I will wash your hair,' Karima said, clearly uneasy. Miryam could be as scorn-

ful as she wished, but most of the slaves took care never
to find themselves alone with Lucy if they could help it.
Whether she was an evil *jinn*, or merely an ignorant
foreigner, her company was better avoided.

Lucy handed over the soap with an absent-minded
murmur of thanks. Why? she thought wildly. Why did
Hashim Khan want to see her again? Certainly not to
take her into his bed. He had never made any secret of
the fact that he found her pale body and curly brown
hair repulsive. Besides, she was twenty-three now, an
old woman. If he hadn't desired her two years ago,
when her skin was still soft and her body plump with
good food, he wouldn't desire her now, when her skin
was tanned to a dark brown and her body was stretched
taut with muscle.

The fear settled into an ice-cold lump at the pit of
her stomach. If not into his bed, then almost certainly
into somebody else's. The Khan would have no other
use for a woman. Even the dancing and singing at tribal
feasts was performed by young boys, dressed up to look
like women.

But whose bed was he planning to send her to? He
had no more brothers, and his eldest son was still a
youth, barely thirteen or fourteen, surely too young
even for Hashim Khan to consider a threat.

So who was he planning to kill this time?

Lucy salaamed, prostrating herself on the tiled floor
and kissing the toe of Hashim Khan's embroidered right
slipper. He wriggled his foot, deciding whether or not
to kick her, then grunted the command for her to rise.
She stood nimbly, taking care never to straighten her
back, or lift her eyes. The Khan liked his subjects to
cringe with appropriate humility. 'The *ferangi* woman
may sit,' he declared loudly.

Lucy thought she must have misunderstood but, only
seconds later, a slave appeared in front of her holding
a small stool. Warily, she lowered herself on to the
seat, expecting at any moment to hear the roar of the

Khan's voice commanding his bodyguard to slit her throat for impudence.

The Khan inspected her huddled figure with undisguised approval, then chuckled. 'She is well-behaved for an Englishwoman, isn't she?' he remarked to a companion outside Lucy's range of vision. 'I had a bit of trouble with her in the beginning but, as you see, she finally understands the true meaning of obedience.'

A deep, rather bored masculine voice replied. 'Indeed, Excellency, it is difficult to believe she is English. The usual arrogance is entirely lacking. I could wish there were more who behaved like her in my own country. You have accomplished much, Most Excellent One.'

Hashim Khan roared his agreement and, while cups of snow-cooled *sharbat* were poured, Lucy risked a lightning-swift glance towards his guest. Other than the fact that he was tall and less than middle-aged, she could deduce little about him. He spoke Pashto fluently, but his accent sounded strange even to Lucy, whose command of the language was not yet perfect.

He's a foreigner, she thought, with a little spurt of excitement. No foreigner had ridden into the valley since her arrival two years earlier.

Her excitement disappeared all too swiftly, replaced by a shudder of foreboding. Please God, she pleaded silently, don't let Hashim be planning to kill this one, too.

The Khan's voice intruded upon her anguished thoughts. 'Well, Man of the Punjab, what do you think of my bargain now you have seen her? I offer her to you with my goodwill in exchange for your guns and your ammunition.'

The boredom in the foreigner's voice became more pronounced. 'I would like to inspect the merchandise before making a final judgement.'

The Khan clicked his fingers. 'Please, help yourself to a view. Be my guest.'

The foreigner — from what the Khan had said, Lucy guessed he must be a Muslim trader from the Punjab

province of Northern India—strolled across to where
she sat. Carelessly, he tossed her veil to one side, then
crooked his finger under her chin, tilting her head
backwards so that her entire face and neck were
exposed to his gaze. Lucy looked up into his dark,
assessing eyes and felt a curious heat flare in her cheeks.
For a moment he was oddly silent, then he drew the
veil back across her face and turned scornfully on his
heel.

'Your Excellency undoubtedly sees fit to jest. Of
what possible value to me is such an old and withered
female? She lacks even the merit of being fair-haired
and blue-eyed, like most of her countrywomen. She
will fetch no price on the slave market, and she doesn't
appeal to me at all.'

'I did not offer her to you for your pleasure,' the
Khan replied irritably. 'Take her to the British authorities in Peshawar. They will reward you handsomely
for her return.'

'If they do not hang me first,' the foreigner remarked
drily. 'Who is she, anyway, and what is she doing here?'

'She claims to be the daughter of one of their high
officials, a man of much importance in the government
of your country. Naturally, I have no way of knowing
the truth of her claim. My warriors, you understand,
found her wandering in the desert, and, out of the
overflowing goodness of their hearts, they brought her
here to my protection.'

'A most understandable decision on their part,
Excellency, since the benevolence of your disposition is
admired throughout Afghanistan.'

Lucy peeked up in time to see the Khan nod a modest
acknowledgement. 'She has caused me nothing but
trouble,' he said through a mouthful of sweetmeats.
'And yet I have continued to feed her throughout the
long months of winter.'

'Indeed, Excellency, one sees the extent of your
benevolence in the fat padding her bones.'

The Khan frowned, but, before he could speak, the
foreigner bared his teeth in a smile. 'It is because of

your famous benevolence, Most Illustrious Khan of
Kuwar, that I take the liberty of pointing out that my
rifles and ammunition have a value we can readily agree
upon. The woman, on the other hand, has no value at
all if the British do not want her. She may be the
daughter of an important man, as she claims. Or she
may be nothing more than the cast-off whore of a
British soldier.' The trader paused, the irony of his
voice unmistakable. 'Since your warriors picked her up
in the desert, alas, we have no way of confirming her
story. And hence, no way of establishing her value to
me.'

The Khan's eyes flashed with anger. He didn't
appreciate having his lies turned so neatly against him.
'Indeed, what you say is true, trader. However, because
of *your* great wisdom I take the liberty of pointing out
that you are not in a position to strike the best of
bargains. Your guards were killed by thieves in the
mountains. You yourself barely escaped with your life.
Furthermore, your weapons—those Enfield rifles
whose value we both agree upon—already repose in
the hands of my tribesmen. In these painful circumstances, a wise trader would take the woman and be
thankful.'

The foreigner spoke tersely. 'Your words offer
enlightenment, Excellency, and of course I bow to your
superior understanding of my circumstances. But, if I
take the woman and return her to the British authorities
in Peshawar, is there not some chance that Your
Excellency may find himself the object of a punitive
raid by their army? I mention such a possibility only
because it is well known how women contrive to twist
even the simplest story into a maze of lies and recrimi-
nations. She may choose to pretend she was abducted,
or something equally outrageous.'

'The British are too busy to launch an expedition
against a humble servant of the Amir such as myself. If
retribution is called for, it will surely be directed against
the Great Amir himself, may he reign forever.'

Dear God, Lucy thought. Hashim Khan hopes to

provoke the British into attacking Amir Sher Ali!
Which must mean that he had switched allegiances,
since he had undoubtedly worked hand in glove with
the Amir at the time of the trade delegation massacre,
and her own capture, two years earlier.

Her mind raced feverishly. Who could the Khan have
allied himself with now? The Russians, whose spies
were everywhere, and whose Imperial armies pressed
at the northern borders of Afghanistan? Or simply one
of the many local contenders for the Amir's throne?

Lucy had no way of knowing if the Indian gun trader
understood Hashim Khan's political intentions. Probably not, she thought, since the intrigues surrounding
the court in Kabul seemed totally impenetrable to most
outsiders.

However obscure the Khan's underlying motives, one
part of his message had been easy to understand. The
trader must realise by now that he would be killed if he
didn't accept Lucy in exchange for his supply of rifles.
She looked up, just in time to see him shrug.

'I will take the woman to Peshawar,' he said, his
voice clipped to the point of harshness.

'I knew you would understand my point of view once
I had clearly explained it,' the Khan murmured, his
chins wobbling with satisfaction. Lucy decided he must
be more anxious to get rid of her than she'd realised,
or he would never have tolerated the trader's curtness.

Belatedly, the trader seemed to realise his danger.
He rose from his chair and salaamed deeply. 'May my
guns serve you and your men faithfully for many years,
Most Excellent Ruler.'

'I'm sure they will,' the Khan replied. 'Allah permit-
ting, you will wish to leave at first light tomorrow
morning.'

'Yes, I think that would be best.'

'You shall have my finest mule as a mount for the
woman.'

'Your Excellency is all kind consideration. And my
own horses?'

The Khan waved his hand in a vague, all-encompass-ing gesture. 'Everything will be taken care of,' he said. 'Trust me.'

Poor trader, Lucy thought wryly. What a rotten deal he's getting. Me and a mule, and maybe the return of his own horses if he's lucky. I hope my stepmother is prepared to pay him a decent reward for bringing me home.

And then the realisation finally struck her. *Home*! Hashim Khan was actually planning to let her go! She swallowed hard, closing her eyes and clasping her hands tightly together in her lap. In the whole two years of her captivity, silence had never been so hard to maintain, but she forced herself to sit unmoving on the hard stool, in case the slightest sound from her might cause one of the men to change his mind.

The gun trader and Hashim Khan engaged in a ritual exchange of compliments to mark the conclusion of their bargain. The three musicians struck up a triumphant and out-of-tune march, and the Khan rose. He walked over to stand in front of Lucy, who curled at once into a humble ball at his feet.

Incredibly, the Khan stretched out his own hand to pull her upright. 'Go in peace, Daughter of a Distant Land, and remember to tell your people of the kindness you have received from the Khan of Kuwar.'

Lucy almost laughed, but the Khan wasn't joking, she realised, or even being sarcastic. He genuinely believed she had much to thank him for. She managed to choke back her true feelings and force out a few words of seeming gratitude. She kissed his slipper, resisting the impulse to take a large bite out of his toe. 'May Allah reward you in proportion to your years of generosity, Most Noble Ruler.'

Hashim Khan was not the man for spotting subtleties unless they hit him over the head. He patted her on the shoulder and sighed as if genuinely sorry to be losing her. Perhaps he was. He was unlikely ever again to find such a perfect scapegoat for his misdeeds.

'You will spend this night with the trader,' the Khan ordered. 'And make sure you do as he bids you.

Remember, a disobedient woman is worse than a pool of dog's vomit in the sight of Allah.'

On this elegant note, he departed for his sleeping chamber, his dancing boys prancing in his wake. At the threshold of his private quarters, he turned and beckoned to one of his bodyguards. 'Show the trader from the Punjab to the chamber we have prepared,' he ordered. 'See that the *ferangi* woman goes with him.'

The guard salaamed and Hashim Khan waddled into his room. A lissom dancing boy closed the curtains, screening the Khan and his entourage from view. Lucy blocked her ears to the ensuing sounds and looked quickly around. Apart from the bodyguard and a couple of slaves preparing themselves for sleep on the floor of the audience hall, she and the gun trader were alone.

He did not seem to consider this a fortunate circumstance, and certainly not an enticement to lust. As she stood, he inspected her swiftly then turned away, his dark brows drawn in a ferocious frown. Before she could decide whether to risk speaking, the bodyguard gestured, indicating that they should both accompany him down a narrow corridor. The trader strode forward without so much as a backward glance.

She was not in the least offended by his indifference. The Khan had compelled him to accept a terrible bargain, and many men would have shown their annoyance by beating her. As soon as he gave her permission to speak, she would try to convince him that a reward would be forthcoming for her safe return. If he believed in that reward, she was less likely to find herself abandoned somewhere in the mountains between here and the Indian town of Peshawar.

The bodyguard pulled aside a heavy woven curtain and gestured to the trader. 'Your room, honoured trader. May you have a restful night and awake refreshed.'

'In the comfort of the Khan's palace, quiet sleep is assured,' the trader replied, entering the guest chamber. He totally ignored Lucy as she slipped quietly to a far corner of the room, but her stomach knotted tight with dread. The chamber was hatefully familiar.

The trader walked across the room, sending a single brief glance in Lucy's direction. Naturally enough, he made no comment on her state of cowering silence. Women never spoke unless spoken to, and slaves were supposed to cower. If the possibility of treachery on the part of the Khan had entered his head, he gave no sign of it. Lucy couldn't quite make up her mind whether he was unbelievably foolish or amazingly wise.

The bodyguard unrolled the thick sleeping pallet and scattered embroidered cushions at one end. Then, from a roughly carved niche in the wall, he withdrew two heavy woollen blankets, shaking them energetically. Fortunately, they were quite new, so not much dust resulted and no scorpions were unexpectedly set free. Lucy had learned to inspect her bedding very carefully before crawling into it. Finally, the guard pointed to the brass pitcher of cold tea, and a tray bearing an assortment of sticky sweetmeats, before bowing himself out of the room.

The trader removed his turban and tossed it on to the pallet, then began to unfasten the buttons of his padded cotton jacket. When all sound of the bodyguard's retreating footsteps ceased, he crossed to the entrance of the room and gently drew back the curtain. Satisfied that nobody lurked outside, he turned and looked directly at Lucy.

'It's quite safe for you to speak,' he said quietly in Pashto. 'There is no one to hear us. Why are you trembling? What is there about this room that terrifies you so?'

Lucy was so astonished by his perception that for a second or two she simply stared at him. On the very brink of blurting out the truth, caution returned. She knew almost nothing about this man except that he was Indian, a trader and a Muslim. Such a man was unlikely to harbour tender feelings towards anyone from England. He had kept remarkable control of his temper so far, but she couldn't risk trusting him. If she warned him that Hashim Khan might already have poisoned him, he was as likely to blame her as to feel grateful.

Lucy took refuge in the pretence of stolid stupidity that had been her defence for most of the past two years. She lowered her head deferentially. 'Forgive me, master. I regret that my woman's brain is feeble. I do not understand your meaning.'

'You understand me very well, Englishwoman. In the great hall when you prostrated yourself before the Khan you pretended to fear him, but deep inside your heart I could see that you despised him.'

She kept her eyes modestly averted, concealing a fresh flare of surprise. 'I regret if my behaviour gave the wrong impression, master. Hashim Khan is the Ruler of all Kuwar, his great wisdom is respected——'

'Spare me your acting, Englishwoman. It isn't very good. Hashim Khan is a greedy fool and we both know it. However, fools can be every bit as dangerous as wise men, and that is why I want to know what you fear about this room. You became afraid as soon as the bodyguard showed us in here. Do not deny it. Your face is pale and your hands still tremble. What is there to terrify you in this simple sleeping chamber?'

Lucy thrust her hands beneath the thick folds of her veil, disconcerted yet again by the acuteness of the trader's observations. He had scarcely seemed to glance in her direction, and yet he had sensed more of her true feelings than anybody else in the entire period of her captivity.

'I was suddenly afraid I might not please you, master,' she said after a moment's hesitation. 'I know you find me old and withered, and I didn't want to be left behind when you set out for Peshawar.'

'That last part, at least, is probably true,' the trader muttered. He pushed his fingers through his hair, which was thick and dark, and oiled to a high shine. 'I suppose the Khan and his men have used your body with roughness,' he said brusquely. 'But you have nothing to fear from me. Unlike the Great Khan, I value my neck, and I have seen what British gentlemen do to men of my race who violate one of their women. I wish to claim a reward when we return to Peshawar, not a personal visit from the hangman.'

'Then you will take me back to India with you?' she breathed. 'If you do, I swear that you will be paid well for your troubles.'

'Don't worry, Englishwoman, I intend to be paid in full. I hope your family is rich.'

When speaking Pashto it was not considered rude to address somebody by the name of their country, but Lucy felt a sudden, inexplicable urge to hear the trader say her name.

'We should introduce ourselves,' she said primly. 'My name is Miss Lucinda Larkin. My friends and family call me Lucy.'

The trader looked at her blankly, then turned his back without answering. Lucy felt unutterably silly. What had she expected, for heaven's sake? English names could be difficult for Indians to pronounce and no self-respecting Easterner would permit himself to appear at a disadvantage in front of a woman. Of course the trader wouldn't say her name.

She was so busy feeling embarrassed that it was late—dangerously late—before she realised that the trader had crossed to the other side of the room and was pouring a cup of tea. She hurled herself after him, knocking the brass cup out of his hands a split second before he could raise it to his lips.

Silence filled the sleeping chamber. The trader picked up the cup and returned it carefully to the tray. Still silent, he retrieved his turban from the sleeping mat and used the loose flap to mop up the tea soaking into his pantaloons. When he finally looked at Lucy, his eyes were hard with anger. 'Is it poisoned?' he asked, his voice cool. 'The preserved fruits, too?'

'I don't know. Perhaps.' Her mouth twisted in a bitter smile. 'I am not in Hashim Khan's confidence.'

'Then why did you knock the cup from my hand?'

She twisted the edge of her veil between her fingers.

'I can't believe the Khan is prepared to let us go. I believe he must have some scheme to kill us.'

'The Afghan code of honour is strict. A host's duty to protect and honour his guest is sacred. Even the Khan wouldn't dare to violate that rule before his people.'

'That's true. But the Khan has convinced the villagers I am a *jinn*, so he cannot be held responsible for what happens to any man left alone with me.'

The trader's brow quirked upwards. 'And are you a *jinn*?'

'Of course not,' she said, exasperated. 'If I had magic powers, do you think I would have spent the last two years as one of Hashim Khan's slaves?'

'Not if you are a sensible *jinn*, certainly. So tell me, Englishwoman, what happens to the unfortunate visitors who find themselves alone with you?'

She drew in a deep breath. 'They die. At least, not visitors. There have been no visitors since I arrived here. But the Khan's brothers all died in this room. With me.'

The trader steepled his fingers and regarded them contemplatively. 'Ah,' he said. 'I see.'

'I tried to save them,' she said tightly. 'I tried everything I knew. But it was always. . .too late.'

'So you did not actually feed them the poison?'

'No! How could you think such a thing?'

'You could have been forced,' he said. 'I imagine the Khan is capable of dreaming up many ways to compel a captive woman to do his will.'

'I didn't poison them,' she repeated. 'His brothers were half-delirious by the time the Khan brought me to this room. The first time, I thought his brother was drunk, although I know alcohol is forbidden to Muslims. But from the way he clutched at my robe. . . I thought. . . I didn't realise. . .'

Her voice tailed away and the trader touched her lightly on the arm. 'Take heart, Englishwoman. I plan to survive the night in good health. I took care to eat only from dishes already tasted by Hashim Khan.'

'Then you suspected him, too!'

'In my travels, I have learned to be cautious.'

'Perhaps he truly means to let us both leave,' Lucy said, still not quite ready to believe such good fortune. Almost to herself, she added, 'I suppose there is no need for him to kill you since he already has all your rifles.'

'That is true. But I wonder why he is so anxious for me to take you back to India?'

'He was obliged to offer you something in trade for the guns.'

'But why you? I should have thought a *jinn* would be very useful to keep around.'

'The villagers blame me for the harsh winter we have just endured. My presence is beginning to cause disagreement among the elders. Maybe the Khan has decided I'm more trouble than I'm worth.'

'That could be, I suppose.' The trader laid his turban on the table alongside the fruit and tea. 'Well, I don't know about you, Englishwoman, but I am exhausted. If the Khan really is going to permit us to set off at dawn tomorrow, I would like to get some sleep. How about you?'

'I am tired,' she acknowledged.

'Here.' He handed her an embroidered pillow and one of the blankets, then stretched himself out on the pallet without waiting for her thanks.

She had expected to be compelled to share his sleeping mat, since the fact that he found her old and unattractive didn't mean that he would refrain from making use of her body. She reflected wryly that she was the only person in Kuwar — probably in the whole of Afghanistan — who was over sixteen years of age and still a virgin. At least her status as a *jinn* had served one useful purpose: it had prevented her from being forced into the role of town whore.

Lucy folded the blanket in half and tucked the pillow against the corner wall, grateful for the trader's generosity in sharing his covers. Tiptoeing so as not to disturb him, she extinguished the lamp. In the privacy of darkness, she unpinned her red woollen veil, took off her slippers, and crept between the welcome warmth of the blanket.

Finding sleep elusive, Lucy lay between the warm layers of her blanket, staring at the unrevealing hump of the trader's body. He was taller than most men of the Punjab, and broad-shouldered. His skin was dark and his hair raven-black, unlike many of the Kuwari tribesmen, whose eyes were sometimes grey and whose hair often had a distinctly reddish glint. When the trader had removed his turban, Lucy had seen a narrow white scar high on his forehead. It looked almost as if he had once suffered a bullet wound. Perhaps he had. The life of a gun-runner who plied his trade between India and Afghanistan couldn't be easy. His life must often be at risk.

Lucy stiffened at the trend of her own thoughts. A gun-runner! Dear God, what a naïve fool she had been! The trader was dealing in *Enfield rifles*. Enfields were Britain's newest and best guns, only recently imported into India. Since the Lucknow Mutiny, twenty years earlier, British officials had made sure no guns ended up in the hands of Indian natives. So the most likely way for the trader to have come into possession of such highly prized weapons was to have stolen them. He must have robbed an army barracks somewhere in the Punjab. Which, Lucy concluded, meant that the British government had almost certainly put a price on his head.

She lay in the darkness, listening to the trader's steady breathing. By the standards she had been brought up with, he was not only a thief, but also a rebel, perhaps even a revolutionary. He might be one of those misguided natives who campaigned against all the wonderful improvements of the British government in India. By any standard at all, he was obviously a man to be treated with extreme caution.

On the other hand, rebel or not, he represented a chance to escape from Kuwar village, and Lucy considered that a powerful argument in his favour. If only she could be sure he was planning to take her with him tomorrow morning! Would an experienced gun-runner risk coming into contact with the British authorities on the off chance of receiving a reward? Would he slow himself down on the difficult journey back to India by allowing a woman to tag along? Lucy could guess the answers to her questions all too easily, and she didn't like them one bit.

The blur of silent movement in the doorway caught her unawares, but her eyes had become accustomed to the darkness and he immediately discerned the shape of a man wielding a knife.

'Trader, watch out!'

Even as she gave the low cry of warning, the trader uncoiled himself from the pallet, lashing out to grab the wrist of the intruder. The knife clattered to the floor and the trader sprang forwards, the momentum of his leap toppling the would-be assassin backwards. The crack of the intruder's skull hitting the tiled floor reverberated through the room.

A beam of light from the corridor refracted from the polished steel blade of the second assassin's knife as he pushed aside the doorway hangings.

'Behind you!' Lucy screamed. 'Another one!'

In a single fluid movement, the trader reached into the cummerbund at his waist, pulled out his own knife, and whirled around to throw. He acted so swiftly that Lucy didn't see the knife pass through the air; she only heard the dull thud as it landed on target. The second assassin clutched his stomach, swayed on his feet for a second or two, then collapsed on to the floor.

The trader picked up the fallen knives of the two assassins, then stood very still in the centre of the room, listening.

Lucy swallowed hard. 'Is he. . .are they both dead?'

'Yes.'

'What are we going to —— ?'

The trader placed his hand flat over her mouth. 'Don't talk,' he murmured into her ear. 'Don't make any sound at all.'

Skirting the bodies, he picked up the brass pitcher of tea and made his way to the door. He carefully closed the curtains then stood there, his body tense with concentration.

After five minutes, his vigil was rewarded by the sound of footsteps creeping along the corridor. The trader silently pressed himself against the left-hand side of the entrance. The footsteps came to a halt and a head poked hesitantly through the curtains. 'Ali? Mohammed?'

The intruder had no time to ask anything more. The trader brought the brass jug crashing down on his head, and the intruder sank to the floor, tea dripping in sticky rivulets over his face.

Lucy gulped.

'He's not dead,' the trader said quietly. 'I took care not to hit him too hard. He was just the look-out.'

'The l-look-out?'

'There had to be one,' the trader explained. He put on his turban and readjusted his waist-sash to accommodate the three new knives he had acquired. 'If the Khan wants to blame you for my murder, he can't very well allow anybody to see his assassins creeping into our chamber. So there had to be somebody posted as a guard. Probably nobody in the village knows of the Khan's plans except these three men.'

'Oh.' Lucy turned away and stared at the corner where she had been sleeping. It was the only place she could look without seeing a body. 'You seem awfully good at — er — '

'At repelling attacks?'

She supposed that was as good a way as any of describing what he had done. 'Yes.'

'In this country, people tend to throw knives first and ask questions afterwards. I've learned to sleep with one ear open, but thank you for your warnings. They made things easier.'

'You're — er — welcome.' The traditional courtesy seemed positively bizarre in the circumstances and Lucy gave an involuntary hiccup of laughter.

The trader looked at her sharply. 'Put on your veil, Englishwoman; there is no time for hysterics. We must go now.'

'Go?' she repeated stupidly. 'How can we go?'

The trader smiled. 'How can we stay? That's surely a better question.'

It was the first time she had seen him smile, and her stomach gave an odd little leap of response. 'I meant that we can't go because the Khan won't let us.'

'If we leave right away, he may not be awake to stop us. At any rate, it is our only chance, so we must take it. Here, let me help you with your veil. We must hurry.'

He picked up the large square of finely woven red wool and placed it over her head. 'Do you have pins?' he queried. 'I'm afraid this is one article of feminine apparel that always defeats me.'

'You need to fold it like this,' she said, demonstrating. As soon as she could, she covered the lower half of her face. For some reason, she felt acutely aware of the trader's nearness, possibly because after two years among the Kuwari she was no longer accustomed to appearing unveiled in the presence of a man.

'Very good, Englishwoman.' For an instant, the trader's gaze locked with hers, then he turned away, removing one of the dead men's turbans and ripping off pieces of cloth to gag and bind the third intruder.

'Fold the blankets,' he ordered as he tested the knots he had tied. 'We'll freeze without them even at this time of year. Now, do you know the quickest way out from here into the compound?'

'I think so, although I haven't been inside this part of the palace very often.'

'You will have to lead the way. I'll follow you and carry the blankets.' The trader paused, as if to emphasise the tremendous concession he was making. Men in this part of the world didn't carry burdens when a woman was around to do the task for them.

'If anybody sees us they will think our behaviour is very strange.'

He smiled wryly. 'If anybody sees us, Englishwoman, we shall be dead.'

She shivered. 'What happens when we reach the outside?' She glanced down at her velvet slippers. 'Are we going to walk all the way to India?'

'If need be, but I trust it won't come to that. When we are outside, you are going to the kitchen area to steal provisions.'

'You speak of stealing very casually, trader. Unfortunately, I have little experience of the art.'

'And I, unfortunately, have no time to train you. However, Englishwoman, if we wish to avoid starvation on the mountain passes, you will need to steal us some food. I trust your untutored skills will prove adequate to the task.'

'Why can't you steal the food?'

'Because I shall be in the stables, acquiring us horses.'

'You cannot possibly hope to steal horses! Slaves sleep in the stables, and the slightest noise will awaken them!'

'Lower your voice, Englishwoman. I don't plan to *steal* the horses. If you remember, two of them are mine, and a pack mule as well. I shall simply demand from the slaves the return of my own animals.'

Lucy doubted very much if the recovery of his horses would be as easy as he made it sound. However, she was resigned to the fact that her life was already forfeit, and she might as well die attempting to escape as cowering in the slaves' quarters. She shrugged.

'If we turn right as we leave this room, I believe there is a door that leads into the kitchen gardens. Will you follow me, master?'

Lucy felt no real excitement when they escaped into the deserted grounds of the palace without seeing a soul. Bludgeoned by the horrible experiences of the past hour, her emotions had reached the point of exhaustion, and she felt only apathy when they reached the kitchen gardens in safety. She knew their amazing good luck wouldn't hold. The only questions were how soon they would be caught, and how much they would be tortured before they were allowed to die.

The trader drew her into the deep shadows of an awning stretched over one of the outdoor ovens. 'Dawn is breaking,' he said quietly. 'We have little time. What's the quickest way to the stables from here?'

'Follow the irrigation ditch,' she said, thinking how totally absurd it was even to be offering such information. The ditch ran straight through the centre of the village. Admittedly the trader wouldn't need to walk far, but he would surely be seen or heard by a dozen people before he was halfway to his destination. 'The stables are to the east of the palace.'

He nodded. 'I recall the layout of the village, although I wasn't given much chance to look around.' He gave her a little push in the direction of the storage huts. 'Go, Englishwoman, and when you have your supplies walk outside the palace wall and wait for me.'

'But of course,' she said.

If he heard the heavy irony of her tone he made no acknowledgement of it. He crept away from her, gliding close to the wall, a silent shadow among the last grey shadows of the night.

Lucy watched him until he disappeared behind the kitchens. Then she walked quite brazenly into the storage hut, so sure she would be discovered that it seemed pointless to attempt any stealth. When several seconds passed and nobody challenged her, she began to feel afraid. Her body shook so violently that her teeth began to chatter.

Lucy clenched her jaw until her teeth stopped chattering, then went to one of the shelves. Woven storage bags, empty at this season of the year, lay in a pile in front of her. She picked up two of medium size. Frantic now with the need to be gone, she began to stuff the bags with provisions: dried apricots and nuts from the distant city of Qandahar, hardened balls of milk curd and strips of smoked goat meat from the village, and stale flat loaves of bread from the palace tables, brought here to be ground up and used as a thickening for soups.

Running for the exit, she almost fell headlong over the wooden chest that contained the Khan's favourite tea, so expensive that nobody else in the village had ever tasted it. As she picked herself up, she defiantly scooped out a generous supply. If by any chance the trader managed to get his horses back, his saddle-bags would contain a pot for boiling water. And if the trader failed to acquire any horses, it didn't matter what she stole. She would be beaten and executed anyway.

Her hands were ice-cold and shaking as she retied the mouths of the loaded sacks with a length of braided goat's hair, then slung them over her shoulder and made for the door. Her luck had held so incredibly long that, try as she might, she couldn't quite quell the wild hope that somehow she and the trader would make good their escape.

She was already outside the palace wall, already allowing the hope to blossom, when Miryam's voice sounded sharply behind her. 'Where do you think you're going, lump of pig's lard? And what do you have in those sacks?'

Lucy stopped dead in her tracks, turning around to bow with abject humility. Please God, she prayed. Don't let anybody have heard Miryam's voice. She placed her hand on her heart and grovelled. For the last time, she promised herself. Whatever happened, for the last time.

'Most Excellent Mistress, I was sent here by the Khan — blessed be his name forever — in search of supplies.'

'Supplies?' Miryam marched aggressively forwards. 'What supplies, you lying good-for-nothing? Why would the Khan send you to get supplies?'

'He could not sleep, Great One.' Lucy held her breath. Two steps nearer, and Miryam would be within range of her head. 'He wished me to brew him some tea.'

'And for that you needed two sacks?' Miryam

demanded. She moved one step closer. Lucy's heart stopped beating. 'Show me what you have hidden away in those sacks, thieving daughter of a dog.'

She moved the final, fatal step and Lucy lunged forwards, using her head to butt the slave mistress in the stomach with all the force she could command. Without a sound, Miryam collapsed at Lucy's feet.

'Well done,' said a quiet voice behind her. 'What an efficient thief you turned out to be.'

'You should know,' Lucy responded tartly.

'I would like to stay here and exchange compliments with you,' the trader said. 'Unfortunately, I estimate we have about fifteen minutes before somebody decides he is brave enough to wake up the Khan. I hope you can ride using a man's saddle.'

Lucy had never ridden anything but side-saddle in her life. 'Of course I can,' she lied.

The trader cupped his hands for her foot, then tossed her up into the saddle. The horse pranced nervously, but she managed to bring it under control. The trader grunted, but made no comment.

'I'll give us each half the supplies,' he said, hurriedly buckling one of the sacks on to the rear of Lucy's saddle, then fastening the other to his. He sprang on to his horse with the ease of somebody accustomed to spending half his life in the saddle. His gaze when he turned to her was quizzical.

'Ready, Englishwoman?'

She drew in a deep breath. 'Ready,' she said firmly.

A great noise of shouting and screaming arose from somewhere deep inside the palace. Simultaneously, Miryam began to groan.

'Dear God! The bodies must have been discovered. What shall we do?'

'Ride as you have never ridden before, Englishwoman.' He handed her a whip, then dug his spurs deep into the horse's flanks.

'Gallop, Englishwoman!' he called, as his horse sprang forwards. 'Ride as if we have the devil at our heels, or we shall very soon find ourselves in hell!'

CHAPTER TWO

THE trader set such a bruising pace that for the first few minutes Lucy concentrated on staying in the saddle. The rough path out of the village quickly gave way to scree and desert scrub, forcing the trader to rein in his horse from an all-out gallop to a fast canter. With profound relief, Lucy did likewise. She quickly realised, however, that, although the danger of her falling out of the saddle was considerably reduced the chance of her horse stumbling and breaking a leg was greatly increased.

Her riding skills were tested to the utmost during the next few miles. They had ridden less than an hour, but the terrain was so difficult that both horses were showing signs of strain when they encountered a fast-flowing mountain stream, crossing their path diagonally. A rough track followed the right-hand bank of the stream, curving away into the horizon.

Thank heaven, Lucy thought, and turned gratefully towards the path.

'Not that way,' the trader said tersely. 'Through the water.'

'But, master, the path will be faster——'

'The water will obliterate our tracks,' he said, urging his horse into the stream. 'Hashim Khan's men have been gaining on us ever since we left the village. We can't outrun them.'

Lucy strained her ears. Faintly, far in the distance, she could hear the thud of horses' hoofs, and her heart pounded faster in response to the ominous sound. Dear God, why was he worrying about tracks when their pursuers would be upon them at any minute?

'The Khan's men won't need to follow our trail once they can see us,' she pointed out, trying not to let her impatience show. 'They can't be more than seven or eight minutes behind us. We must get on to dry land and gallop again! Hurry, master. Please, hurry!'

The trader totally ignored her, concentrating instead on urging his horse to move faster through the ice-cold, swirling water.

Lucy scowled at his back. She hadn't really expected him to bring her to safety, so there was no logical reason to feel disappointed by his slow-wittedness. The important question was whether she should resign herself to death at this pigheaded man's side, or put her gelding to the gallop in a last desperate bid for freedom.

The trader spoke without turning around. 'The Khan's men will catch you before you have gone five miles, Englishwoman. You had better stay with me.'

'Listen to their horses, you obstinate oaf!' Lucy was too frightened to waste time wondering how he'd once again managed to read her thoughts. 'They're gaining on us! Five minutes more and they'll *see* us!'

'And if you shout much louder, they won't have any need to see us,' he retorted grimly. 'They will be able to hear with great precision which direction we have taken. Follow me, Englishwoman, and endeavour to keep your suggestions to yourself. Fortunately, the wind is at our backs and they are riding hard. With luck, and Allah's mercy, they won't have heard you.'

A couple of minutes later, he guided his horse out of the water on to the far bank of the stream then quickly dismounted. 'Come,' he said to Lucy. 'This is the place. Pray they do not know of it.'

The place was a patch of ground less than fifty feet square, since in this area the rocky base of the mountain reached within a few yards of the water. Their pursuers were coming closer by the second. The pounding of horses' hoofs had already swollen to a threatening crescendo. Four minutes, she thought frantically. Four minutes and they'll see us.

The trader, his face impassive, tugged a knife from his waistband and hacked off a branch from the solitary, half-dead bush growing between two large boulders.

He looked up, and she could have sworn she detected

a gleam of amusement in his dark eyes. 'Dismount and
lead the horses straight ahead,' he said. 'Quickly! You
will find a cave behind that outcropping of rock. I will
follow and erase with this branch any footprints we
leave.'

Her legs were shaking when she slid off the horse, as
much from fear and hope as from fatigue. By now, she
could hear the jingle of harness on the pursuing horses,
and she ran with desperate urgency toward the rocky
outcroppings that marked the base of the mountain.
How could the trader have known about a cave? He
had supposedly been robbed and then had ridden
headlong into Kuwar seeking protection. When had he
found time to explore the area around the village?

She walked around the needle-nosed outcroppings of
rock and discovered that the cave actually existed!
True, it wasn't much of a cave, but at this moment
Lucy thought it looked beautiful.

With the trader close at her heels, she forced her
gelding's head down so that they could pass through the
low, narrow entrance. The space inside was no bigger
than a large horse stall but the ceiling rose over ten feet
so they could stand upright.

She leaned against the gelding, resting her cheek
against his sweating neck. The familiar smell gave her
comfort. If she closed her eyes, she could almost
imagine she was a child again, back in the stables of
Hallerton, her home in the English countryside.

The sounds of pursuit became louder, crushing her
daydream in the thunder of galloping hoofs. Six or
seven horses at least, Lucy calculated, all travelling at
breakneck speed. She held her breath as the Khan's
men raced past the cave, the noise of their horses' hoofs
deafening despite the muffling effect of the rock in front
of the cave. Their pace, thank God, didn't slacken.
They must have realised their quarry had stepped off
the path to ride in the water, but they weren't wasting
time searching for tracks. They obviously expected to
overtake the runaways at any moment, and, given the
speed of their pursuit, that was a logical conclusion.

Lucy hoped they would keep galloping and avoid thinking for a very long time.

When every last echo of sound had died away, she closed her eyes and leaned back against the wall of the cave to relish the silence. Eventually, she opened her eyes. 'Are we going to ride downstream?' she asked. 'We'd better hurry, master, in case they decide to turn back.'

'No, we will stay here until our pursuers return. The path they have taken is the route we ourselves must follow.'

She understood at once what he intended. He planned to wait until Hashim Khan's men headed back towards Kuwar village, then she and the trader would emerge from their cave and ride serenely on to India, free of pursuit. The scheme, elegant in its simplicity, was so likely to succeed that she found herself smiling.

'You are amused, Englishwoman?'

She shook her head. 'Admiring,' she said. 'How did you know of this cave, trader?'

'It is a long story and a boring one as well.'

'But we have time to spare if you would care to recount it.'

'Tell me rather how you came to be a captive of the Khan of Kuwar. You must be one of the very few Englishwomen ever to set foot on the soil of Afghanistan.'

'I am the daughter of Sir Peter Larkin,' she said, then stopped. She hadn't spoken her father's name in two years, and her throat suddenly felt tight. Her voice was thick with unshed tears when she continued speaking. 'He was murdered here in Afghanistan two years ago, along with all his colleagues.'

'I have heard of this man,' the trader said softly. 'His loss occasioned much grief to the people of the Punjab. It is rumoured in the bazaars that the British authorities still have no idea what caused the massacre of this man and his delegation.'

'There is no mystery,' she said bitterly. 'Their deaths were caused by the treachery of Amir Sher Ali. The

Amir received my father and the other officials with great courtesy, but he never intended to honour the agreements he signed. We had travelled less than five hours on our return journey to India when we were attacked. Everybody was killed except me — and the Amir's camel drivers.'

'You believe Amir Sher Ali ordered the massacre, even though you were taken captive by the Khan of Kuwar?' he asked.

'I'm *certain* Sher Ali ordered the massacre. The day before our delegation left Kabul, he apologised to my father, saying that our horses had become sick and that they wouldn't be strong enough to survive the journey home. So that we wouldn't be delayed, he graciously provided our entire delegation with camels.' She smiled, a smile lacking all trace of humour. 'We would have done infinitely better without such graciousness. When the Khan's men attacked our caravan, several of the tribesmen were riding horses I recognised as belonging to our delegation. Hashim Khan's brother, who led the attack, was riding my father's stallion.'

'And you concluded, naturally, that your horses had never been sick.'

'They had rarely looked more splendid. Amir Sher Ali simply needed them to use as a bribe. He knew the Khan of Kuwar would not provide his murderous services free of charge.'

The trader scratched his forefinger up and down the white blaze above his horse's nose and the animal rolled its eyes in silent ecstasy.

'The Enfield rifles the Khan stole from me have some very interesting properties,' he said meditatively.

'They are British army rifles,' Lucy said stiffly. She didn't understand the trader's abrupt change of subject, nor did she like this reminder that he had probably come by his stock illegally.

The trader seemed unperturbed. 'Yes, that is true,' he said. 'Unfortunately, these particular rifles do not live up to the usual British standard of excellence. It is most regrettable, but after a few rounds have been fired the hammer will jam on the percussion cap, and the rifles will never work again.'

'You mean they're *defective*?'

The trader winced. 'Let us not use such ugly words, Englishwoman. A trader never likes to hear his merchandise described in such terms. Let us say rather that the rifles need a modified firing mechanism in order to work properly. And that mechanism, I fear, can be obtained only in England.'

After a moment of stunned silence, Lucy burst out laughing. 'Are you telling me, trader, that the Khan has acquired two dozen absolutely useless weapons in exchange for me?'

The trader's gaze lingered for a split second on her mouth before he glanced away. He shrugged apologetically. 'Alas, Englishwoman, I fear it is so.'

'Thank you for telling me,' Lucy said, her laughter ending. 'My heart rejoices in the knowledge that for once Hasham Khan's treachery has not been rewarded.'

The trader seemed preoccupied with adjusting the sacks attached to his horse's saddle. He didn't look at Lucy when he spoke.'You converse in Pashto with the elegance of a native-born Easterner, Englishwoman. Do you speak my language also?'

'Urdu? Much less than I should, given that I spent four years in India. I speak Pashto fluently because it is the language I have used every day for the past two years.'

'Then we shall continue to speak to each other in Pashto.'

'You do not speak English, master?'

'I prefer not to,' he said shortly. Perhaps realising his abruptness, his voice was friendlier when he continued.

'Much has happened in India since you were taken captive by Hashim Khan. Last year, Queen Victoria of England was crowned Empress of India, and Lord Lytton has become India's first viceroy. Your Prime Minister, Mr Disraeli, is very busy pursuing his dream of a British Empire that spans the entire globe.'

Lucy was silent for several minutes, absorbing the

news. 'It is curious how strongly our minds resist the idea of change,' she said at last. 'My life after the Khan captured me became utterly different from everything that had gone before, and yet I somehow expected the world outside Kuwar village to stand still.'

The trader responded quietly enough, but his voice was laced with passion. 'India was not changed, Englishwoman. Not in the last two years, not in the last two centuries. It would take more than the coronation of a distant queen to alter the way of life among the people of my country.'

'Perhaps that is a pity,' she replied tartly, irritated by his attitude. Didn't he appreciate the efforts the British government was making to civilise India? She lifted her chin. 'A country that forces widows to throw themselves on the funeral pyre of their dead husbands is not so perfect that it can safely ignore the need for progress.'

'That custom concerns only the Hindus,' he said dismissively, reminding her forcibly of the great gulf between the different religious faiths in India. 'We Muslims have never required our women to commit *suttee*. We do not need such dramatic demonstrations from our wives in order to be sure of their devotion.'

'Well, bully for you,' she muttered in English. 'I suppose you just keep them locked up in the *zenana*.'

He quirked a brow enquiringly and she gave him one of her best and most insincere salaams.

'My words are not important, master.'

'But please do repeat them; I insist.'

'If that is your wish, master. . .'

'I believe you said something about the *zenana*.'

Two years in Kuwar, Lucy reflected, had transformed her into a skilful liar. She smiled ingratiatingly. 'I said merely that the women of your *zenana* must be very happy, master, because your wisdom as a husband is written on your face for all to see.'

'Is that so? How odd, considering that I am not married.'

'You're not married?' Lucy was shocked out of her fake humbleness. The trader could not be a day less than thirty years old, and according to the customs of his people he should have been married for at least a decade.

The trader placed his finger to his lips in a warning gesture. 'Hush, I hear hoof beats. And this time the wind is not in our favour. Try to keep your horse and your mouth quiet, Englishwoman.'

She fell silent at once, and after a minute or two she heard the distant clip-clop of horses' hoofs. This time, the little cavalcade of searchers moved at no more than a fast trot, and from the unevenness of the sound she guessed that one of the horsemen occasionally broke away from the group to inspect the ground for hoof prints or other signs of the runaways' trail.

She and the trader were in much greater danger than they had been before, Lucy realised. If any of the tribesmen chose to cross over the stream and look more closely at the rocky ledge in front of the cave, they would be discovered, because the horses would never remain quiet.

She looked across the small cave towards the trader, seeking reassurance. Oddly, his sardonic gaze brought comfort.

He must have sensed her anxiety, because he turned towards her, meeting her eyes for a few brief seconds before looking away. She watched as he silently drew two knives from his cummerbund. Still in silence, he turned one knife inwards, pointing the tip toward the bottom of his stomach but leaving an inch of space between the blade and his clothes. With a swift slash of his hand, he whipped the knife upwards over the middle of his body.

He offered the knife to Lucy. 'If the Khan's men stop outside the cave, you will need to do what I have just shown you, Englishwoman.' His voice was expressionless, and so low she could scarcely hear it.

'I think. . .I could not. . .'

'You must, Englishwoman. Hashim Khan will not grant you so merciful a death.'

She looked down, ashamed of her weakness. 'You

are right, master, but I'm afraid my hand would betray
my will.'

'Then you must stand here next to me so that I can
perform the task for you if need be.' Quickly, silently,
he switched places with his horse. 'Hurry,
Englishwoman, come here beside me. You do not want
the tribesmen to find you alive.'

She copied his manoeuvre, slipping around her horse
to join him in the centre of the cave. Her horse shifted
his hindquarters, jostling her against the trader. She
jerked back from the unexpected contact as if she had
been scalded. The trader looked at her, his gaze typi-
cally ironic, and for no reason she could think of the
blood crept into her cheeks, making them flame with
heat.

He turned away. 'There is grain in my saddle-bags,'
he said. 'Scoop some out so that you have something
with which to pacify the horses if they become too
restless.'

She was about to answer when he shook his head
sharply. 'Be still. The Khan's men will soon be upon
us.'

The search-party rode inexorably nearer until Lucy
could actually hear the voices of the tribesmen and the
laboured snorts of their horses. Dear God, how she
wished sound travelled in only one direction! She
divided her grain into two hands, held one serving out
to each horse, and prayed as she had never prayed
before.

The cavalcade of disgruntled searchers was almost
opposite the mouth of the cave.

Lucy's gelding, scenting the other animals, backed
into the wall of the cave, pawing his agitation. The iron
of his shoe struck with a metallic thud against a piece
of stone.

'What was that noise?' somebody demanded.

'It was a *jinn*, trying to get out of his bottle,' another
voice answered sarcastically. 'This search is a waste of
time and I want some food. Those two must have

doubled around and left the village from the west. The other search-party will have found them by now.'

To Lucy's profound relief, there was a general murmur of agreement. The horsemen broke into a slow canter and the sound of their voices faded rapidly into the distance. At last even the echo of their hoofbeats was swallowed up in silence.

The trader tucked his knives back into his cummerbund. 'Another hour to wait, and then I estimate it will be safe for us to start on our way.' A tiny smile lightened the habitual severity of his expression.

'What do you say, Englishwoman? Shall we eat some breakfast while we wait?'

Once the trader deemed it safe to emerge from the cave, they rode for eight hours without stopping, and darkness fell long before they finally tethered the horses for the night.

When the exhausted animals had been fed and watered, the trader built a small fire while Lucy searched along the riverbank for a flat stone she could heat and use to bake a loaf of unleavened bread. She kneaded flour and water together, then smeared the heated stone with a lump of hardened mutton fat. The sizzle and delicious aroma made her stomach rumble with anticipation. Wrapping raisins and strips of dried goat meat in the heated dough, she bowed as she handed the food to the trader.

He ate in silence, accepting everything she offered with a brief nod.

'You may eat that yourself,' he said, when she offered him the third envelope of dough.

Lucy was surprised. 'You have finished, master?'

'No, but you must be hungry. I can wait until you have eaten something.'

She bowed low. 'Thank you, master,' she said, taking a huge, luxurious bite of the food. She chewed slowly on the stringy meat, letting the raisins burst with sweetness on her tongue. What a strange man he was, to be sure. She had never heard of any Indian or

Afghani man allowing a woman to eat before his own hunger was completely satisfied. She licked her fingers and decided to stop worrying about his motives. At the moment, she was simply grateful for his consideration.

As she had hoped, the trader's saddle-bags contained a small pot for boiling water, and so they were able to top off their sumptuous meal with a bowl each of the Khan's favourite imported China tea. The delicate, floral scent of the tea drifted pleasantly beneath their nostrils before floating away on the chill of the night air.

Replete with warmth and good food, Lucy drew her knees up to her chin and stared into the embers of the fire. In two years, she couldn't remember eating and drinking so well.

'How did you know of the cave, master?' She was so relaxed that she didn't realise she had spoken the question aloud until he answered her.

'My trading partner was a Ghilzai, a nomad from near Jalalabad. His family used to travel this route every spring with their flocks of sheep. He showed me the cave only a few hours before he was killed.'

She yawned. 'We were lucky he knew of it, master.'

'Yes, we were.' He got to his feet. 'Wash the bowls in the stream, Englishwoman, and I will unroll our blankets. It is late, and we should leave at first light tomorrow. We cannot be sure that Hashim Khan won't send a more efficient search-party after us.'

When she returned, the fire was banked with stones and the trader was already curled up in one of the blankets, asleep. The other blanket, neatly folded in half, lay about five feet away from him.

Lucy checked the blanket for snakes and spiders, then crawled between the warm folds. Unpinning her veil, she shook out the trail dust and fashioned a small pillow. She lay down with a small sigh of contentment.

The trader's voice started her. 'Sleep well, Englishwoman.'

'Thank you, master. May Allah grant you peaceful repose.'

'I live in hope, Englishwoman.'

There was something distinctly odd about the way in which the trader addressed her, Lucy decided. Something about his tone of voice, or perhaps the words he used. . . Something that wasn't quite right. She really ought to decide what it was. . .

Lucy slept.

The next three days passed uneventfully, apart from minor mishaps. The trader maintained a relentless pace, driving the horses to the limit of their endurance each day. However, since he had stolen a plentiful supply of grain, and Lucy had stolen a plentiful supply of food, the journey didn't seem particularly arduous to her. The horses recuperated each night, and her energy actually seemed to increase as the days passed. For the first time in two years, she was eating three full meals a day, and her body responded eagerly to the extra nourishment.

'I'm glad you brought the tea,' the trader commented on the fourth day of their journey, as she brewed a pot to accompany their noon meal of dried fruit and stale bread toasted over the fire. 'It makes mealtime a little more bearable.'

She was obscurely disappointed by the implication that he hadn't enjoyed their peaceful moments sitting by the fire. They rarely spoke as they rode, but once seated by the fire they usually chatted in a friendly way about nothing in particular. She had told him about England, describing all the harmless pleasures of a carefree childhood on a prosperous country estate, and he had seemed to listen with interest. True, he had imparted very little personal information in return, but he had always seemed willing to talk about the latest political developments in India.

He was surprisingly well-informed about international politics — surprising because Lucy knew from her father and from other British officials how difficult it was to interest the natives in affairs outside their village, let alone in the alien world beyond India. She supposed that it was the trader's precarious life as a gun-runner that sparked his interest in world affairs. After all, he would need to know who was getting ready to fight if he wanted to find the best markets for his merchandise.

'You are amazingly silent, Englishwoman. What have I said or done to offend you now?'

She glared at him. She had almost stopped worrying about his uncanny ability to sense her moods and read her thoughts, but occasionally she found it disconcerting.

'You have done nothing, master. I am only sorry that my humble efforts to prepare satisfactory meals have not met with your approval.'

He poured himself another cup of tea, his eyes gleaming with definite amusement. 'Have you noticed, Englishwoman, that you only call me "master" when you are angry with me?'

'Master, how can you believe such a thing when I am all gratitude for your kind ——?'

'Do be quiet, Lucy,' he said casually.

She stared at him open-mouthed. He pronounced her name Loo-sie, with a slight break in the middle, but his accent gave the ordinary name a curious appeal.

She wrapped her arms around her knees and stared at him over the top of her veil. 'You remembered my name.'

'Of course.'

'But you never used it before.'

'It is the English way to leap into intimacy, jumping into situations without weighing the consequences. Here in the East, we realise that time will take care of many things.'

'And now you have decided it is time for us to be. . . intimate?'

'I have decided only that it is time, with your permission, to use your given name.'

'You know you have my permission,' she said haltingly, although somewhere deep inside she acknowledged that she had grown almost fond of the sardonic way in which he called her 'Englishwoman'.

He poured boiling water on to the tea-leaves in her bowl and handed it to her.

'Thank you, trader.'

'My name,' he said, 'is Rashid.'

They had been travelling for almost a week when the rough, beaten-earth tracks that criss-crossed the mountains began to converge in a single southerly direction. Lucy, for the first time in days, felt the sharp bite of fear. Below them, in the valley, the Kabul River flowed peacefully toward India's northern frontier, but Lucy drew little comfort from the knowledge that she was nearly home. The sun shone as brightly as ever, but its warmth failed to relieve her inner chill.

She scowled at the trader's back, which appeared annoyingly unconcerned, just as it had done all morning. The tilt of his head seemed positively merry, and Lucy wouldn't have been surprised if he had burst into song. His heedlessness infuriated her. Didn't he realise that the closer they came to the Khyber Pass, the more vulnerable they were to attack? Until now, he had chosen a route that avoided the scattered settlements of Afridi tribesmen who controlled access to the Pass. But soon they would have to ride into the open, where they would be at the mercy of any tribesman whose gun-finger itched on the trigger.

So far, Lucy hadn't spotted a single warrior anywhere within shooting distance, but her fear remained. She and Rashid had encountered so little danger over the past few days that she expected each bend in the road to bring them face to face with disaster. As her panic increased, the trader's stolid, unhesitating ride forwards became more and more provoking.

The distant sound of horses honed Lucy's fear into immediate, razor-sharp terror. They were being pursued, she was sure of it, and by a troop of horsemen riding at a fast canter. Who could it be if not Hashim Khan's men? Now that she had tasted freedom, it

would be impossible to return to slavery. The chill
inside her froze into an icy block of desperation. She
urged her mount forwards.

'Do you hear them?' she asked Rashid, drawing
alongside him on the narrow path. 'I knew Hashim
Khan wouldn't let us escape so easily! He has sent an
army to catch us! Dear God, where shall we hide?'

'There is no need to hide. The sounds you hear are
not from Hashim Khan's men.'

She didn't doubt his judgement, and the relief was
overwhelming until she realised the ease with which he
had calmed her fears. Then relief was replaced by
anger.

'How do you know it isn't the Khan's men?' she
demanded. 'Are you gifted with magic ears that recognise one set of hoofbeats over another?'

'Not hoofbeats,' he answered absently. 'Harness.
These riders have no bells on their harness.'

'And the lack of a few bells is sufficient to convince
you the riders aren't part of Hashim Khan's army?'

'You know that the men of Kuwar pride themselves
on the decorative silver bells embedded in their reins.
Besides, these horses approach from the west, and
Kuwar village lies to the north-north-east.' With no
change of tone, he added, 'I think this ledge looks like
a good place to stop. The sand and those boulders
make a natural resting place.'

'Resting place? Here — where the horsemen are certain to come upon us? Are you run mad, trader?'

He was silent for a moment, then he said, 'I gave you
the gift of my name, Englishwoman. Do you find it so
difficult to use?'

She didn't answer. A week ago the habits of slavery
had still been deeply ingrained and she wouldn't have
dreamed of defying him, even by silence. But adequate
food — and perhaps something in the trader's own attitude — had restored her sense of personal dignity. She
watched him dismount, frowning her disapproval and
refusing to join him.

'Do you plan to sit on your horse and scowl all afternoon?' he enquired mildly.

'Unless you tell me why we're stopping here.' She paused for a moment. 'Please, Rashid.'

He acknowledged her use of his name with the faintest of smiles. 'Because the horsemen will catch up with us sooner or later. Better here, where we can control the situation.'

'How can we control it?'

'We shall pretend to be nomads. We are on our way to rejoin our tribe, having been separated from them by mischance last winter. Whoever these horsemen may be, our best defence is to pretend abject poverty and total ignorance.'

'But which tribe shall we claim as our own? I speak only the language of Kuwar valley, none of the other Afghani dialects.'

'You are a woman. There will be no reason for you to speak.'

'And you? How can you avoid speech? Will you pretend to be dumb?'

He ignored her sarcasm. 'No. I shall simply claim brotherhood with whichever tribe the horsemen are least likely to know.'

Lucy made a move toward dismounting, but he forestalled her, reaching up and lifting her from the saddle.

'Praise Allah that you look much like any other woman from this part of the world,' he said, setting her on the ground and tilting her face up in a cursory inspection. 'Although you are definitely too clean.'

He dug up a handful of dust and rubbed it into her forehead, sprinkling the residue over her headshawl and grinding it into the weave of the fabric. He stepped back to admire his handiwork, then gave a grunt of approval. 'Fortune smiles on us. At least you are brown-eyed and dark-skinned, unlike most of your countrywomen. There is nothing in your appearance to arouse suspicion.'

She watched meekly as he removed their depleted

supplies from the back of his saddle. Unfastening the
sack, he scooped up a handful of raisins and tied them
in a grubby piece of cloth, along with a bag of flour and
a lump of mutton fat. The remainder of the food,
including the precious tea, he stuffed back into the
sack.

'Here, tie these beneath your *kamis*,' he said, holding
the provisions out to Lucy.

She stared at him blankly.

'There is no other way to safeguard our supplies,' he
explained, hacking at one of the blankets with his knife.
'We must pretend you are with child. It is because of
your condition that I am forced to waste time resting in
the middle of the day. Like any self-respecting husband,
I am not pleased with the weakness you are displaying.'

'And whose fault is it that wives become pregnant?'
she demanded.

Rashid grinned. 'A husband proves his virility. A
wife takes care of the consequences. That is the way of
the East. Make haste, wife of mine, the horsemen are
almost upon us. Use this strip of blanket to tie the sack
and the blanket over your stomach. Endeavour to keep
the mound smooth.'

She turned her back as she pulled up her overdress
and tried to comply with his instructions. Incon-
gruously, she found herself wondering how it would
feel to carry the child of a man she loved within the
warmth of her body.

Rashid spoke from behind her, his voice impatient.
'The men are almost upon us. I can smell their horses.
Why are you taking so long, Englishwoman? Do you
need me to help you?'

Before she could reply, she felt the coolness of his
fingers at her back. Oddly enough, his coolness merely
increased her sensation of heat. He crossed the makeshift cord around her waist, then turned her around so
that he could knot the ends over the sack and the folded
pad of blanket. In a couple of seconds he was finished.
He pulled her straining *kamis* down over the resulting

bulge and looked at her with a faint gleam of
amusement.

'At least seven months along, I would think. From
the wealth of your feminine experience, does that seem
right to you, Englishwoman?'

'A little more,' she replied evenly. She looked up,
meeting his gaze with a hint of challenge. 'I gave you
the gift of my name, trader. Will you not use it?'

For a moment she thought he would not answer her,
then he smiled wryly. 'There can sometimes be much
danger in a name, Loo-sie, have you not discovered
that?'

'How can my name be dangerous? I don't —
understand.'

'No, I suspect you do not. Perhaps it is better so.'

The strange silence between them was broken by a
crescendo of sound as a dozen or more horses and
riders cantered into view. With much shouting from the
men and snorting from the horses, the miniature cavalcade plunged to a halt.

'Remember, say nothing at all,' Rashid murmured in
her ear, making a great show of pulling her veil lower
down on her forehead. 'No Afghani woman would
speak to strangers when her husband is present.'

Lucy nodded, huddling within the dirty folds of her
veil as Rashid moved forwards to greet their pursuers.
They were soldiers, Lucy realised, but not Afghanis, or
British soldiers, as might have been expected this close
to the Indian border. They were Cossacks in full
uniform, with two officers leading a dozen men.

The senior officer, recognisable from his myriad rows
of gold braid, withdrew his sabre from its sheath, rattled
it menacingly, then hurled some remark in Rashid's
direction. Lucy had no idea what he said, but she could
hear the contempt in his voice even through the barrier
of an unknown language.

Rashid bowed very low, looking both worried and
humble. 'I am honoured to be of service,' he said in
Pashto, the most commonly used dialect of the region.
'But unfortunately this feeble brain of mine is not

clever enough to understand the wisdom of your discourse, Most Excellent Horseman.'

The officer frowned, gestured irritably to his junior, then barked out some command. The junior officer edged forwards, and addressed Rashid in mangled, thickly accented Pashto.

'My good fellow, we are important peoples from the Great Motherland of Russia, and we wish to know of where we have been lost.'

'Most Excellent and Honoured Visitor, this is the Safed Koh Mountain range,' Rashid replied.

'We know that,' the Russian declared curtly, making no effort to indicate that Rashid should rise from his obsequious bow. 'We have journeyed from Qandahar and we have been lost. We wish to find our path forward.'

'The servants of the Great White Queen live just over the Khyber Pass,' Rashid offered with an air of supreme innocence. 'Most Honoured and Noble Russian, Son of the Motherland, do you seek to journey into the lands of the Great British Queen? She is, perhaps, also the Queen of Russia?'

'Of course she isn't, you fool! And of course we don't want to go to India!' The officer drew in a deep breath and lowered his voice.'We wish to find the valley of Kuwar, and the palace of Hashim Khan, ruler of the valley.'

Lucy only just managed to conceal a start of surprise. Rashid, still staring meekly at his toes, gave not the slightest indication that the Russian's words shocked him.

'The Palace of Hashim Khan is not easy to find, Most Honoured Stranger to Afghanistan.'

'You do not tell us something new, old fellow. We have been seeking this valley of Kuwar in many days. We have urgent messages from our great emperor to give to your Khan.'

'Most Illustrious Traveller, I fear that Hashim Khan is not my Khan. He is not even known to me. To my regret, I confess that my ignorant eyes have never feasted upon the beauty of his palace. But my cousin's cousin—blessed be his wandering feet—has told me of the wonders of Kuwar.'

'And did he tell you how to get there?' The young lieutenant's supply of patience was clearly becoming exhausted. He looked longingly at the whip coiled on his saddle, and Lucy found herself almost sympathising with his frustration. The flowery rituals of Afghani courtesy made the straightforward exchange of information almost impossible.

Gritting his teeth, the officer tried again. 'We have messages from Prince Mohammad Ayub, which must be delivered to Hashim Khan immediately.'

Lucy gave a startled exclamation before she could stop herself. Without warning, Rashid's arm lashed out, landing a sharp blow across her shoulders. 'Silence, wife!' he thundered.

She covered her face with her hands and bowed low. 'I beg your pardon, husband,' she said. 'Your unborn son caused me a moment of pain.'

Rashid did not deign to acknowledge her apology. Bending abjectly toward his knees, he addressed the Russian officer. 'Forgive the unseemly behaviour of my wife, Most Excellent Leader of Men. She did not mean to intrude her presence upon your eyes, but she is old, and for many years was barren. In her condition, she sometimes forgets her manners. Now what was it that you told my ignorant ears?'

The lieutenant glanced at Lucy with a mixture of disdain and pity, then shrugged. 'I said that we have messages from Prince Mohammed Ayub that must be carried to Hashim Khan immediately.'

Prince Mohammed Ayub was the son of Amir Sher Ali. Ayub had tried to seize power from his father and had been exiled to Persia on charges of treason. Extraordinary as it was for Russians to venture so close to British territory, it was surely even more extraordinary for them to carry messages to Hashim Khan from a rebellious son of the Amir. Hasham Khan had always declared himself a friend and close ally of the Amir.

Moreover, the Russians had never given any indication that they wished to topple Sher Ali from his throne.

Lucy wondered if the Russians had decided to invade Afghanistan and were hoping to provoke internal rebellions as an excuse for crossing the border. She stole a glance at Rashid, but the trader gave no indication that he recognised the importance of the information he had just gleaned. It was possible that he didn't realise its significance, Lucy reflected. A gun-runner presumably didn't care who was fighting whom as long as the battles continued to rage and his profits to soar. She had seen much evidence of Rashid's cunning and his ability to survive, but perhaps she had been wrong in assuming that his quick thinking was based on an overall understanding of the complex politics of Afghanistan. With an effort, she returned her attention to what Rashid was saying.

'Prince Mohammed Ayub is undoubtedly a man of great importance, Most Excellent Son of Russia. Unfortunately, my ignorance has such a wide extent that the prince's name is unknown to me. I trust you left him in good health, Excellency?'

The officer rolled his eyes heavenwards, obviously muttering some Russian imprecation for patience. 'The Prince's health has never been better. Now, I want an answer. The route to Kuwar. How do we find the palace of Hashim Khan?'

'I will tell you, Most Noble Foreigner. Unfortunately, Allah's command that his servants should always be truthful forces me to inform you, Excellency, that you and your honoured companions ride in the wrong direction. Your noble steeds carry you directly away from the valley of Kuwar. The palace of Hashim Khan lies in the direction of the setting sun. You must go down from these mountains along the path that curves to your left. When you are in the valley, you must follow the River Kabul to the west.'

Rashid's directions would take the Russians directly to the fortified city of Jalalabad, and Lucy found herself wondering what his motives might be. Was he simply directing the Russians along the quickest route to Kuwar, not even realising that he was sending them into danger? Or did he know that Amir Sher Ali's deputies in Jalalabad would very likely arrest the soldiers as they approached the city? The Russians and the British had been snarling at each other across Afghanistan for the past thirty years. From the British point of view, Lucy knew it would be better for this troop of Russian soldiers to be penned up in Jalalabad rather than out creating mayhem with Hashim Khan. But would the trader care about the outcome of a quarrel between Britain and Russia? As an Indian native, might Rashid actually hope that the Russians would win in any dispute with the British rulers of India? Lucy acknowledged that she would probably never know the answer to her questions.

The lieutenant finished translating Rashid's directions for his superior officer. Scowling ferociously, the captain sheathed his sabre and wheeled his mount around, obviously giving the command for his men to fall in behind.

'My captain thanks you for your help,' the young officer said, tossing a couple of silver coins on to the ground at Rashid's feet. 'We go now.'

Rashid slid forwards to cover the coins with his feet, giving every appearance of being thrilled to receive them. Removing the dirty cloth pouch from his belt, he made haste to open the package. The lump of fat, the bag of flour and the pile of raisins lay exposed to the Russian lieutenant's view.

'Most Excellent Visitor, as a parting gift please help yourself to your choice of my humble provisions.'

The young officer eyed the dusty pile of supplies with horror, but he had obviously been in Afghanistan long enough to know that it was a mortal offence to refuse food when it was offered. Gingerly, he reached out to select three or four raisins. He chewed them slowly, as etiquette demanded, keeping his eyes carefully averted from the grey lump of mutton fat. His ordeal over, he thanked them curtly and rode up to join his captain at the front of the troop. Within a minute, the soldiers had retreated around the bend.

Once they were out of sight, Lucy would have spoken, but Rashid put out his hand, gesturing her to silence. When the last hoofbeat had faded into oblivion, he turned to face her, his expression grim.

'Show me your shoulder. I tried to restrain the force of my blow, but it was necessary for my anger to look convincing. I trust I didn't hurt you too much?'

'I have survived much worse, trader.'

'But not at my hands.'

She heard regret in his voice and for some reason it disturbed her. She turned abruptly away, lifting her *kamis* and tugging at the knotted blanket so that she could remove the bulge of her false pregnancy. Playing the role of his pregnant wife had been an unsettling experience. She pulled irritably at the makeshift rope, until the knots finally opened, and the sack and blanket fell to her feet. She turned around, shaking the veil back from her shoulders. 'You did not hurt me, trader. Your blow merely reminded me how glad I am to be an English lady. Thank God I shall never have to endure the humiliations suffered by an Eastern wife.'

'True. But you will also never know the pleasures.' His voice became arrogant. 'Unlike the men of my country, the English are not known for their skill as lovers.'

She blushed hotly. 'English ladies seek companionship and loyalty from their husbands. They do not wish for skilful. . .for. . .what you said.'

'How boring,' he murmured, his voice soft and somewhat amused.

'We would say sensible rather than boring,' she returned loftily. 'An English lady sees no pleasure in becoming her husband's slave.'

'You have, I think, much to learn about the subtleties of my country,' Rashid said. 'A man in love is as deeply enslaved as the woman who partners him. But we don't have time to discuss the rival merits of eastern- and western-style marriage. Come, we have a long way to go if we are to cross the summit of the pass during daylight tomorrow. Let me help you remount.'

For the first few miles after their encounter with the Russians, Lucy waited impatiently for an opportunity to broach the subject of the rebellious Prince Mohammed Ayub and his possible alliance with the Russians. By the time the afternoon shadows had lengthened into evening, wiser thoughts prevailed. What would she gain by voicing her suspicions to Rashid? She had no knowledge of where the trader's loyalties might lie, but from tiny hints in his conversation she suspected he disliked the increasing power of British rule in India. As she prepared their evening meal, she reminded herself that Peshawar was no more than three days' ride away. Her discoveries—and her worries—would much better be discussed with the officials of the British Raj, rather than with a merchant whose first loyalties must lie with his guns.

CHAPTER THREE

THE night after they had successfully crossed into British India, Rashid told her that armed Afridi tribesmen had tracked them across the entire thirty-mile length of the Khyber Pass. When Lucy wanted to know why the pair of them had been left unmolested, Rashid replied laconically, 'The Afridi know me. I have brought them gifts from time to time.'

'I suppose I should be grateful your gifts to them worked properly,' she muttered. 'Otherwise, no doubt, I would have been slaughtered in payment for your past misdeeds.'

He laughed. 'Never fear, Englishwoman. Even I am not so foolhardy as to give malfunctioning weapons to the Afridi. The warriors guarding this pass have always received the very best I have to offer.'

'You have given them Enfield rifles? Is that what you mean by "the best you have to offer"?'

Rashid looked at her through a drift of smoke from the camp-fire. 'It is illegal for a native of the Punjab to have such advanced weapons in his possession. Did you not know this, Englishwoman?'

She looked away. 'Yes, I knew. I realised long ago that you must have stolen the rifles you sold to Hashim Khan.'

'Do you not think it rather dangerous to reveal such insights to me, Englishwoman?'

Lucy busied herself with sliding the cooked dough off the stone and on to a tin plate. 'I trust you not to harm me, Rashid. Am I wrong?'

He took the food without answering her. 'Everything is not always as it seems on the surface,' he said finally. 'But you are right to believe I will not harm you. I shall return you safely to Peshawar.'

'Is it dangerous for you to enter the city, Rashid?'

'I am not at risk from officials of the Raj. I do not steal my merchandise and I do not work against your country, Englishwoman, even though I despise much of British policy in India.'

'Why do you despise my government, Rashid? What's wrong with our policies? Most Punjabis welcomed the arrival of the British authorities. Your rulers invited us in. Nobody from my country fought to conquer your lands.'

'A mouse may sometimes choose to live under the rule of an elephant rather than a tiger. At least with an elephant in control he can see when danger approaches. The fact remains that it will take my people generations to undo the harm well-meaning Britishers have done to them.'

'How can you talk of harm when we have achieved so much in the last hundred years?' Lucy asked passionately. 'My country has given your people a legal system that is the envy of the world. The courts here are no longer susceptible to bribes, and peasants have the hope of true justice for the first time in their history. We have brought schools to villages, water to barren land, and doctors to care for your sick. The roads we have built unite your cities. The telegraph lines we have laid link India to the rest of the world. In every province where the British have ruled, progress has followed.'

'All this is true. And in exchange you have demanded nothing from us save our souls.'

'Indian natives are permitted freedom of religious expression,' Lucy retorted angrily. 'We are amazingly tolerant of your superstitions, except where they are dangerous or wicked.'

His smile seemed almost sad. 'And who is to decide what is wicked, Englishwoman? What to you are superstitions, to my countrymen are profound expressions of belief. Is it so hard for you to accept that your Christian churches do not encompass all that is good in humanity's religious experience?'

'Have some tea,' Lucy said, gritting her teeth. 'The water has boiled at last.'

The trader threw back his head and laughed. 'Ah, I had forgotten! English ladies do not discuss religion or politics, is that not right? Such discussions are reserved exclusively to the gentlemen.'

'Certain topics are better suited to the masculine mind,' Lucy said primly. 'The feminine mind, by contrast, is naturally inclined to domestic matters. A well-brought-up lady doesn't enjoy political or religious arguments. Her most intense pleasure and interest is always aroused by matters concerning her family and her home.'

'If you believe that, Englishwoman, then you are as much a slave to your heritage as any Indian child bride. You must also be blind to the reality of your own self. You are living proof that a woman's interests can be as wide-ranging as any man's.'

Lucy ignored the odd little quiver of pleasure Rashid's remarks generated. The closer they got to Peshawar, the more vividly she began to recall the strictures of her old life. As her stepmother had often reminded her, Lucy had never fitted well into conventional society. And after two years as Hashim Khan's slave, she wondered if she would ever again manage to adapt to the rigid proprieties of life in colonial India.

'Surely I have not shocked you into silence, Englishwoman? Do you have no angry response, no stinging rebuttal to prove to me the error of my thinking?'

'Of course not, Rashid. It's not appropriate for me to try to prove you wrong. I realise it's difficult for us to understand each other. We come from very different backgrounds and you have never been to England. And naturally, in your profession, you cannot have met many English ladies or gentlemen. . .'

Her words tailed away as she heard the note of condescension in her voice. She hadn't intended to sound so patronizing, and she hurried into speech, her voice determinedly cheerful, her smile artificially bright. 'Shall we be in Peshawar tomorrow? If so, we have more than enough of the Khan's special tea to brew ourselves a second pot.'

The glance he threw at her was disconcertingly sympathetic, but all he said was, 'With Allah's blessing, we shall be in Peshawar tomorrow. Another pot of tea would make a welcome celebration to mark the end of our journey.'

Lucy felt an emotion akin to sadness as she carried a fresh supply of water from the stream and set it on the hot stone. She stared into the red heart of the fire and allowed her thoughts to drift.

'What do you think of, Englishwoman?'

'The end of our journey.'

'You are happy to return to your people.'

'Yes. Yes, of course I am.'

'But your face holds sadness, Englishwoman, and many doubts.'

Rashid had divined her mood correctly; Lucy's feelings were oddly ambivalent. The days spent travelling with the trader had been some of the most enjoyable she had ever experienced. Their escape had been dangerous and their path rugged, but Rashid's presence had provided a sense of security and many moments of quiet mutual content. His conversation — infuriating at times — had stimulated new ideas and fresh perspectives. Their meals had seemed tastier and more satisfying than a gourmet dinner prepared by a master chef. In Rashid's company she had felt more alive than at any time in her life before.

Lucy knew she would never be able to express such feelings once she returned to Peshawar. Tonight was the last night for honesty, the last night for an admission of how much she had enjoyed the trader's company. Perhaps, even now, it was too late. Civilisation already loomed too close. English inhibitions, English propriety reached out their tentacles, reasserting their claim upon her.

'The journey from Kuwar has not been unpleasant,' she said carefully. 'And I am grateful to you, Rashid, for the protection you have given me since we escaped

from Kuwar. I know you would have journeyed more
swiftly if you had abandoned me along the way.'

In the darkness she could see his grin. 'Ah, but then
I would have had nobody to cook my supper,
Englishwoman.'

'I believe you are quite capable of cooking your own
meals, trader.'

'Perhaps. But I'm sure my culinary efforts would lack
your elegant touch.'

She looked down at their final ball of hardened
mutton fat, sitting on a battered tin plate surrounded
by some withered strips of smoked goat's meat. Their
eyes met across the fire and she burst out laughing.

The trader watched her, his gaze lingering on her
mouth. 'The kettle boils, Loo-sie,' he said at last, his
voice husky. 'Shall we have our second bowl of tea?'

Normally, Lucy fell asleep the moment she crawled
between the folds of her blanket. Tonight, sleep
remained elusive, hovering tantalisingly beyond her
grasp. She stared at the stars, brilliant points of silver
light in the surrounding blackness, and listened to the
steady rhythm of Rashid's breathing. The dangers of
his lifestyle certainly didn't seem to interfere with his
rest. Lucy had told the trader endless stories about her
own childhood. He, she now realised, had told her only
that his father didn't approve of his politics or his
profession and that they were barely on speaking terms.

The distant howl of a hungry jackal jolted her into a
sitting position. Even though she didn't cry out, Rashid
threw off his blanket and crouched at her side almost
before the sound of the jackal's howl died away. The
moonlight reflected off the steel blade of the knife he
held ready in his hand.

'What is it?' he asked quietly. 'What troubles you,
Englishwoman?'

'I suppose it was the jackal. Did you not hear it?'

'Yes, I heard it. The jackal has never awoken you
before. What causes your wakefulness tonight,
Englishwoman?'

'Nothing,' she said, looking down at the knife and at his long brown fingers curled over the handle. 'Nothing at all.'

'Or perhaps you should more truly say *everything*.' Lucy didn't reply and the trader continued, 'Tomorrow you will return to your friends and family. After two years living among the people of Kuwar, you will take time to feel comfortable again in English society. It is only natural that you should feel nervous, Englishwoman.'

She looked up at him, smiling uncertainly, wanting to make light of her worries. 'You call me "Englishwoman", Rashid, almost every time you speak to me. But I'm not sure how English I feel any more. Sometimes. . .sometimes. . .I think that the woman who was Hashim Khan's slave will always crowd out the memories of my earlier life. I am not Lucinda Larkin any more. How can I be? I have lost her innocence.'

Slowly, he slipped the knife back among the folds of his cummerbund. He cupped his hand under her chin, gently tilting her face upwards. She had folded her veil to use as a pillow, so her head was uncovered. She made no protest when he reached out with his other hand and slowly pushed back a lock of hair that had fallen across her cheek. They stared at each other in silence. Lucy could read little of what Rashid was thinking, but she sensed that he was troubled and wondered why. Their silence became so intense that it seemed as if the entire world waited for something to happen.

Finally, he touched her lightly on her cheek. 'There is no shame in anything you did while you were held as Hashim Khan's prisoner. You know that, don't you Lucy? You did what you needed to do in order to survive. Be proud that you possessed the courage and the strength of will to keep yourself alive.'

She smiled ruefully. 'At this moment I don't feel very courageous. There will be so many questions to answer once I am home again. The men will want to know

every detail of the massacre that killed my father. The
ladies won't want to hear a word about anything so
brutal, but they'll be twice as anxious to assure themselves that I haven't adopted any indelicate native
customs like eating with my fingers or. . .' She stopped
abruptly.

Rashid squeezed her hand in a fleeting gesture of
reassurance. 'However prying they are, the good ladies
of Peshawar surely cannot be more intimidating than
Hashim Khan and his band of cut-throats.'

'Huh! That shows how little you know about it,' she
muttered. 'On most occasions the ladies of Peshawar
are more intimidating than an entire army riding into
battle.'

The trace of amusement faded from his expression
and his eyes darkened. He leaned towards her until
they were almost touching. 'Take heart,
Englishwoman,' he muttered. 'You will find that you
have more strength than you know. I predict you will
outwit the ladies of Peshawar as successfully as you
outwitted Hasham Khan's soldiers.'

'You outwitted the Khan's men, Rashid, not I. You
saved my life.'

'Did I?' He laughed somewhat oddly. 'Then certainly
I must claim my reward before it is too late. It seems I
have earned it.'

She was obscurely disappointed by his remarks, even
though she had always acknowledged that he deserved
compensation. 'I have promised that you will be well
paid for your services, Rashid.'

He gave another odd laugh. 'Well paid? Perhaps.
But tonight I do not speak of money. Tonight I find
myself in need of other rewards.' His words were no
more than a breath of sound against her mouth. He
brushed his thumbs across her eyelids, closing them,
and a moment later she felt his lips cover hers in a
gentle kiss.

Lucy's mouth began to tremble beneath Rashid's,
although she wasn't frightened, and she felt the strangest urge to press herself closer to his chest. As soon as

she leaned against him, he made an odd, groaning sound deep in his throat and wrapped her inside the circle of his arms, crushing her against his chest. His lips became hard against hers and, with a little sigh of astonishment, Lucy opened her mouth.

She had no idea what she expected to happen next, but at the touch of Rashid's tongue against hers a wave of excitement swept through her. His day's growth of beard rasped against her skin, but the prickles of pain seemed almost pleasurable. Lucy reached up to twist her hands in the thickness of his ebony-dark hair, wanting to feel the strands twined around her fingers. A delicious langour stole through her limbs and she lay back on her blanket, instinctively seeking the support of hard ground for her boneless body.

Rashid followed her down on to the blanket. His lips moved urgently over her mouth, sliding down the slender column of her throat, parting the strings of her *kamis* so that he could taste the soft, delicate skin above her breasts. Lucy almost stopped breathing. The night stood still and hushed as he pushed the threadbare cloth from her shoulders and eased it down towards her waist.

Her nipples sprang erect in the cold night air, but she scarcely felt the cold. His fingers caressed and stroked until her entire body was throbbing and warm beneath his skilful touch. When his mouth finally replaced his fingers at her breast, she shuddered in response, yearning for some unknown but more intense form of the pleasure he was arousing.

His lips burned their way back to her mouth, a scorching flame against her skin. He kissed her again and again, until even her innocence could not protect her from the knowledge of how deeply the passion had begun to blaze within him — and within her.

Suddenly, she felt fear: fear of the unknown, fear because her body's response had raced so far out of her control. Her mind tensed, and her body stiffened in an automatic effort to regain control over the unfamiliar sensations that threatened to consume her.

Immediately, Rashid became very still. They lay together, unmoving on the blanket, his face wiped clean of all expression. Then he sat up, pulling her *kamis* back onto her shoulders, and drawing away from her. 'I am sorry,' he said, his voice hard, and somewhat cool. 'I did not intend to bring back evil memories.'

'You didn't. There are no memories——'

'One day you will find a husband who deserves you, Englishwoman. A man who can give you the home in the country that you long for. A man who will be at your side when your children are born. It will be for him to overcome the darkness of what lies behind you in Kuwar. It will be for him to show you how much joy there can be between a man and a woman. Do you understand what I am trying to say, Englishwoman?'

'I feel — cold.'

He didn't take her in his arms to warm her. He got up and dragged his blanket a few inches closer to hers. If she had reached out her hand only a little way, she could have touched him. But she didn't. She lay absolutely still.

'I will put some more wood on the fire, Englishwoman.'

'Thank you.'

'Sleep, now. Trust me, Lucy. You need not fear the jackals tonight, nor the ladies of Peshawar tomorrow.'

No, Lucy thought, she had nobody to fear save herself. Defiantly, she stretched out her hand until she could touch him.

After a long, silent moment, he turned his hand palm upward, entwining his fingers with hers.

Lucy felt two tears trickle out from beneath her eyelids and roll down her cheeks. Rashid's fingers closed a fraction more tightly around hers.

'The time with you has been good, Lucy.'

Warmed by his words, she slept.

The trader chose to approach the city of Peshawar through the chaotic streets of the local market. With great difficulty, Lucy followed him through the narrow, dung-splattered passage he forged between rows of gourd sellers, rice-cake vendors, and fried-fish pedlars.

'Why are we taking this ridiculous route?' she demanded as a young boy darted almost under the horses' hoofs in pursuit of his spinning top.

Rashid avoided a group of children chasing a pet monkey that had slipped its chain. 'It is the shortest way to the British compound.'

His reply sounded abstracted, and Lucy looked at him questioningly. He returned her gaze, his eyes dark and without any trace of their usual mockery.

She drew in a quick breath. 'What is it, Rashid?'

'We have reached the end of our journey, Englishwoman. It is time for us to part company.'

'But we haven't reached my stepmother's house——'

The trader didn't answer. In a single swift movement, he jumped from his horse and tossed the reins towards her. 'Catch, Englishwoman!'

She instinctively reached out to grab the reins. By the time she had controlled his skittery horse, he had already crossed in front of her mount and begun to walk at her side. For the briefest of moments he laid his hand against hers in a gesture that was almost a caress. 'We must say goodbye, Englishwoman. Our paths diverge here.'

'Rashid, no! You can't leave me alone in a place like this!'

He stared ahead, his profile expressionless. 'You have no further need of me. You know your way home.' He bowed his head, touching his hand to his heart in a formal, graceful salute. 'Go with God, Lucy Larkin. May your life be long and blessed with many children.'

Her stomach plunged as if she were suddenly falling from a great height, and her throat constricted. 'But why would you leave me when we are so close to my home? What about your reward from my family?'

'The promise of money always interested you much more than me, Lucy Larkin.'

'But where shall I find you? For God's sake, where are you going? *Rashid!*'

He ducked behind a passing wagon without answering her frantic shout, dodging back toward the centre of the market-place. She called his name again, but she couldn't even be sure he heard her voice over the cacophony of merchants' cries. It was impossible to turn the horses around on the narrow pathway, and her gaze managed to track him for no more than twenty yards before he was swallowed up in the thick, milling crowds — one dusty, turbaned head among a score of others.

Lucy knew she had no real hope of finding him. Nevertheless, she dismounted and hunted doggedly on foot for more than an hour before she finally acknowledged that her search was pointless: the trader didn't want to be found.

Suddenly bone-weary, the task of controlling both horses seemed insurmountable. She escaped from the crowded market as quickly as she could, a hand on the bridle of each animal. Her arms ached and her eyes smarted from the dust as she lashed the horses together, then climbed back on her own gelding.

Hours of riding over harsh, mountainous terrain had never seemed so exhausting as the stretch of smooth gravel road leading to the British compound. She could feel herself swaying in the saddle by the time she reached the familiar driveway leading up to her father's bungalow. Her weariness lifted at the sight of the neat, white-painted buildings. The scent of jasmine wafted pleasantly over the high garden wall and she drew in a deep refreshing breath. Home. Dear God, she had come home!

Lucy didn't recognise the gatekeeper, but that was almost a relief. She wanted to get inside the house before she had to cope with the pandemonium her return would naturally inspire. She gave a polite nod to the servant, thinking how difficult it was to find the right words to announce that you weren't dead.

'Good day,' she said, after a brief hesitation. 'I am Miss Larkin, the daughter of the sahib, Sir Peter Larkin, who died in Afghanistan. Please open the gates.

I am very tired and would like to rest after my long journey.'

The gatekeeper barely glanced at her. 'Be off with you, brazen hussy! We don't let the likes of you into the house of my master.'

Brazen hussy? Belatedly, Lucy gave some thought to just what sort of bizarre appearance she must present. She resisted the impulse, born of fatigue, to snap at the servant. 'I know it must be difficult for you to recognise me,' she said. 'But despite these clothes, I am English. Lady Margaret Larkin, the memsahib, is my step-mother. She will be most angry when she hears that you have kept me waiting outside the walls of my own home.'

'My master and his memsahib are called Rutherspoon, not the name that you say. Why do you waste my time with your foolish lies?' the servant replied.

'Rutherspoon? The people who live here are called Rutherspoon?'

'Of course. Everybody knows it. The sahib is district officer and a most important man. Now be off with you.'

Lucy stared at the servant, torn between wry amuse-ment and a terrible feeling of anticlimax. Good heav-ens, how foolish she'd been to expect to find her stepmother and stepsister still living in their old bunga-low! Lady Margaret and Penelope had loathed India from the day they first arrived. Lady Margaret would never dream of staying in Peshawar, not when she had the exciting option of returning to London as a griev-ing — and wealthy — widow. She had undoubtedly taken the first ship home after hearing of Sir Peter's death.

Lucy felt the urge to cry, but instead a choked gurgle of laughter emerged from her dust-cracked lips. One part of her mind recognised the hysteria that lurked far too close to the surface. Another part no longer cared.

The servant frowned. 'There's nothing to giggle about, young woman. Mr Rutherspoon is a most excel-lent sahib, of great consequence in this region.'

'I'm sure he is. I'm sorry.' Lucy regained her composure with a struggle. 'Well, gatekeeper, if Mr Rutherspoon lives here instead of Lady Margaret Larkin, then it is Mr Rutherspoon I must see. Please open the gates. We have business to attend to, your master and I.'

The gatekeeper hesitated before deciding that discretion was the better part of valour. He lifted the heavy bar that locked the gate, then turned his back, symbolically denying responsibility for her penetration of the bungalow's spacious grounds.

Lucy cantered through the gates and rose swiftly to the white marble entrance steps, not giving any of the outdoor servants a chance to stop her. Taking a leaf from the trader's book, she tossed the reins of the horses towards a startled gardener, who had been enjoying a snooze in the shade of a palm tree. 'Catch!' she called.

She slid from the saddle and dashed for the front door, making it halfway down the hall before the startled doorkeeper gathered his wits sufficiently to chase after her. She sprinted towards the drawing-room, a gaggle of shouting, gesticulating servants snapping at her heels.

Lucy burst into the crowded drawing-room. Peshawar's British ladies, assembled for afternoon tea and the polite exchange of slander, returned their teacups to their saucers in perfect unison, their mouths gaping in identical lines of outrage. Seeing herself with their eyes, Lucy became embarrassingly aware of the fact that her clothes were in tatters.

A large-bosomed lady, tightly encased in salmon-pink satin, rose to her feet. 'What is the meaning of this?' she enquired haughtily. 'Mahbub, remove this. . .this *person* at once.'

'Mrs Rutherspoon?' Lucy shook off the servant's restraining hand. 'Mrs Rutherspoon, forgive me for intruding upon your tea-party like this, but I am Lucinda Larkin. I've just escaped from two years of captivity in Afghanistan. This used to be my home. I thought to find my stepmother and stepsister here.'

Mrs Rutherspoon sank back on to her chair, her colour alarmingly high. 'Lucinda Larkin? *Sir Peter's daughter*?' She peered at the dirty, brown-skinned woman in front of her. 'But you were reported dead! I attended memorial services in the cathedral myself! Mr Rutherspoon was there with me, and even the Governor General came!'

'I'm honoured to have been the recipient of such a splendid funeral, Mrs Rutherspoon, but, as you can see, the services were somewhat premature. Happily, I am not dead.'

Mrs Rutherspoon closed her eyes, and clasped her hands to her ample bosom, then decided that rather than fainting, which might crumple her new dress, she would summon her husband.

Inwardly congratulating herself on this brilliant solution to a difficult problem, Mrs Rutherspoon opened her eyes. 'Mahbub, send a boy to fetch the sahib home. Tell him he is to come at once.'

Gathering strength from the silent approval of her audience, Mrs Rutherspoon braved another direct glance at the intruder.

'Miss—er—Larkin, if indeed you should by any chance happen to be Miss Larkin, although that is most difficult to conceive of since Miss Larkin is dead and even if she had been captured would surely never have survived the horrors of her captivity——'

'I am Miss Larkin.'

Mrs Rutherspoon was not accustomed to being interrupted. She bridled angrily. 'So you have told us, Miss Larkin, if you are indeed Miss Larkin. In any case, whoever you. . .that is to say, I am sure you must realise that your extraordinary claim raises many difficult matters, which will all need to be sorted out.'

Mrs Rutherspoon rose to her feet, and glared at Lucy from her commanding new height. 'I have sent for Mr Rutherspoon. Mr Rutherspoon is the district officer.'

'And therefore able to resolve everything,' Lucy said.

Mrs Rutherspoon was not a lady to be troubled by subtle undertones of sarcasm. 'Of course,' she said, relieved to feel the conversation moving on to firmer ground. 'The district officer is the Queen's representative. He is able to resolve everything that does not need to be referred to higher authority.'

'In matters of a return from the dead, one wonders who the higher authority might actually be. Although if the district officer is considered an adequate substitute for Queen Victoria I dare say God has no cause to quibble.'

The assembled ladies gave a gasp of horror, and Mrs Rutherspoon was once again rendered speechless. By good fortune, Mr Rutherspoon himself arrived before the intruder could utter any further blasphemies — either against God or His earthly representatives.

'Good afternoon, ladies. Delightful to see you all.' With consummate skill — not for nothing had he been promoted to district officer — Mr Rutherspoon made himself heard over a babble of agitated feminine voices. 'Harriet, there are two horses eating the roses outside the front door, and Mahbub has been telling me the most ridicul——'

Mrs Rutherspoon regained her voice. 'This woman claims she is Lucinda Larkin.'

'What!' Goggle-eyed, the district officer swung around to face Lucy. 'Have you run mad, young woman? Lucinda Larkin is dead!'

'No,' Lucy said quietly. 'I am not dead. I have been held captive for two years in Kuwar valley, in central Afghanistan.'

Mr Rutherspoon glared at her. 'Young woman, you are offending the memory of a noble British family. Miss Larkin and her father were massacred two years ago. The bodies. . .the remains of the bodies. . .were brought back to India by soldiers of the Fifty-Ninth Light Infantry.'

'No,' Lucy said again. 'My father was massacred, together with all twenty of the men who formed part of Britain's trade delegation to the Amir of Afghanistan. But I was not killed. I was taken prisoner by the Khan of Kuwar. And now I have escaped.'

The drawing-room fell ominously silent. Dead, Miss Larkin had been a martyr killed in service to the Empire. Alive, she seemed destined to become an embarrassing blot on the purity of English womanhood. Mr Rutherspoon mopped his brow.

'I think we should discuss this — er — this return in my office. M'wife's drawing-room is not the place, you know.'

If she was Lucinda Larkin, Mr Rutherspoon would get her shipped out of here on the next available boat, before she could start causing trouble. Let the authorities in England sort out the legalities of the situation, whatever they might be.

Mr Rutherspoon possessed considerable organisational skills, and he used them now to excellent effect. His wife was summoned to action with a single brisk nod. 'Harriet, you will no doubt wish to escort our — er — visitor to a guest room so that she can refresh herself. I will join you in your sitting-room in just a moment.' He smiled at the assembled ladies. 'I know your charming guests will understand why we must cut short your tea-party.'

Lucy, escorted by a phalanx of servants, was led towards the rear of the bungalow. By nightfall, every servant in the British compound, right down to the boys hired to twirl the ceiling fans in the various drawing-rooms, had heard the dramatic story of her arrival at the district officer's gates, and her subsequent claim to be the long-lost Miss Lucinda Larkin. Most found the story unbelievable, but were willing to hold off final judgement until seeing the intruder dressed in English clothes. English clothes were notorious for their powers of transformation.

In this decision, the servants were joined by their masters, and by the district officer himself. 'Let's see how she cleans up,' Mr Rutherspoon commented to his wife over an evening glass of sherry.

'I've offered her one of Rosamund's good dresses,' Mrs Rutherspoon said, sounding astonished by her own

own generosity. 'And all the necessary — er — accoutrements.

'She didn't say a single word to me except please and thank you,' Mrs Rutherspoon burst out, overcome anew by the injustice of it all. 'I tried to offer my sympathy, to let her confide some of the horrors of her enslavement to me. After all, I am a married woman and I was determined to be brave, however shocking her revelations. But all she did was thank me for the lavender soap and tell me that she was quite capable of taking a bath alone. She is an impostor, she must be. No English lady would be so curt with the first white woman she has seen in two years.'

'She may feel a very proper reserve, m'dear. Even though you are married, with me as your husband you have naturally been shielded from the full demands of man's lower nature.'

Mrs Rutherspoon did not look as grateful as might have been expected. She was frowning when Mahbub appeared at the entrance of the drawing-room. 'Miss Larkin would like permission to join you and the memsahib, sahib.'

'Send her in,' Mr Rutherspoon said heartily. 'We are waiting to see her.'

Quick, soft footsteps sounded in the hallway. Mr Rutherspoon rose to his feet as Lucy walked gracefully into the drawing-room, head high, shoulders straight, one hand controlling the movement of her draped skirts, the other lightly clasped around the fan. She halted in front of Mrs Rutherspoon, dipping into the slightest of curtsies.

'Ma'am, I must apologise for interrupting your tea-party this afternoon. When I rode up to the bungalow I had not considered the many months that have passed since my father's death. I assumed that my stepmother and stepsister would still be living here. When the gatekeeper informed me that the new district officer was in residence, I could think of nothing to do other than bring my plight to his attention.'

Mrs Rutherspoon fanned herself. 'That you have certainly done.'

'Yes, I'm afraid I have.' Lucy's huge eyes softened with rueful laughter. 'Sir, I realise that my arrival on your doorstep has caused a great deal of trouble for your family. I also realise that my years in captivity have altered my appearance greatly. However, there must be several people still living in Peshawar who would recognise me. Perhaps Mr Chester, the vicar, or Mr Smythe, from the local school?'

Was it just coincidence that she had chosen two people who no longer resided in the region? Mr Rutherspoon scrutinised her intently. 'I'm sorry to say that Mr Smythe is no longer with us. He passed away at Christmas.'

'Oh, I'm sorry, that is sad news. He was a good man and an excellent teacher. Is Mrs Smythe still here?'

'Unfortunately not. She was advised to take the children back to England, to live with her late husband's brother.'

'The climate never agreed with her,' Lucy commented. 'She probably made a wise decision. Well, if Mrs Smythe is not here, how about the vicar?'

'Mr Chester is now archdeacon of the cathedral and so neither he nor his wife live in Peshawar.'

'Oh, bother!'

'Bother, indeed. However, take heart, Miss Larkin. I dare say, in these special circumstances, Mr Chester would be prepared to journey here to make a positive identification.' Mr Rutherspoon tugged at his moustache. 'Yes, that is what I shall do. I shall send a telegraph message to the cathedral tomorrow. I dare say Mr Chester might be here with us in as little as three days.'

Mr Rutherspoon could detect no sign of alarm at these words and he decided to abandon all hope of resolving the issue of her true identity that evening.

Summoned by an urgent telegram, the Very Reverend Archdeacon Otis Chester arrived in Peshawar only three days later. 'Good of you to notify me so promptly, Rutherspoon,' he said, on being ushered into the district officer's study. 'I knew Sir Peter and his eldest gal very well. This is a bad business.'

'You suspect my guest is not the real Lucinda Larkin?'

The Reverend Mr Chester gave a short bark of laughter. 'On the contrary, my dear sir. The Lucy Larkin I knew was just the sort of woman to survive two years of captivity in darkest Afghanistan. I was thinking of the difficulties ahead of the poor gal. She's not going to be welcomed by her stepmother, nor by her stepsister. Lady Margaret inherited a great deal of money from Sir Peter; now all that money reverts to Lucy. Not a happy situation.'

'Indeed not.' Mr Rutherspoon paced uneasily. 'Mrs Rutherspoon insists this woman is an impostor, but I don't agree. Still, you shall judge for yourself. . .'

Lucy followed the servant downstairs, outwardly composed, inwardly trembling. When making her escape from Kuwar, she had never considered there might be doubts about her identity once she returned to India. It would be ironic — more than ironic — if the Reverend Mr Chester failed to identify her as Lucinda Larkin. He had once been a good friend, but she needed only to glance into the mirror to know that even good friends might have difficulty in recognising her. The weight she had lost had affected the contours of her face, so that, whereas her cheeks had once been round and rosy, now her cheekbones stood out high and stark, making her eyes seem enormous, and draining every vestige of pink colour from her darkly tanned skin.

'Missy is here, sahib.'

Lucy squared her shoulders and held her head extra high as she walked into the study. She barely had time to register the presence of an elderly white-haired gentleman standing next to Mr Rutherspoon before the Reverend Mr Chester strode across the room and clasped her in his arms.

'My dear girl, my very dear Lucy.' He kept hold of her hand, shaking it repeatedly. 'What a pleasure this is! What a most unexpected pleasure! Only the sight of your father standing at your side could make the occasion more perfect.'

Lucy's smile was more than a little tremulous. 'He died as bravely as you would have expected, with no word of reproach for his murderers.'

'And now enjoys the heavenly reward to which he is so justly entitled. Sir Peter was one of God's most loving servants. Take comfort from that knowledge, my dear.'

'I do. But sometimes I am selfish enough to wish that he were still here with me.'

'You were close and loyal companions as well as father and daughter. Such feelings are natural, Lucy. It would be odd indeed if you did not miss him. The good Lord does not require you to be odd.'

'Ah, dear Mr Chester! You always make me feel that I am less unworthy than I had feared.'

'That is one of the requirements for keeping my job. My Employer has strict rules about it. It is written into my employment contract. I am to make His congregation feel worthy.'

Lucy astonished herself by giving a little laugh. 'And to think I was afraid you wouldn't recognise me!'

'There could be no danger of that, my dear. Your eyes have not changed, nor the stubborn tilt of your chin. You are a little thinner to be sure, but remember my hobby!'

'Your hobby? Oh, of course, sketching! You are a talented artist.'

'Well, that is being too kind, perhaps, but I do pride myself on my artist's eye.' He patted her hand, his smile becoming teasing. 'I always knew there was a classic oval face hiding behind those plump schoolgirl cheeks of yours.'

Lucy laughed again, surprising herself with the sound. '*Classic oval*? Come, dear sir. I'm afraid you have acquired a flatterer's tongue to go with your artist's eye.'

'I hope not,' Mr Chester said quietly. 'Flattery is false coin that does not enrich the giver or the receiver. But you must tell us what has been happening to you, my dear, while we all imagined you dead. Why do you not make yourself comfortable on the sofa beside Mr Rutherspoon, and tell us how you managed to make the journey across Afghanistan without losing your life? That is surely the greatest miracle in a whole series of miracles.'

'I had an escort,' Lucy said. 'A Muslim trader by the name of Rashid. He claimed to be from Lahore, and he seemed very familiar with the safe routes out of Afghanistan.' She held her breath, waiting for the district officer to jump in with the information that just such a man was wanted for the crime of stealing Enfield rifles from a British garrison.

However, the name Rashid seemed to conjure up no immediate images of a villain. Mr Rutherspoon said merely, 'These native merchants are the only people who really know the safe passages into Afghanistan, and into Tibet, too. I am forever telling our military fellows that they need merchants, not scouts, to get them safely across the mountains.'

The Reverend Mr Chester looked puzzled. 'But why did the Khan of Kuwar suddenly allow you to leave, Lucy, when he had been holding you prisoner for two whole years?'

'He didn't exactly allow us to leave,' Lucy said drily. 'On the contrary, he seemed quite determined to kill both me and the merchant.'

'So you managed to escape?'

'Yes, because the trader had horses and I was able to steal a supply of food. Otherwise we would never have survived the journey.'

The archdeacon and Mr Rutherspoon were both full of questions, which she answered willingly, giving the two men an account of her trek with Rashid across the mountains to the Khyber Pass.

'You are lucky the Afridi tribesmen didn't attack you,' Mr Rutherspoon commented as she finally drew her tale to a close. 'Our soldiers have been having a lot of trouble with them over these past few months. There's trouble brewing in Afghanistan, and all of us living in this part of India know it.'

'Do you think the Russians are stirring the pot?' Lucy asked.

Mr Chester coughed. 'Why did you ask about the Russians, Lucy? Do you have any special reason for supposing that the tsar is sticking his fingers into the Afghani pie?'

'Yes. The trader and I encountered a troop of Russian soldiers quite close to the Khyber Pass. They told us they were travelling from Qandahar to Kuwar and had lost their way. They mentioned they had messages to carry from Mohammed Ayub to the Khan of Kuwar.'

'Mohammed Ayub?' Mr Rutherspoon wrinkled his brow. 'You mean the exiled son of the Amir?'

'Yes, and from what the Russians told us it seems that he has ventured back into western Afghanistan.'

'I'm sure the viceroy's office would be most interested in that piece of news,' the archdeacon murmured. 'Could I ask you, my dear, to write an account of any political information you may have gleaned during your time in Afghanistan? I will take it back with me to Lahore and see that it is carried personally to the viceroy.'

'I am very willing to help in any way I can, but, other than this one incident, and my first-hand knowledge that the Khan of Kuwar is totally untrustworthy, I really had no opportunity to learn anything of significance during my period of captivity. Neither the Khan nor the elders of the village trusted me with their political opinions. Women in Kuwar are not considered thinking human beings, and I was a foreigner, which made matters worse.'

Mr Rutherspoon winced. 'I'm sure the archdeacon doesn't wish you to recount any horrors of a personal nature,' he said hurriedly. 'We realise there will be many — events — that occurred during your captivity that you will wish to banish from your memories entirely.'

'That is certainly true,' Lucy rose to her feet. 'For what it's worth, Mr Chester, you shall have your account of my imprisonment and of our meeting with the Russian soldiers.'

'Thank you, my dear.'

Lucy stared down at her hands. 'Now that we have established who I am, what do you suggest I do, Mr Chester?'

He smiled gently. 'Why, that is simple, my dear. I recommend that you go home as quickly as we can book you comfortable passage on a fast ship. You must go home to England, and to your family. The past is finished. The rest of your life awaits your homecoming.'

CHAPTER FOUR

ABDULLAH jumped from the top of the high wall surrounding Rutherspoon Sahib's garden and landed safely on agile, mud-encrusted feet. Rashid would have been pleased with his pupil's skill at evading detection. Abdullah had timed his arrival well. The travelling carriage was already waiting, hood down, silk-fringed parasols raised in protection against the sun. The doors of the bungalow stood open, and Abdullah craned forwards, parting the leaves of the bush for a better view.

A voice sounded in the doorway. A soft murmur of laughter drifted into the garden. Abdullah peered through the roses. A slender dark-haired woman was descending the steps, speaking quietly to the assembled servants. This is the one, he thought immediately. This is the Englishwoman who has stolen the heart of my master and carries it away with her across the ocean.

Rashid had left Peshawar two weeks ago, but he had been explicit with his instructions, and Abdullah chose the moment to carry out those instructions carefully. He waited until the groom and outriders were mounted on the carriage box and Rutherspoon Sahib had escorted the other two women back to the shade of the veranda. Then he jumped over the marble lion and took three swift strides to kneel at the feet of the Englishwoman.

'A present for you from Rashid, my master,' he murmured in Pashto, and pressed the little draw-string package into her gloved hands.

He waited only to be sure that she had clasped the gift, and then he was off, running across the garden on winged feet. The wall loomed ahead, but the rough plaster offered plenty of finger- and toe-holds to a boy of Abdullah's skill. Safely at the top, he straddled the wall for a split second, looking back towards the carriage.

The Englishwoman had opened the tiny leather bag and had seen what lay inside. She held the bag pressed close to her heart as she looked up at Abdullah. He saw tears sparkle at the corner of her eyes and spill over on to her cheeks. He watched in grim silence as her lips slowly formed the Pashto words for 'thank you'.

The comfort and convenience of travel between India and England had been greatly increased since Lucy's outward journey seven years earlier. The recent completion of the Suez Canal, linking the Mediterranean Ocean with the Red Sea, meant that ocean liners of virtually any tonnage could now pass from Asia to Europe unhindered by stretches of land. Lucy blessed the achievements of modern science, and the miracles of modern engineering, as the gleaming new Pacific and Orient steamship traversed the hundred miles of man-made waterway.

The endless, tranquil days at sea gave her ample time to rest and recuperate from the rigours of the past two years. Gripped by a lethargy that she didn't attempt to analyse, Lucy would have been content to stay drifting at sea forever.

Her detachment remained firmly in place until Mr Upton, the ship's captain, announced that they were crossing the Bay of Biscay and would soon be entering the English Channel. Within twelve hours, the ship would dock in the port of Southampton. Lucy realised that she was dreading her arrival in England, and the forthcoming meetings with her stepmother and stepsister. Wryly, she reflected that she was probably the only person on board who wished that the journey home from India still took several months, as it had done in the bad old days of sails, mutinous crews and precarious provisions.

Alone in her cabin, Lucy walked over to the dressing-table and sat down in front of the mirror. The candle-light flattered her brown skin, making it appear soft and tinted with pink. But even in candlelight she looked nothing like a blushing virgin, which was a mite unfair since she was precisely that.

Lucy sprang to her feet, impatient with the narcissistic trend of her thoughts. She was determined to make a useful life for herself continuing some of her father's charitable projects. Later on, she might even go back to India. . . Many activities forbidden to a young girl were permissable for a spinster who would soon celebrate her twenty-fourth birthday.

A spinster. The word stuck in her throat, echoing with loneliness. Unbidden, her hands moved to the tray on the dressing-table where a soft leather pouch rested next to her hairbrush. Lucy picked up the little bag, pulled open the neck cords, and allowed the object contained inside to drop into her hand.

The diamond eyes of the exquisitely wrought gold camel stared up at her arrogantly, but there was no cruelty or malevolence in the beast's expression. The craftsman who created this camel had worked with love and good humour, so that the animal appeared comic in its bad-tempered, cross-gaited dignity.

She stood abruptly, stuffing the costly trinket back inside its pouch. She took the cloak from the hook inside the small closet and wrapped it hurriedly around her shoulders. She would go up on deck and take a walk. It was the way most of her insomnia-plagued nights had ended during this voyage, and it seemed fitting that for these last few miles at sea her thoughts should once again be filled with Rashid. Heaven knew, his image had been with her on every other stage of the journey. She might as well accept the inevitable and carry him with her for these final hours. Tomorrow she would land in England and she would bury the memory of Rashid deep in her heart where it could no longer pain her. Tomorrow her love-affair with a Muslim trader from the Punjab would finally be over.

The boat-train arrived in London's Victoria Station from Southampton shortly after luncheon. Lucy, more

excited than she had expected to be, allowed a porter
to take her cases, then scanned the station for a glimpse
of Lady Margaret and Penelope. Now that the moment
of greeting was finally here, she realised how much she
was looking forward to seeing her family again.

She spotted her father's old housekeeper waiting on
the platform, and happiness surged through her. Lucy
had been less than three when her mother died in
childbirth. Mrs Burt, far more than any of Lucy's
nursemaids, had filled the role of mother. Lucy felt a
huge smile curve her mouth upwards.

'Burtie!' She covered the twenty yards of platform
that separated them at a run. 'Burtie! You haven't
changed a bit! How wonderful to see you.'

The housekeeper dipped into a curtsy, then gathered
her former charge into her arms. 'And it's wonderful to
see you, too, Miss Lucy.'

Lucy emerged breathless from the hug. 'Have you
been waiting long?'

'Only a few minutes. The train arrived right on time.
Wonderful how punctual these trains are, isn't it?
Thousands of miles of travelling and you arrived almost
to the minute; it hardly seems natural, does it? And
you look a fair treat, Miss Lucy.'

'It's good to be here. I don't even mind the rain!'
Lucy smiled. 'But where are my stepmother and stepsister? They are brave to sit in the carriage on such a cold
day.'

Mrs Burt avoided Lucy's eye. 'I hope you're not
feeling chilled, Miss Lucy. 'Tis miserable, wet weather
for June.'

They had reached the main exit to the station before
Mrs Burt could bring herself to tell the truth. 'There's
the carriage, Miss Lucy. Unfortunately, Lady Margaret
and Miss Penelope had luncheon arrangements and
they couldn't be here to meet you. I dare say they'll be
back at the house by the time we get there.'

The excitement in Lucy's face died. 'Oh, yes. Of
course. It was foolish of me not to realise they would
be busy.'

Lucy was accustomed to the noise and chaotic activity of Indian cities, but she still found herself overwhelmed by the size and busyness of London. Through the grey mist of rain, she peered out of the window at the huge shops, listening to Mrs Burt give a running commentary on the merits and failings of the various establishments. Farmer and Roger's Great Cloak and Shawl Emporium on Regent Street seemed to extract the housekeeper's highest measure of praise, and Lucy resolved to pay a visit there soon.

A little thrill of pleasure lightened Lucy's mood. Shopping for a new wardrobe in this city would undoubtedly be fun. And when she stopped to think about it, it was several years since she had had the chance to do anything just for fun.

'We've arrived, Miss Lucy. We're home.'

Even as the housekeeper spoke, one of the grooms opened the door of the carriage and let down the steps. Lucy scarcely had time for more than a quick glance around the quiet, tree-lined square before a footman with an open umbrella rushed to escort her into the house.

She stepped into the entrance hall.

'Good afternoon, Miss Lucy.' The butler greeted her with his most regal bow, snapping his fingers to indicate that the footman should take off her damp cloak and relieve her of her gloves. 'On behalf of all the staff, Miss Lucy, may I say how delighted we are to have you back in England?'

'Thank you, Fletcher. It's good to be back.'

'If there is any way I can be of service, Miss Lucy, you have only to ask.'

Seven years had added at least seven inches to his waistline, and she smiled mischievously. 'Well, I distinctly remember the last occasion on which you offered me your services, Fletcher. But I'm afraid that next time I get stuck halfway up the apple tree I won't be able to call on you to rescue me. Your *embonpoint* would prove disastrous to us both.'

Fletcher stared straight ahead. 'On the contrary,

miss, I could be of great assistance. Now that I am such an important personage, I could send one of my underlings to fetch a ladder.'

Lucy saw the twinkle in his eye and laughed. 'So you could! Ah, Fletcher, I have missed all my friends from the servants' hall these past few years.'

'The feeling is reciprocated, Miss Lucy.' The butler cleared his throat. 'Lady Margaret and Miss Penelope are waiting for you in the drawing-room, Miss Lucy.'

She drew in a deep, fortifying breath. 'Thank you, Fletcher. I shall join them now.'

Lady Margaret, ravishing in a day gown of dove-grey challis, and Penelope, equally ravishing in pale blue, rose to their feet as soon as Lucy entered the drawing-room. Penelope, looking sulky, stayed by the sofa, but Lady Margaret held out her hands and glided across the room, every movement delicate and graceful. At forty-four, she was still a stunningly attractive woman.

'My dearest, dear Lucy!' Lady Margaret bent her cheek in the direction of her stepdaughter's face, trailing a waft of ladylike violet perfume.

'My dear, let me look at you!' She stepped back, her china-blue eyes gloating as she summed up Lucy's damp and travel-stained appearance and contrasted it with her own daughter's pink-and-white prettiness. Well satisfied with what she saw, Lady Margaret smiled.

'Well, perhaps you are not quite in *bloom*, but you are here and that is the main thing. We must not be greedy, must we, Penelope?'

'No, Mama,' Penelope replied dutifully, although she hadn't the faintest idea what her mother was talking about.

Lady Margaret stretched her smile a little wider. 'Dearest Lucy, I'm sure it is miracle enough to have you home with us. We could not hope you would return looking as fresh and unspoiled as you did on the day you left for that ill-fated mission to Afghanistan. After such dreadful experiences as you have endured, it is only to be expected that you would appear so thin and wretched.'

'I take heart, Stepmama, from the fact that I am nowhere near as thin and wretched as I was a month ago.'

Lady Margaret's smiled hardened. 'Such bravery! Such determined cheerfulness in the face of disaster! I am all admiration, and so is your sister, isn't that so, Penelope?'

'Yes, Mama.'

'And you, Lucy, you absolutely must not worry about *anything*. My dearest child, take my word for it, we will soon have you restored to perfect health.'

'My health is excellent, thank you. The weeks on board ship——'

'Your courage is a lesson for us all, but I beg you, Lucy, do not lie awake at night worrying about your bizarre appearance. Don't fear that I shall force you to go about in society until you are completely recovered. I would not *dream* of asking you to expose yourself to public view at this point in time. Above all, you mustn't despair about your complexion, whatever other people may have said to you. Even though you are so dreadfully brown that one might mistake you for. . . That is to say, Dr Burberry's patented cucumber lotion has been known to improve *far* worse cases than your own.'

'That is certainly an enormous relief,' Lucy said, producing a smile as broad and insincere as Lady Margaret's own. She decided there was something almost reassuring in the fact that her stepmother had changed so little. The difference was that Lucy no longer found her stepmother's barbs wounding.

A tiny frown marred the otherwise unwrinkled perfection of Lady Margaret's brow as she observed her stepdaughter's amusement.

'Much has happened in your absence, Lucy. Your sister is on the verge of forming a most eligible connection.'

'Penelope, I'm so pleased for you!' Lucy crossed the room and kissed her stepsister with genuine warmth. 'Whoever the man is, he is lucky to have found somebody so pretty to be his wife.'

'He says I am a perfect English rose,' Penelope reported proudly, fluffing her curls.

'A gentleman of acute perceptions, I can see,' Lucy teased her gently.

Penelope merely looked blank, so Lucy tried again. 'Goodness, it's hard to believe you were in the schoolroom when I last saw you, and now you are old enough to fall in love!'

'He is a baron,' Penelope said, as if this explained everything. 'His uncle is under-secretary of state for eastern affairs. He is going to be an important man in the government, and I shall be a Society Hostess.' There was no doubt that the words were capitalised in her mind.

Lucy struggled to contain her amusement. 'I hope I may be invited to one of your dinner parties. And who is this soon-to-be-important man in the government?'

'Lord Edward Beaumont, third Baron Ridgeholm.' Lady Margaret breathed the words on an ecstatic sigh. The daughter of an earl herself, she had never quite forgiven a world which required her to marry first an elderly baronet and then Sir Peter Larkin—a mere knight, whose title had been awarded as a result of his unaristocratic talent for making money. Her daughter's success in snaring the attentions of a peer of the realm had kept Lady Margaret in a state of tingling excitement for days.

'Is the engagement already announced?' Lucy asked.

'Not precisely, but we expect the Baron to make his declaration at any moment,' Lady Margaret said. 'He has been overseas for the past six months on an assignment from the foreign office. He returned only three weeks ago and sent a message to us *immediately*. We understood the significance of his prompt attentions, of course——'

'It means he is interested in me,' Penelope interjected, anxious for her sister to share this understanding.

Lady Margaret directed a withering glance towards her daughter. 'As I explained to Penelope, we must honour Lord Ridgeholm's scruples in not seeking to pay his addresses before he went overseas. Naturally, it would not have been proper to seek a promise from her when he was going so far away.'

'He went to India,' Penelope remarked. 'I would not have liked to go there with him, even though he is a baron. I *hate* India. It smells.'

'Was it Baron Ridgeholm's first visit to that country?'

'Not at all. He was there shortly after your father died and was assigned to discover the truth about precisely what had caused the massacre of the British trade mission to Amir Sher Ali.'

'He apparently had little success.'

'That cannot be wondered at,' Lady Margaret said. 'Everybody knows there is no understanding the Afghanis. I'm sure Lord Ridgeholm did his best. He dealt with all the people who move in the *highest* circles of the Raj. He was invited to spend a weekend in Lahore with the viceroy himself.'

'Very impressive, but perhaps not the most useful way to occupy his time if he was trying to uncover what had occurred in central Afghanistan?'

Lady Margaret dismissed the complaint with an airy wave of her hand. 'He was *most* attentive to me and to your poor sister, helping to arrange our passage back to England and taking care of a hundred annoying details for us. We saw him several times upon his return to England, but then he was sent abroad again and has only just returned. In view of our hopes for Penelope, we could not consider refusing when he invited us to join him and his uncle for luncheon today.'

'Naturally not.' If there was irony in Lucy's voice, neither her stepmother nor Penelope heard it. 'But am I understanding you correctly? Lord Ridgeholm hasn't actually proposed marriage to my sister, or even declared that his affections are engaged?'

'Mama is confident we'll be able to bring him up to scratch any day now,' Penelope confided.

Lady Margaret winced. 'Darling, I have explained before that we don't refer to the Baron's intentions in those vulgar terms. A lady does not anticipate a gentleman's declaration. She simply behaves towards him with her usual innocent charm.'

Penelope didn't blink an eye at this outrageous untruth. 'Yes, Mama. I understand, Mama.'

'Do you love him?' Lucy asked quietly. 'You are still only nineteen, Penelope. There is plenty of time for you to make a love match, you know.'

Penelope stared at her stepsister in astonishment. 'Of course I love him,' she said. 'He is a *baron* with estates all over the country.'

Lucy sighed. 'Of course,' she said. 'I can see at once what a lovable person he must be. Is he handsome?'

For the first time, Penelope appeared uncertain. 'He is. . .he is very distinguished-looking,' she said. 'And he is fun to talk to. I can always understand what he's saying, not like some of the other gentlemen who prose on for ever about international relations, and parliamentary elections, and all those horrid, boring things. He just talks about my clothes and I tell him where I have been shopping. He knows everything about the latest fashions, and he always notices when I have a new fan or when I have changed my hair-style.'

In view of his employment at the foreign office, Lucy hoped that Lord Ridgeholm also knew at least a little bit about the Indian sub-continent, although from her sister's description she was not optimistic.

'Perhaps it is time for us to speak of your late father,' Lady Margaret said.

'He did not suffer at the end, Mama. The bullet struck him in the heart and his death was almost immediate.'

Lady Margaret breathed deeply. 'I do not wish to discuss the manner of your father's end. I advised him repeatedly not to go to Afghanistan. He chose not to listen to me and the consequences were inevitable.'

Lucy walked over to the windows and clutched one of the heavy gold tassels tying back the crimson velvet drapes. She was not going to shed tears in the company of people who cared so little about her father's murder.

'If not his death, then what did you wish to discuss in regard to Papa?'

'When you go to your bedroom, Lucy, you will find several communications waiting for you from the family's solicitor. I cannot help but remark that your late father disposed of his estate in a remarkably odd fashion.'

'Oh?'

'For reasons I shall never understand, your father chose to leave all his capital and property to you.'

'To me?' Lucy turned around. 'But what about you and my sister?'

'He provided an. . .adequate. . .dowry for Penelope and a small lifetime income for me. However, I am sure you can see that this is yet another occasion where your father's quirks and starts have created a most unsatisfactory situation.'

Lucy didn't doubt that it was extremely unsatisfactory for her stepmother, whose tastes ran from the merely costly to the super-luxurious. It would be interesting to see what size of lifetime income Lady Margaret chose to designate as 'small'.

Still, the terms of her father's will shocked Lucy greatly, since it had never occurred to her that she would inherit his entire estate. Lady Margaret was looking at Lucy anxiously, a hectic flush staining her cheeks. No wonder her stepmother's earlier barbs had been sugar-coated, Lucy thought with a flicker of amusement. In effect, Lady Margaret and Penelope were both her pensioners, a reversal of roles she found almost comic.

'There is another matter,' Lady Margaret announced, each word obviously costing her pain. 'Since you are not dead, the monies I have expended over the past two years were not actually mine to spend.'

Lucy could not dispel an ignoble desire to pay her stepmother back for countless moments of previous humiliation. She produced a smile, kinder and sweeter than one of Lady Margaret's own.

'Please, dear Stepmama, I beg you not to give the

matter another moment's thought. I would not *dream* of prosecuting you for spending *my* money. I shall speak to the solicitor first thing tomorrow morning and arrange matters so that the purchases you and Penelope have made during my absence are not deducted from your next quarter's allowance. Of course, I rely upon you in the future not to exceed the income Papa allotted you.'

Lady Margaret, for once in her life, was bereft of speech. Lucy was ashamed to discover that she felt no guilt.

Penelope, however, was anxious to get priorities taken care of. 'Will the money Papa left me be enough to pay for my trousseau?' she demanded.

'I'm sure it will,' Lucy said, 'although I can't promise since I haven't yet read the correspondence from the lawyers.'

'You won't have time to read their letters before tea,' Penelope said. 'It's nearly three o'clock, which means you have only an hour to change. Lord Ridgeholm is coming especially to meet you.'

'Please make my apologies for today,' Lucy said. 'I need to deal with all the correspondence from the lawyers, and besides, I have nothing suitable to wear.'

Her stepsister nodded seriously. 'You could come to dinner,' she suggested. 'The Baron won't be here. He has to attend some silly old reception at the Russian embassy, so we shall be dining alone.'

'In that case, I shall look forward to joining you. Is it eight o'clock, as always?'

'Eight o'clock,' Lady Margaret agreed faintly. 'We shall be dining strictly *en famille* for the next few days.'

'You may start inviting guests again quite soon, Stepmama,' Lucy remarked kindly. 'I plan to go shopping tomorrow and I dare say by the time I have bought some new clothes you will be able to present me almost anywhere without disgracing yourself. Fortunately, two years as Hashim Khan's slave didn't destroy my memory of which fork I must use, or how to drink soup. It's only my memory of how it feels to be loved and wanted that has been destroyed.'

She left the room before either Lady Margaret or Penelope could summon up a reply.

The first few days of Lucy's return to London were crammed full of visits from lawyers, estate managers and bankers, all anxious to convey to her the news that she was a very wealthy woman. A wealthy woman, moreover, who could dispose of her riches in virtually any manner she chose, unhampered by the constraints of a male guardian.

To the relief of her various advisers, this extraordinary state of affairs did not seem to unhinge her. Aside from fulfilling several charitable bequests outlined in her father's will but not yet funded by Lady Margaret, Lucy made only minor changes in the administration of her estates. These, her advisers noted happily, were all designed to enhance efficiency.

It was the height of the season, so that Lady Margaret and Penelope were frequently absent from the house. At night, however, the three ladies invariably dined together, and without company. After a week of meals where the conversation centred almost exclusively on Baron Ridgeholm's pronouncements concerning Penelope's various gowns, and Lady Margaret's calculations of how soon he might be induced to propose, Lucy decided that it was past time for her to meet this eligible prospect.

'When can we expect to see this elusive Baron at dinner?' she asked. 'I am so much looking forward to meeting such a paragon.'

Her stepmother and Penelope exchanged conspiratorial glances. 'Penelope and I both agree that you should become acquainted with her future betrothed, and we believe we have the perfect occasion in mind. We think you should meet Lord Ridgeholm at a ball.'

'Do you have any particular ball in mind?'

Lady Margaret rushed to explain. 'The fact of the matter is, Lucy, dearest, that before we heard you were still alive Penelope and I had already spent a great deal of time planning a ball to be given here in the grand ballroom. It has never been used since your father bought the place, and it's really a shocking waste to have all that gilt and crystal waiting upstairs unseen and unused.'

'I'm sure Papa would want us to have the ball,' Penelope explained. 'Remember how he was always telling us "Waste not, want not"? Just think how wasteful we are being with his ballroom.'

'I'm not absolutely sure that was the sort of wastage he had in mind,' Lucy murmured. Seeing her stepsister's crestfallen face, she relented. 'Did you get as far as setting a date for this ball?'

'Oh, yes! We sent out invitations as soon as we knew Lord Ridgeholm was back in England. Mama said even you could not be so mean-spirited as to refuse to pay the bills for a function that was so important to my future.'

Lady Margaret winced. Lucy choked back a little laugh. 'I'm delighted to know you have such faith in my basic good nature,' she said. 'May I know when I am hosting this ball so that I can take care of one or two trivial details, such as ordering a ballgown for myself?'

'A week on Saturday,' Lady Margaret confessed. 'My dear, I'm sure you will enjoy the occasion and find the Baron a most delightful prospective brother-in-law.'

Lucy was, she admitted to herself, somewhat curious about this man who so completely dominated the conversations of their household. She looked at Penelope, who was holding her breath, and found herself smiling with shared anticipation. 'A ball sounds wonderful,' she said. 'How many arrangements do we have left to make?'

On Saturday morning—the day of the ball—the Larkin household awoke to a brilliant blue sky, a refreshing breeze and a warm burst of golden sunshine. As far as Lady Margaret and Penelope were concerned, the glorious weather added a final promise of success to an occasion they were already convinced would be the hit of the season. Lucy was far more nervous about the ball than either her stepmother or stepsister could have guessed from her calm demeanour. London might be a more sophisticated city than the border town of Peshawar, but Lucy didn't doubt that she would still be the object of much behind-the-hands gossip.

There was one advantage at least to the fact that her reputation was irreversibly sullied: she had no obligation to dress herself in virginal white. Set free to choose the most dazzling of her Indian fabrics, Lucy had indulged herself with a formal gown of peacock-green silk, tantalisingly draped around the bustle with sea-foam-coloured gauze draperies.

Madame Renier had avoided the mistake of dipping the neckline of the ballgown obviously low, and Lucy, relieved that her shoulders were not completely naked or her bosom excessively exposed, neglected to notice that the gown contained little of the whalebone stiffening and padding that normally disguised the true shape of the wearer. Peering into the looking-glass merely to frown over her tanned complexion, she never noticed that the cut and trim of the bodice not only flattered her tiny waistline but also emphasised the generous curve of her breast. Delighted with the soft rustle of her skirts, she twirled around her bedroom without the faintest clue that she looked like an exotic bird of paradise preparing to take its place among a cluster of sparrows.

'You look magnificent, miss,' her dresser murmured, fixing a jewelled aigrette into Lucy's hair. 'What necklace are you going to wear tonight, miss?'

Lucy picked up a diamond pendant that had been her mother's, then set it down again on its velvet bed. Her gaze turned to the leather pouch that lay, as always, on the dressing-table. Before her conscious mind could reject the action, her fingers reached out and pulled the little gold camel from its home. Its diamond eyes winked at her mockingly, as if it had known all along that tonight it would come to the ball.

'I'll wear this instead of a necklace,' she told the dresser. 'Could you pin it in the centre of my dress, here?'

The dresser fastened the final button on Lucy's obligatory kid gloves, then handed over her fan. 'Here you are, miss. I'm sure you'll be the belle of the ball.'

Lucy laughed with wistful amusement. 'Thank you, Rose.'

Lady Margaret and Penelope were waiting in the drawing-room when Lucy arrived downstairs. Penelope wore a white tulle gown, scattered with seed pearls and looped with satin rosebuds.

'Oh, there you are, Lucy! Do you like my dress?' She held out the skirts as she executed an expert waltz-twirl. 'Mama says I look like every man's dream of innocence.'

'You look wonderful,' Lucy said, banishing an unworthy twinge of envy. 'You, too, Stepmama. That shade of lilac is most becoming.'

Lady Margaret condescended to smile. Secure in the knowledge that she and Penelope represented all that was most desirable in English womanhood, she felt inclined to be generous.

'And you look quite nice, too, Lucy. Your new gown is a most — er — interesting colour.' A happy thought struck her. 'Indeed, you will show off Penelope to excellent advantage as we greet our guests. Perhaps it is as well that you didn't attempt to gloss over realities by wearing white.'

'Yes, that was my own opinion entirely,' Lucy said, realising that for once Lady Margaret had no intention of being rude.

'What is that brooch you are wearing?' Penelope asked. 'Do you see, Mama? It's a camel, isn't it, Lucy?' She shuddered. 'Ugh, I hate camels.'

'In that, sister, dear, we are in total agreement.'

'Then why do you wear the brooch?'

Because it makes me feel that perhaps Rashid has not totally forgotten me. Because, as he plans his next foray into Afghanistan, I wonder if he will think of those nights we spent in the mountains. . .and the night when he took me into his arms and kissed me and made me understand what it means to be a woman.

Lady Margaret spoke absently. 'Yes, Lucy, why did you choose to wear something so singular?'

'The. . .person who gave me the brooch knew how much I loathed the beasts and it became something of a joke between us. Do you see how the camel's eyes twinkle with a mischievous light?'

'They are diamonds,' Penelope said, bewildered. 'Of course they twinkle. That is what diamonds do.'

Fortunately, Lucy was spared the need to attempt any further explanation by the arrival of their first guests for the pre-ball dinner.

The guests were all assembled when Fletcher finally announced the arrival of the under-secretary for eastern affairs, Lord Triss, and his nephew, Edward Beaumont, third Baron Ridgeholm. Lucy's head jerked up sharply, curious to see the man who had caused such flutterings of hope and speculation within her family circle.

A tall, lean, aristocratically featured man stood in the doorway, immaculate in formal evening attire of white tie and tails. Although he was doing nothing more remarkable than crossing the room to greet his hostesses, he seemed to command attention by the sheer power of his physical presence.

Involuntarily, Lucy's hand reached up to clutch the camel nestled at her breast. For a moment, she swayed on her feet as the room spun around her in a dizzying whirl. Gripping the back of a nearby chair for support, she willed herself to remain upright. She looked again at Lord Ridgeholm.

The Baron was bowing low over Lady Margaret's hand. 'Dear lady, what a treat this is for us all to be here in your home on such a jolly evening. You even procured us the perfect sunset to admire as we stepped out of our carriages at your front door.'

Lady Margaret tittered. 'The sunset required *all* our powers of organisation, my lord. Penelope and I are so pleased you were able to accept our invitation.'

'Ah, yes, Miss Penelope.' Lord Ridgeholm screwed a monocle into his left eye, and took Penelope's hand. 'How charming you look, to be sure, Miss Penelope. An English rose, encircled by rosebuds. Such a jolly sight!'

Lucy didn't bother to listen to any more of Lord Ridgeholm's drivel. Her breathing slowed, her heart ceased pounding, and the world slowly righted itself on to a normal axis. Dear God, but she was becoming obsessed! Her memories of Rashid were beginning to dominate her powers of rational observation. For a split second — for one wild, insane instant — she had actually thought Lord Ridgeholm was Rashid!

The Baron and Penelope were still engaged in conversation, so Lady Margaret introduced Lucy to Lord Triss.

The under-secretary, a middle-aged man of average height and keen eye, shook her hand with enthusiasm. 'I'm delighted to make your acquaintance at last, Miss Larkin. You are a young lady of outstanding courage, and it is a privilege to meet you. I knew your father, you know, and he was a fine man. He is sorely missed by his colleagues and by his country.'

'Thank you, my lord. I miss him, too. He was my friend as well as my father.'

Lord Triss gave her hand a final, brisk shake. 'Some time very soon we must have a long talk about your experiences in the East. We have too few people in our government who know anything about Afghanistan, and I warn them that it is a country which will likely cause us trouble.'

'I should be happy to share with you any insights that I have, my lord. I agree with you completely about the potential danger our country faces in Afghanistan. As long as the Russian Emperor persists in sending troops to annex territory in central Asia, I fear that the borderlands of India can enjoy no peace.'

Lady Margaret's silvery laugh barely concealed the underlying thread of her displeasure. 'Now, now, Lucinda, you must not tease Lord Triss with your advice on how to run the government of India. Despite your long exile from civilisation, you must know we cannot have political discussions at one of my parties.'

'The fault was entirely mine,' Lord Triss said. 'I apologise, Lady Margaret, for introducing unseemly topics into your drawing-room. Miss Larkin, I shall look forward to speaking with you at a later date but, in the meantime, may I introduce my nephew, Edward Beaumont, Baron Ridgeholm?'

Lucy sank into the requisite curtsy, experiencing a ridiculous sense of disappointment when she lifted her gaze and found herself staring straight into the distorted, bulging left eye of the baron. She had never before had any opinion about gentlemen who used monocles. Now she discovered that she found them absurd.

'I understand we have each returned recently from the same country,' Lord Ridgeholm remarked. 'India. Tedious, hot sort of place, isn't it? Demmed flies are enough to drive a fellow demented.'

Lucy was determined to be polite. 'Not all of India is hot, my lord. In the hill country, the climate can be quite pleasant.'

Lord Ridgeholm lowered his voice confidentially. 'Tell you the truth, Miss Larkin. It isn't only the climate that tries a fellow, it's dealing with the demmed natives. From the highest to the lowest, they're all the same. You can't trust the traders in the bazaar, and you can't trust those wretched maharajas. Sign a treaty with an Indian maharaja, and by Jove he'll break the terms before the ink on the paper is dry.'

'Maybe if we didn't constantly force the maharajas to sign treaties they would prefer not to sign, we would find their honour longer-lasting,' Lucy snapped.

'Oh, I say, that's jolly good.' Lord Ridgeholm removed his monocle and polished it busily. 'But misguided. Natives never want to sign *any* treaties, Miss Larkin, that's the trouble. There's no pleasing them, you know. They're not in favour of progress like we more enlightened people are. Why, I met one old fellow who told me that what his village needed wasn't a telegraph office but more buffaloes!'

Lucy had a guilty suspicion that before she met Rashid she, too, might have thought telegraphs more important than buffaloes. She fixed her mouth into a polite smile, grateful for once to retreat into feminine inanity.

'I'm sure you would know better than I how to deal with the Indian natives, Lord Ridgeholm. Naturally, I have no experience in negotiating with maharajas.'

'Naturally not.' The Baron gave a short bray of laughter. 'The world would be a sorry place if we had the ladies negotiating our treaties for us, wouldn't it, Miss Larkin?'

'Since I cannot imagine the men ever allowing us such a privilege, Lord Ridgeholm, I had not speculated on the outcome.'

'Indeed, speculation can sometimes lead to dangerous conclusions, can it not, Miss Larkin?' The inanity of the Baron's smile belied the sudden seriousness of his tone. Apparently losing interest in her views of treaty negotiation, he adjusted his monocle and peered intently at her bosom.

'I say, that's a most interesting brooch you're wearing, Miss Larkin, if I may make so bold. Saw a lot of camels in India, of course, but never could get accustomed to them, myself. Preferred the elephants. Quite comfortable to ride an elephant once you get used to the sway. Unusual piece, that brooch.'

'It was a gift from an Indian friend,' Lucy said stiffly, hating the reminder of Rashid in the presence of this oaf who seemed to exemplify precisely the type of Englishman Rashid had so often mocked.

'Quirky creatures, those natives. They make carvings of the oddest things. Inside some of their temples. . .'

Lord Ridgeholm obviously recalled just in time that the statuary inside Indian temples was rarely a fit subject for an English lady's ears. He cleared his throat. 'Ahem; I should say, the workmanship on your camel isn't bad at all, despite the odd choice of subject.'

He reached out and very delicately lifted the camel
for closer inspection. At no point did his finger touch
Lucy's dress, let alone brush against the bare skin
above the lace-bordered neckline. For some inexplicable reason, however, she found herself holding her
breath, and when Lord Ridgeholm let the brooch fall
back against her dress she was literally shaking.

'A jolly little piece, isn't it?' he said, turning to greet
the hovering Penelope with a broad if vacuous smile.
'It's been delightful chatting with you, Miss Larkin. We
must talk some more about India very soon.'

Not if she had any choice in the matter, Lucy
thought, sighing with relief as she heard the butler
announce that dinner was served.

Lord Ridgeholm was the dominating figure at the
table. On his way home from India, he had served as
the official British observer at the signing of a treaty
between Turkey and Russia. Having spent three whole
days in the company of Turkish and Russian diplomats,
he now considered himself an expert on the subject of
central Asia. Despite Lady Margaret's edict against
political discussion, he seemed determined to expound
his conclusions for the benefit of the dinner-table at
large. Lucy soon realised that his opinions were com-
pounded chiefly of ignorance, liberally interspersed
with the worst sort of imperialist dogma.

By the end of the meal Penelope, who had barely
concealed her yawns during her beloved's discussion of
British imperialism, was bubbling and smiling again as
Lord Ridgeholm devoted his attention exclusively to
her. Having delivered himself of fifteen minutes of
nonsense about Asia, Lord Ridgeholm seemed all set
to spend the rest of the evening discussing Penelope's
clothes.

They will make ideal marriage partners, Lucy
decided. Good-looking, but with scarcely a brain to
share between them. Heaven help their children!

Lucy had no idea why the thought of Penelope's and
Lord Ridgeholm's children depressed her so pro-
foundly, unless it was because she could detect not the

smallest sign that either potential parent was actually in love with the other. Her hand crept up to the neckline of her gown, and her fingers closed around Rashid's camel. The gold felt warm, almost vibrant, from contact with her body. Unaccountably, her gaze flew to Lord Ridgeholm at the other side of the table. His head was in profile and he seemed fully engaged in talking with her sister, but Lucy could not shake the odd impression that he had, in fact, been looking at her. Heat — which must have been caused by too much champagne — flamed in her cheeks as Lord Ridgeholm leaned closer to Penelope, bending his head to hear some murmured confidence.

She would have to swear off champagne for the rest of the night, Lucy decided. The unaccustomed alcohol was giving her a most irrational desire to weep.

CHAPTER FIVE

THE guests gathered for Lady Margaret's ball agreed it was destined for success even before the musicians struck up the notes of the first waltz. Lucy was relieved to discover that she did not lack for partners, and for a few dances she revelled in the harmless, almost forgotten pleasures of light flirtation. The covert glances and snide comments that had followed her in colonial India did not seem to be a problem here in cosmopolitan London. It was Cedric Ffoulkes who enlightened her to reality. Lucy knew him only as the brother of one of Penelope's friends. They had scarcely taken a single turn around the ballroom when Ffoulkes's hand crept upwards from her waist, splaying out against her spine and propelling her so close that the requisite twelve inches between her body and his was precipitously narrow.

'Mr Ffoulkes, you are crushing the front of my gown,' Lucy said, smiling to soften the impact of her words.

Ffoulkes's hold became tighter and more overtly lecherous. 'No need to pretend with me, m'dear, I'm a man of the world. Your stepmother explained how you managed to stay alive out there in Afghanistan. Tonight's entertainment must seem pretty tame in comparison to what you've been accustomed to over the past few years.'

'If you consider it entertaining to tend a vegetable garden with your bare hands, to wash clothes in an ice-cold mountain stream, and weave goat-hair into car-pets, Mr Ffoulkes, then indeed the last two years of my life have been one long round of reckless gaiety. I myself never managed to find much that was amusing in such occupations.'

Cedric Ffoulkes was no longer smiling. 'Cut line, Lucinda. If the tribesmen had wanted gardeners, they wouldn't have enslaved a woman. We all know how those savages love to get their hands on a white woman. Tell me, m'dear, were they very — rough?'

Lucy was shaking so hard she was afraid her knees might not support her, but she refused to give Ffoulkes the satisfaction of seeing her distress.

'I do not recall that I gave you permission to use my Christian name, Mr Ffoulkes. I would be grateful if you would escort me back to my stepmother. Let me assure you that you labour under several misapprehensions.'

Ffoulkes totally ignored her request to leave the dance-floor. 'No need to get on your high horse, m'dear. Nobody's blaming you for seeking re-entry into society. After all, it wasn't your fault you were captured.'

'You're too generous, Mr Ffoulkes.'

He preened. 'It's a pleasure to be generous to a woman like you, Lucinda. You just need to understand that if you re-enter society it will be on our terms. Your gown shows that you're a woman who knows how to make the most of yourself, and you will receive plenty of offers. I want to get mine in first. I will show you the best of good times, m'dear, inside the bedroom and out.'

Some miracle of self-preservation prevented Lucy from slapping his face. Despite her anger, she realised that if she precipitated a scandal on the dance-floor her reputation would be shattered beyond repair. Refusing to respond to any of his conversational gambits, she counted out the remaining bars of music, then tore herself from his arms and marched off the floor without once looking to see if he followed.

'Oh, Lucy, isn't it a lovely ball?' Penelope asked, her cheeks flushed, her smile pretty.

'Delightful.'

'Lemonade, Miss Larkin?' the Baron asked politely.

She could barely control her trembling sufficiently to speak, much less hold a glass. 'Thank you, but not at the moment.'

'I think you would find the taste refreshing, Miss Larkin. Pray, allow me.'

The cold glass was placed firmly in her hand and her fingers wrapped around it. She took a sip simply because it was easier than arguing and found, to her surprise, that the sharp tang of the lemons did serve to calm her. She jumped when she realised that Lord Ridgeholm had moved much closer to her and was talking again.

'It is very warm in here with so many candles blazing, isn't it, Miss Larkin?'

Dear heaven, didn't the man ever talk about anything save clothes and the weather? Lucy sighed, forcing herself to respond politely.

'Yes, it's surprising, but somehow ballrooms always seem to become overly warm.'

'That being the case, Miss Larkin, would you care to accompany me out on to the balcony for a breath of fresh air?'

The prospect of breathing some cool night air was suddenly more than appealing.

'Thank you,' she said, with real gratitude. 'Some fresh air would be welcome.'

Once outside, the Baron leaned against a stone support pillar and stared down at the moonlit garden.

'Are you pleased to be back in England, Miss Larkin?'

'Well, yes, I had thought so.' She sounded so hesitant, even to herself, that she added briskly, 'Of course I am delighted to be home.'

Lord Ridgeholm did not seem to hear the subtle undertones of doubt in her reply.

'Have you had a chance to explore any of the London shops as yet, Miss Larkin? I'm sure it's a pleasure for all of us who have spent time in primitive countries like India to discover that within a half-mile walk we may purchase new boots, select the style of a new overcoat, and admire the latest fashion in Parisian hats.'

To her amazement, Lucy found herself responding to his smile. 'I have explored *dozens* of London's shops,

my lord. The most delightful thing is that I still have so
many more left to visit!'

'If I may say so, Miss Larkin, your purchases have
been made to delightful effect. Your gown is exquisite.'

Lucy put down her empty lemonade glass, her smile
fading as she remembered Cedric Ffoulkes's insulting
comments about her dress. Her voice stifled, she admitted, 'I fear that the cut and the vivid colour may create
a. . .a wrong impression.'

Lord Ridgeholm examined her gravely. 'Not to any
man of discernment, Miss Larkin. The cut merely
reveals the skill of an expert dressmaker. As for the
colour, it is the perfect complement for the auburn high-
lights in your hair and the creamy colour of your skin.
The impression is altogether delightful, I do assure you.'

Lucy felt her lacerated pride begin to heal itself
under the baron's soothing words. No wonder Penelope
liked to listen to him talk about clothes, she thought
with wry amusement. 'Thank you,' she said. 'I am
honoured to have pleased such a connoisseur of feminine fashions.'

Lord Ridgeholm beamed. 'If you are cooler, Miss
Larkin, perhaps we might take a toddle around the
dance-floor? I believe the musicians are getting ready
to play another waltz.'

Lord Ridgeholm might have the vocabulary of a
schoolboy and the political understanding of a gnat,
Lucy reflected, but his manners were superb. Her sense
of perspective returning, Lucy dismissed Cedric
Ffoulkes as an oaf and a scoundrel.

'I would love to dance,' she said, placing her gloved
fingertips lightly upon the Baron's outstretched arm.

'Jolly good,' he replied. 'Shall we go in?'

Lucy soon discovered another reason why her sister
Penelope so much enjoyed Lord Ridgeholm's company:
he was, quite simply, the best dancer she had ever
partnered. Unlike Ffoulkes, his hand seemed barely to
touch her spine and yet he managed to convey every
nuance of his intentions. Asking occasional courteous
questions about her journey home from India, the

Baron twirled her around the ballroom in an odd, half-dazed state that she could not properly identify. She supposed that it must be the reaction to her horrible experience with Cedric Ffoulkes that caused her to focus so obsessively upon Lord Ridgeholm's dark, aristocratic features.

Lord Ridgeholm did not look in the least like a typical Englishman. More like an Arab or even a man from further East. . . Lucy broke off her wild thoughts. Lord Ridgeholm's skin was slightly tanned, as might be expected with somebody who had just returned from six months in India. He was, of course, nowhere near as dark as Rashid, nor did his hair have the same glistening sheen. . .

A ripple of unease coursed down Lucy's spine as she realised how consistently her thoughts returned to the same bizarre fantasy. Lord Ridgeholm must have felt the slight tremble of her body. He looked down at her, and she stumbled, missing the beat of the dance.

Lord Ridgeholm eased her back into the simple rhythm. 'Are you cold, Miss Larkin? I trust you didn't take a chill while we stood talking on the veranda.'

'No, I'm not cold.' And indeed she was not. The surface of her skin had begun to burn with little prickles of heat.

The Baron guided her into a final, dazzling spin and for a split second she felt his gloved hand against the naked skin of her back. She sank into a curtsy. He bowed, as protocol decreed, over her hand. 'Jolly good show, Miss Larkin. That was a splendid dance, what?'

'Yes, splendid. Thank you.'

When Lucy walked off the dance-floor, she was shaking again, but this time it wasn't with rage, or even with fright. It was with desire.

Lucy spent the rest of the night wondering who was the fool. Lord Ridgeholm, Baron, about to become engaged to Penelope Deveraux. Or Lucinda Larkin, spinster, obsessed by the memory of a vanished Punjabi trader.

* * *

During her two years in Kuwar valley, Lucy had learned much that was usually kept hidden from young, unmarried English ladies. With these insights to guide her, Lucy had long since realised that Rashid attracted her. For some reason, the Punjabi trader aroused emotions and passions within her that no other man had ever evoked. She supposed it was inevitable that Lord Ridgeholm should provoke some of the same passionate feelings as Rashid, given that her mind kept making a bizarre connection between the two men. The comparisons churned around in Lucy's head until she eventually dropped into a light, uneasy doze.

'Your tea is getting cold, miss.'

Lucy dragged open her eyes and sighed. 'What time is it, Rose?'

'Almost noon,' her maid replied, 'and there is a gentleman from the foreign office waiting in the drawing-room to speak with you.'

Lucy's heart gave a little leap. 'Lord Ridgeholm?'

'No, Miss Larkin. 'Tis a Mr Percy. He's personal secretary to Lord Triss, so he says. I've brought hot water up, so's you can wash, miss.'

Half an hour later, Lucy was downstairs. The affable and deeply apologetic Mr Percy explained that the new British ambassador to Russia was about to leave for St Petersburg, and Lord Triss very much wanted Miss Larkin to discuss her impressions of Afghanistan before the ambassador left England. This afternoon at two o'clock was the only time the ambassador could spare from his hectic round of pre-departure engagements. Could Miss Larkin join the under-secretary at the foreign office in Downing Street for a brief discussion?

'I have explained to Lord Triss that my experience in Afghanistan was very limited. I was confined to a small valley and, like the other women, I was not allowed to be present at any of the village elders' discussions. However, such impressions as I have I will be happy to pass on. Two o'clock this afternoon will be quite convenient.'

'Lord Triss will be most grateful. He realises you must be tired after last night's ball.'

'Since I escaped from Kuwar valley, I have scarcely known the meaning of the word tired. The lives of the Afghanis, particularly of the women, are unimaginably hard by our standards. I find that after two years of constant labour, I crave activity. I shall be glad to have something constructive to do this afternoon rather than sitting at home and receiving endless courtesy calls.'

'Lord Triss will send his carriage for you, Miss Larkin. He insists that you should not be put to the inconvenience of bringing out your horses. It will be here at half-past one.'

The room Lucy was escorted into later that day appeared more like a pleasant sitting-room than an office. Only the papers overflowing on the corner desk indicated that business was indeed conducted in this congenial setting.

Lord Triss and three other men rose to their feet as the footman closed the office door behind Lucy. The under-secretary came forwards and took her hand.

'My dear Miss Larkin, I am most grateful to you for accepting my invitation at such short notice. May I introduce His Excellency, the Viscount Merton, who will shortly become our ambassador in St Petersburg? And you already know Lord Ridgeholm, of course, and Mr Percy, whom you met this morning. If you don't mind, Percy will take a few notes to remind us all of what we say.'

Lucy acknowledged the introductions, while Mr Percy pulled up a chair for her and saw to it that she was provided with a cup of tea. As soon as Lucy was settled Lord Triss began to speak. 'Forgive me if I seem to lecture you, Miss Larkin, but I want to explain why I am so anxious for our ambassador to hear your story. As you know, Mr Disraeli, the Prime Minister, is an ardent proponent of what has become known as the "forward policy".'

'I am familiar with the term,' Lucy said quietly. 'In

contrast to Mr Gladstone, his predecessor, Mr Disraeli believes that we should protect our imperial rights in India by vigorously asserting control over all neighbouring and buffer states, particularly in the north. He considers Afghanistan a legitimate sphere of British influence, and that was one of the reasons my father was asked to head a trade mission to Amir Sher Ali.'

'Very concisely put, Miss Larkin. You may not know that Mr Disraeli has warned Amir Sher Ali that he may not sign any treaties without first getting approval from the British government. In other words, Great Britain will consider any attempt by Afghanistan to exercise an independent foreign policy as an act of aggression.'

'Unfortunately,' Viscount Merton interjected drily, 'the Russian Emperor believes in the identical policy, except with a Russian twist. He believes that Imperial Russia should protect its southern borders by vigorously asserting control over all neighbouring and buffer states. He considers Afghanistan a legitimate sphere of Russian influence. That is why he is attempting to sign "friendship" treaties with the Amir of Afghanistan. The Emperor considers any undue British interest in Afghanistan to be an act of aggression. So far, he has not defined what he means by "undue interest".'

Lucy could not help thinking that the policy of both Britain and Russia had more in common with small boys arguing over who owned which toys than with sensible adults resolving important world issues.

Lord Triss tugged at his moustache. 'The problem is, of course, that Afghanistan cannot be both a Russian and a British sphere of influence at one and the same time. And at the moment we have no idea whether the Amir favours signing a treaty with Great Britain or with the Russian Tsar.'

Lucy could no longer keep silent. 'I would guess, my lord, that his preference would be to sign nothing. I imagine the Amir dreams of an Afghanistan which is free to make its own decisions, unhampered by the power-plays of two alien giants.'

Lord Ridgeholm spoke for the first time. 'What

would give you such an idea, Miss Larkin? Do you have any reason for supposing the Afghanis don't appreciate our honest offers of trade, industry and the other benefits of modernisation?'

'The best of good reasons, Lord Ridgeholm. They murdered my father and his entire delegation rather than honour the treaty we had required them to sign.'

'Then why did they sign the treaty in the first place?' the Viscount demanded irritably. 'Your father didn't ride in with an army of soldiers at his back, demanding compliance.'

'The Afghanis don't like to argue with their guests, and they viewed the trade delegation as guests. Just as we neither understand nor trust the Afghanis, so they neither understand nor trust the people of the western world. The Afghani code of honour is extremely strict. It merely operates on quite different principles from the ones on which we Britishers base our behaviour. Agreement between our governments is likely to prove very difficult to achieve simply because quite often we genuinely won't understand each other.'

'If the Afghanis have such high regard for their guests, then why was your father's delegation ambushed while still under the Amir's protection?'

'By Afghani standards, the Amir had no part in that ambush,' Lucy explained quickly. 'We know that the Khan of Kuwar was paid to do the deed by the Amir, but that is no offence as far as the Amir is concerned. We had never been guests of the Khan, so no rules of hospitality were broken.'

'A meaningless distinction, surely.'

'Not from the Amir's point of view. I have listened to many conversations between Afghanis, and I understand the rules. Few things are ever stated directly. I would be willing to stake my life on the fact that the Amir never openly expressed his wish that our trade delegation should be murdered. The Khan of Kuwar merely read between the lines and drew the correct conclusions.'

The ambassador frowned. 'If Amir Sher Ali is so

anxious to remain independent, why has he recently
sent out unmistakable signals indicating that he would
be willing to sign some sort of mutual defence agreement with the Tsar?'

'Perhaps because he wishes to have some counter-
weight to the overwhelming and threatening power of
the British Raj in India?'

The ambassador stiffened. 'The British Raj is no
threat to any peaceful nation!'

'But the Amir may not understand that. He is like a
mouse, wondering how best to hide from the two
elephants fighting over his head. If he cannot dig into
the ground and remain invisible, what choice does he
have but to climb on the back of whichever elephant
seems less threatening?'

'A very vivid description, Miss Larkin, but what if
we do not want the mouse to climb on the back of this
particular elephant?'

'Then I dare say we could crush it. But is that really
necessary? Our government sees every move made by
the Amir as a threat to our position in India, whereas I
suspect that much of what the Amir does is related to
his position *within* Afghanistan.'

Lord Ridgeholm spoke again. 'Could you clarify for
us, Miss Larkin, why you have this impression? Are
you aware of specific incidents that you feel threaten
the Amir's control over his own country?'

Lucy was surprised to discover just how many political opinions she had formed during her two years in
Afghanistan. Aided by skilful questioning from Lord
Triss, she explained about the fierce tribal and personal
loyalty which motivated most Afghans. 'The idea of a
nation is alien to them,' she said finally. 'It is a foreign
idea, imported less than a hundred years ago. Any ruler
in Kabul will have to win the loyalty of local tribal
leaders by repeated acts of valour, or at least by proving
that it is more profitable to be part of an Afghan nation
rather than simply a member of, say, the Kuwari tribe.'

'And, in your opinion, has Amir Sher Ali won that
loyalty?' Lord Triss asked.

'I think not. He has merely succeeded in putting down local rebellions, usually with the help of foreign weapons, and that is not the same thing as earning personal loyalty. Afghani tribesmen can be bribed into fighting for the Amir on a short-term basis, as I believe the Khan of Kuwar was bribed to murder my father. But in the end the vast mass of Afghani people will require more than threats and bribery to keep them loyal to a central government. They will need pride in the man who leads them.'

'In the meantime,' Lord Triss muttered, 'loyalties can be bought by whoever holds out the promise of the biggest bribe. And at the moment I fear it is the Russian Emperor who is dangling the most enticing carrots. Our government is intent upon offering threats, not promises.'

The ambassador sounded worried. 'We certainly don't want the Russian Emperor taking over control of Afghanistan. He has already seized power in far too many of those central Asian states. Can you imagine the consequences if there were Russian soldiers garrisoned all along the northern frontier of India? There's no guessing what mischief the Tsar would get up to once he had a toe-hold on the Indian subcontinent.'

'And the Tsar is certainly stirring the Afghan pot,' Lord Triss said. 'We have evidence of his meddling in the internal politics of the country. Miss Larkin, please explain to the ambassador about your encounter with Russian soldiers almost at the foot of the Khyber Pass.'

'You know about that incident?' Lucy asked in some astonishment.

There was a tiny silence, then Lord Ridgeholm rose to his feet. 'More tea, Miss Larkin?' He took her cup without waiting for her reply. 'The Reverend Mr Chester reported your experience to the appropriate officials in Lahore,' he explained. 'The report was eventually transmitted to London and came across my uncle's desk.'

'But we would appreciate a first-hand account,' Lord

Triss emphasised. 'If you could tell us your impressions of exactly what happened, Miss Larkin?'

To the best of her ability, Lucy described the encounter, the roles she and Rashid had played, and the Russian lieutenant's revelation that his troops of soldiers had been in contact with one of Amir Sher Ali's exiled and rebellious sons.

'The Amir's hold upon his throne is shaky,' Lucy concluded, 'and like any other cornered animal he is likely to prove dangerous. He will use any means he can find to protect his position.'

'And you think a treaty with the Russian Emperor is one method he may use?' the ambassador demanded.

'Either that, or the Russian Emperor may decide to dispense with Amir Sher Ali altogether and install one of his own puppets on the throne. The presence of Russian soldiers so far south suggests that the Tsar has decided to take an active interest in who sits upon the throne of Afghanistan.'

Lord Triss and the ambassador continued to question Lucy closely for another half-hour, at which time the ambassador was forced to leave for another appointment. He shook hands with Lucy, offering generous praise for the insights she had provided.

'I will send for my carriage,' Lord Triss said as soon as the ambassador had left the room. 'Miss Larkin, I echo the Viscount's compliments. I cannot thank you enough for all the information you have provided. Your first-hand observations will prove invaluable not only to the ambassador but also to me when I present my recommendations on Afghanistan to the foreign secretary.'

Lord Ridgeholm rose languidly to his feet. 'With your permission, Miss Larkin, we won't send for my uncle's carriage. A walk home through St James's Park would be very jolly, if you would allow me to escort you.'

Lucy happened to be looking at Lord Triss, and she thought she detected a hint of laughter in that gentleman's shrewd grey eyes. She turned somewhat uncertainly toward the Baron, but could detect no cause for his uncle's amusement. Lord Ridgeholm, monocle and vacuous smile both in place, looked exactly as he always did.

Nevertheless, even in the Baron's sometimes tiresome company, a walk through the park promised to be pleasant. Since returning to London, Lucy had felt her body stiffening from lack of exercise.

'Thank you,' she said. 'It's a lovely afternoon and a walk would be refreshing.'

The long, soft twilight of an English summer day had barely begun as they entered the park, and a few children were still bowling hoops along the paths. The lake gleamed silver in the setting sun. Ducks squawked as they surfaced from the mud with tasty water-snails or other delicious bugs, and a royal keeper threw fish to the waiting pelicans. Strolling alongside Lord Ridgeholm in an unexpectedly peaceful silence, Lucy felt herself seized by the same odd mixture of contentment and restless expectancy that had gripped her last night when she waltzed with him.

'I trust you are quite recovered from the exertions of the ball?' he queried politely.

'Quite recovered, thank you. Enjoying oneself is hardly an exhausting occupation.'

'Indeed not. But as hostess you had several irksome situations to take care of. Making sure the good bishop did not doze off into his soup-plate must have required a certain amount of ingenuity.'

Lucy swallowed a gurgle of laughter. 'Last night he remained awake to listen to you, my lord. He seemed to find your remarks on Turkish and Russian politics most enlightening.'

'And you, Miss Larkin? I gather you did not share the bishop's admiration for my views.'

'There is no reason for you to suppose that, my lord.'

'On the contrary, Miss Larkin, there is every reason.' He laughed softly. 'Shall I tell you why? Although you always remember to keep your expression fixed into a miracle of polite blandness, you never remember to control your voice. Believe me, it speaks volumes.'

Lucy clasped her hands in front of her in an effort to disguise the odd trembling that had begun to overtake her. Only one other man had ever possessed the uncanny ability to read her thoughts. She stared up at the Baron, looking for. . .looking for she knew not what.

'Very well, my lord, if my voice has already betrayed the truth, I will admit it. I am not convinced that three days in the company of a few diplomats qualifies you as an expert on the aspirations and motives of two large and complex empires.'

'I have also read several good books on the subject,' Lord Ridgeholm offered mildly.

Could that possibly be laughter she saw lurking behind his concealing monocle? But surely the Baron didn't have sufficient intelligence to mock himself in such a subtle fashion? Lucy shook her head to clear it of a sudden dizziness.

'I saw my sister at luncheon today,' she said, feeling an obscure need to remind herself that this man was shortly destined to become her brother-in-law. 'Penelope was in raptures over the exciting time she had last night at the ball. She mentioned particularly how much she enjoyed your company and the several dances she shared with you.'

'Miss Penelope is still young,' Lord Ridgeholm replied. 'If she marries the right man, I am sure she will become a happy and loving wife. At the moment, she needs constant encouragement about her own good qualities, so that she will not feel so desperately inadequate in relation to you.'

'*In relation to me?*' Lucy could not have been more astonished if the Baron had suggested that Penelope felt inferior to the local crossing sweeper. 'But she is probably the most beautiful débutante in London this year!'

'And a widgeon whose mama has not allowed her to develop a single independent thought on any important topic. Have you never noticed how intimidating she finds your exceptional intelligence?'

'I never thought. . . She is so pretty. . .' Lucy stumbled to a halt, and once again turned to look at her companion. The Baron returned her gaze with a flash of his monocle and a typical, meaningless smile. Unbidden, a vivid memory flashed into Lucy's mind of Rashid dealing with the Russian soldiers. He, too, had disguised his quick-wittedness and his acute perceptions behind a façade of blank stupidity.

'My lord. . .' Her tongue suddenly felt too thick and clumsy to voice the questions that buzzed insistently in her head. How could she ask a respectable English nobleman to remove his monocle and sweep back his hair so that she could check for the scar that had run high into a Punjabi trader's hairline? She looked down at his hands. They were gloved, of course. What else had she expected? It would have been the height of bad form for a gentleman to walk out in public without his gloves. Why hadn't she thought to look at his hands when they were in Lord Triss's office? Now it was too late.

'Is something bothering you, Miss Larkin?'

She drew air into her constricted lungs. 'Yes, something bothers me. I want to know. . . I need to know if you are. . .'

If you are the Punjabi trader who rescued me from the Khan of Kuwar. If you are the man who kissed me that night under the stars. I want to know if you are the man I fell in love with, despite all the barriers that should have kept us apart.

She sought desperately for some words that might be more socially acceptable, then seized on them gratefully when they finally came to her. 'I would like to know if we have ever met before, my lord. In Afghanistan, or in India, or. . .or somewhere like that.'

There was an infinitesimal pause before he replied. 'If we had met before, Miss Larkin, I am quite certain I would remember the occasion.'

Lucy was too accustomed to the subtle evasions of

Afghani conversation not to notice that Lord Ridgeholm hadn't precisely answered her question. Her heart began to hammer at suffocating speed.

'My lord, will you please answer me directly? I must have a straightforward reply. Have we ever met before?'

They were passing under the spreading arch of two rows of ancient horse-chestnut trees, and the Baron's face was in shadow, his voice flat and uncompromising. 'No, Miss Larkin, we have never met. Whatever gave you the idea that we had?'

His denial could hardly have been more absolute. Lucy tried to ignore the wave of desolation sweeping over her. 'A feminine fantasy, my lord. It was nothing important.'

They walked in silence for a few hundred yards, until Lord Ridgeholm gave a bark of inane laughter. 'We've made excellent time, by Jove! Look — we're almost back at your house, Miss Larkin.'

Lucy smiled grimly. 'Jolly good show,' she said.

On Monday morning Lucy decided it was time to take a stern grip on her wandering imagination. Rashid was a gun-runner plying his trade somewhere in the Punjab. Lord Ridgeholm was an English baron, about to propose marriage to Penelope. Clearly, no connection between the two men existed save in Lucy's overwrought mind.

'Do you accompany us to Amelia Ffoulkes's morning concert of harp music, Lucinda?' asked Lady Margaret.

'Thank you, Stepmama, but unfortunately I still have a great deal of legal correspondence to catch up on. I fear I must forgo the treat of hearing Miss Ffoulkes play.'

Lucy escaped to the cosy tranquillity of the room that had once served as her father's study. She read through several papers, then walked over to the empty fireplace and curled up in the leather armchair that still bore the imprint of her father's body on its worn surface.

She had many advantages, she realised, in planning

for her future. Few women ever enjoyed the degree of independence that Lucy had acquired under the terms of her father's will. She pondered her situation all morning, and by lunchtime had reached her decision. Her father had always wanted to bring the benefits of free schools and skilled doctors to the people of India. She would dedicate her life to making the projects he had dreamed of a living reality. In the process, she would provide herself with a useful, stimulating way to occupy her time.

Her goals might be idealistic, but Lucy's experience had taught her to be practical in pursuing those goals. She had been ostracised by the Kuwari villagers for the crime of being a foreigner. She had been ostracised by the ladies of Peshawar for the crime of surviving a massacre. And she had been insulted by Cedric Ffoulkes for the crime of living unprotected among Afghani tribesmen. Despite her wish to bring improvements into the lives of the less fortunate, she had no desire to spend the rest of her days as a social outcast. She didn't want to be forever excluded from intimacy with the people living around her, and from the warmth of everyday friendships.

Mulling over the problem as she sipped a cup of coffee, Lucy reached the only logical conclusion. If she was not to remain an outcast, she would need to redeem her reputation, and the best way for a woman of any social level to redeem her reputation was to marry. Therefore, she would marry.

Fortunately, Lucy saw no particular obstacle to achieving her goal. She didn't rate her personal charms especially highly but she placed great faith in the power of her father's fortune. She felt confident that a generous enough payment would entice any number of impoverished aristocrats to overcome their moral scruples about marrying a fallen woman. Her only dilemma seemed likely to be which impoverished aristocrat she should choose as her lifelong partner.

At lunchtime, Penelope dropped the news that Lord Ridgeholm was once again coming to tea.

'His attentions become more marked every day,' Lady Margaret exclaimed. 'Dearest child, I live in *hourly* expectation of receiving his request to pay you his addresses.'

Lucy's resolve to settle her own future hardened. Spurred on by a curious inner urgency, she visited her lawyers that very afternoon. Only with the greatest reluctance was Mr Dunstead finally persuaded to arrange interviews with one or two suitably impecunious scions of the aristocracy.

Three interviews were accordingly arranged, during which a drunken earl and two pompous viscounts made it plain that they considered Lucy's money barely adequate payment for the honour of bestowing their names and bankrupt titles on the daughter of a man who had made his fortune in trade. Lucy rejected them all, well aware that her rejections were met with nothing but relief. Her dark beauty and all too evident intelligence had not been considered assets by any of the three prospective husbands.

Lucy's unsuccessful foray into the husband-market left her depressed but not defeated. She soon decided that she had aimed her sights in the wrong direction. What she needed was a prospective husband who shared her goal of service to humanity. Clearly, what she needed was to marry a minister of religion. What better way to restore her respectability?

Penelope's betrothal to Lord Ridgeholm still had not been announced, but the aura of breathless anticipation throughout the Larkin household had reached oppressive proportions. On Tuesday afternoon, less than a week after her interview with the drunken earl and the two viscounts, Lucy set off in pursuit of fresh quarry.

Reading in the morning newspaper that the foreign missionary society was holding its quarterly meeting, Lucy dressed herself in sober grey linen, and set off for the genteel suburb of Brixton where the headquarters were located. She passed through rooms crowded with ministers recently returned from darkest Africa, and ladies sorting garments intended to clothe naked savages. Eventually she came upon the small room filled with missionaries dedicated to the task of bringing salvation to the peoples of India.

They were all, every one of them, good, kind men, Lucy decided two hours later. Unfortunately, their enthusiasm for converting heathens was equalled only by their total ignorance of the culture they planned to supplant.

Exhausted by her inability to bring any touch of reality to the missionaries' discussions, Lucy sadly abandoned her hopes of finding a soul mate and, leaving a large donation, summoned her carriage for the drive back to town.

Her mood as she changed for dinner was distinctly gloomy. She would not have believed that finding a husband could prove such a difficult business.

Lucy's mood was not improved when she reached the drawing-room and discovered that her stepmother was hosting an 'intimate' dinner party for at least thirty people. The only guests Lucy recognised were Cedric Ffoulkes and Lord Ridgeholm. A charming choice for a pre-dinner chat, she decided acidly. She could either be propositioned or driven crazy by fantasies.

Lord Ridgeholm solved the problem of deciding which man represented the lesser evil. Leaving Penelope surrounded by a coterie of admirers, he sauntered over and cornered Lucy by the punch bowl.

She made no attempt to hide her displeasure. 'Good evening, my lord. I did not expect to find you dining here again tonight.'

'And I am delighted to see you, too, Miss Larkin.'

His tone of voice was so bland that she wondered if he understood the irony of his own remark. She searched his face for any hint of laughter but could find none. With a small inner sigh, Lucy reached for the punch ladle.

'Allow me,' Lord Ridgeholm said, expertly filling a glass and passing it to her. His hands, she noted, were as smooth and manicured as the hands of any other British aristocrat. She sighed again, angry at her inability to stop searching for non-existent clues. The Baron didn't seem to hear her sigh. He smiled cheerfully. 'There has been no sign of rain for the past week. It seems as if we are going to enjoy a dry spell ——'

'Do not,' she said, her voice low and passionate, 'do not, I beg of you, talk to me about the weather.'

Lord Ridgeholm adjusted his monocle. 'Not even the weather in India?' he asked.

'*Especially* not the weather in India.'

Lord Ridgeholm appeared nonplussed. 'But I am such a poor conversationalist, Miss Larkin.'

'Then now will be an ideal opportunity for you to improve your skills.'

'But what if I make some grievous error, Miss Larkin? If I may not talk about clothes or the weather, I fear I may stumble on to some subject which a gentleman should never discuss with a lady. For example, I might find myself telling you that you are particularly beautiful when you are angry and that your eyes sparkle with the richness of warm sherry when you look at me. Worse yet, I might tell you that one small curl has escaped from your carefully arranged chignon and now nestles against your cheek in a way that makes me yearn to see your hair spread out on my pillow. My powers of conversation are so limited that I might even find myself telling you that your lips have parted as you listen to me, and when I see them tremble I wonder if you long to kiss me as much as I long to kiss you. Would you care for some more punch, Miss Larkin?'

Lucy's heart was pounding so hard that she felt as if she would suffocate. 'Who are you?' she demanded. '*Dear God, who are you*?'

Lord Ridgeholm thrust his glass into the hands of a passing footman. 'A fool,' he said, his voice harsh with self-condemnation. 'I am an arrogant, unthinking fool. I beg you will accept my apologies.' He dipped his head in a curt nod. 'Your servant, Miss Larkin.'

He swung on his heel and pushed his way across the crowded drawing-room. Only the butler's stentorian announcement that dinner was served prevented Lucy from running after him.

At ten o'clock, the ladies retired to the drawing-room to drink tea and suppress boredom by gossiping about any acquaintances not present to defend themselves. The gentlemen remained at the dinner-table to drink port, smoke cigars, and regale each other with bawdy stories.

Etiquette decreed that no lady could stand up as the men entered the drawing-room, but tonight Lucy had no interest in obeying the dictates of convention. Murmuring that she had spent too much of the day sitting down, she stood on guard by the door, ready for action. Since her reputation was already tattered, she felt it scarcely mattered if the guests were confirmed in their opinion that Miss Lucinda Larkin was unacceptably 'fast'.

Lord Ridgeholm was the fifth gentleman through the door. With a quick glissade, Lucy thrust herself in front of her stepmother and bared her teeth at the Baron in a predatory smile.

'My dear Lord Ridgeholm!' she proclaimed, linking her arm through his as if they were the best of bosom friends.

'Miss Larkin.' There was a certain wry resignation in the Baron's acknowledgment.

'My lord, you simply must come and see the interesting photographic plates my father produced during his stay in the Punjab. I know you would find the pictures he took with the Maharaja of Jaipur utterly fascinating.'

'I'm sure I would, Miss Larkin. Is it absolutely necessary to see them now?'

'Yes.' She didn't bother to elaborate, but simply propelled the Baron out of the drawing-room into the hallway. Lucy marched the Baron along the hallway and into her father's study. She indicated the small sofa.

'Please sit down, my lord.'

He complied without comment.

'Here are some pen and ink sketches of Calcutta,' she said. 'You will see that my father has captured the mood of the bazaar to perfection.'

Lucy carried the portfolio over to the sofa. Deliberately clumsy, she managed to trip over a bump in the Turkish carpet. The portfolio of sketches scattered in a wide arc over the Baron and the sofa.

'Oh, my goodness!' Fluttering her hands, Lucy sank on to the sofa alongside the Baron. She clutched at various floating pieces of paper and succeeded in wafting several sketches on to the far side of Lord Ridgeholm.

'Allow me,' the Baron said, moving to get up.

'Oh, no, please don't disturb yourself!'

Lucy plucked up the necessary final ounce of courage and leaned across Lord Ridgeholm's lap, pretending to reach for a flimsy tissue tracing. Abandoning any pretence at the last moment, she reached up and pushed back the lock of hair that always seemed to flop forward over the left side of his forehead.

She found the evidence that she had longed for — and dreaded. Disappearing into the Baron's hairline was a narrow white scar that looked as if it had been etched by the path of a bullet. Lucy sat motionless on the sofa, her hand resting against the Baron's forehead, blood coursing like wildfire through her veins. The silence thickened, filling with bittersweet memories.

Slowly, the Baron reached up and covered her ice-cold fingers with the warmth of his own hand. 'Ah, Loo-sie,' he said, his voice soft with rueful laughter. 'You did not have to go to such lengths to discover the truth.'

She finally managed to speak. 'You told me we had never met.'

'I lied. For both our sakes.' He removed his monocle, tossing it impatiently on to a side-table, no longer tolerating the disguise. Then he turned and cupped her face with his hands. His eyes burned with a fever she had seen in them once before. 'God in heaven, Loosie, what am I going to do about you?'

'Kiss me?'

She could not believe she had actually said the words out loud.

He stared at her as if mesmerised. 'Dear God, I must not. Do not let me commit this folly, Lucy.'

Even as he spoke, his head bent closer to hers, his dark gaze betraying the intensity of his desire. Her lips parted in breathless anticipation until finally — finally — he claimed possession of her mouth.

The moment she felt the hard, seeking pressure of his kiss, Lucy was lost. The months of separation vanished in a flash. Her body became flame, her mind a spinning void. Reality began and ended with the sensations that consumed her. Her body remembered the pleasures of Rashid's touch, and her breasts grew heavy with need. She reached out, twining her hands in the thickness of his hair, urging him closer. When his fingers reached inside the ruffled neckline of her gown, her pleasure intensified until she moaned softly.

He bent to kiss the swell of her breasts where they crested above the lace of her gown.

'Lucy, help me.' He murmured the plea against her skin, his voice harsh with need. 'Lucy, tell me that I must stop. Tell me that I must not use you so.'

For answer, she clasped her hands more tightly around him and kissed the top of his head while he nuzzled her breasts.

'Do not stop, my lord,' she whispered. 'My lord, please do not stop.'

The significance of the muffled shriek she heard took several seconds to penetrate Lucy's passion-clouded brain. Only when the Baron stood up and walked over to the window did she grasp the fact that they had been discovered — and by her stepmother of all people.

'And what, may I ask, is the meaning of this utterly *shocking* display?'

CHAPTER SIX

LORD RIDGEHOLM had remained silently by the window ever since Lady Margaret entered the study. He appeared lost in thought and hadn't once turned to look at either woman. Lady Margaret was on the very brink of speaking when his voice interrupted the strained silence of the room.

'Lady Margaret, I think it would be helpful if Miss Larkin were permitted to retire.'

'Lord Ridgeholm has the right of it, Lucinda. Go to your room, please. I will make your excuses to our guests and speak with you later.'

Lady Margaret was considerably relieved when her stepdaughter, after one anguished glance in the direction of the Baron's uncommunicative back, left the room without saying a word.

'You will already have deduced, my lady, that I have a high regard for your stepdaughter. I am aware of the fact that you are not officially Miss Larkin's guardian. However, since you stand in the role of her mentor, I would like to ask your permission to request Miss Larkin's hand in marriage.'

'My lord, I appreciate your offer for my stepdaughter's hand but, as I have said before, it is unnecessary. You have not ruined Lucy's reputation, she has no reputation to ruin. I plan to recommend that she leave for Hallerton tomorrow in order to make a prolonged stay in the country.'

Lifting his monocle, Lord Ridgeholm surveyed Lady Margaret with a cool scrutiny she found extremely disconcerting. 'Let me say, my lady, that I understand you very well,' he remarked at last. 'Allow me to assure you that nothing would deter me from offering marriage to Miss Larkin if it were not for the fact that I believe she will be far better off without me.' He paused for a

Relax with
FOUR FREE
Temptations

plus two FREE gifts!

Temptations offer you all the age-old passion and tenderness of romance, now experienced through very contemporary relationships. And to introduce to you this powerful and highly charged series, we'll send you **four Temptations plus two FREE gifts** when you complete and return this card. We'll also reserve you a subscription to Reader Service which means you could enjoy:

■ **FOUR BRAND NEW NOVELS** sent direct to you each month.

■ **FREE POSTAGE AND PACKING** we pay all the extras.

■ **FREE MONTHLY NEWSLETTER** packed with special offers, competitions, author news and much more.

■ **HELPFUL FRIENDLY SERVICE** telephone our Customer Care team on 081-684 2141

Turn over to claim your
FREE Temptations and FREE gifts.

FREE books
and gifts claim

Yes! Please send me four Temptations and two FREE gifts without obligation. Please also reserve me a subscription to Reader Service; which means that I can look forward to four brand new Temptations for just £7.40 each month (subject to VAT). Postage and packing is FREE. If I decide not to subscribe I will write to you within 10 days. Any free books and gifts will remain mine to keep. I understand that I may cancel or suspend my subscription at any time. I am over 18 years of age.

7A3T

Ms/Mrs/Miss/Mr _____

Address _____

_____

_____ Postcode _____

Signature _____

Offer closes 31st March 1994. The right is reserved to refuse an application and change the terms of this offer. One application per household. Overseas readers please write for details. Southern Africa write to Book Services International Ltd., Box 41654, Craighall, Transvaal 2024. You may be mailed with offers from other reputable companies as a result of this application. Please tick box if you would prefer not to receive such offers. □

Mills & Boon
Reader Service
FREEPOST
P.O. Box 236
Croydon
CR9 9EL

moment, then added, 'Unfortunately, I am not really in a position to offer marriage to Miss Larkin.'

'What do you mean?' she asked worriedly. 'Why are you not in a position to offer marriage, my lord?'

For a moment it seemed he would not answer, then he shrugged. 'I shall be leaving shortly on another mission for my uncle. I am likely to be overseas for some time in a rather remote part of the world.'

'Oh, is that all?' Lady Margaret smiled in relief. 'My dear, *dear* Lord Ridgeholm. A trip overseas is no reason to abandon all thoughts of matrimony. Knowing that the *right* wife waited loyally for your return would make your months overseas fly by on wings of happiness. If you were married to somebody suitable to your station — a young, innocent, beautiful girl like Penelope, for example — your future would be settled. Think how delightful it would be to know that your faithful helpmeet waited quietly for your return in the cosiness of your own dear home.'

'Beaumont Hall has twenty-four bedrooms,' the Baron commented neutrally. 'It could more easily be described as an oversized, under-heated railway station than a cosy little home.'

'My lord, do you not realise that under the ministrations of the right woman even a railway station may begin to feel like a home?'

'I realise precisely that,' Lord Ridgeholm said quietly. 'It is one of the reasons I have found it so damnably difficult these past few weeks to prevent myself from begging Lucy to marry me. She can not only make a mountain campsite feel like home, she is also the most beautiful and courageous woman I have ever met. However Lucy deserves far more than I am able to give her, and in my calmer moments I accept that fact. But now, if you will excuse me, Lady Margaret, I wish to remove myself from temptation before I take some action we shall both regret. I bid you good evening.'

Lady Margaret pulled feebly on the bell rope. 'I will ask Fletcher to show you out, my lord.'

'Thank you.' The Baron inclined his head in a curt nod. 'With your permission, Lady Margaret, I will await my carriage in the hall. I think we have little left to say to each other.'

Next morning, summoning Rose, Lucy politely requested the maid to pack for an extended stay in the country, and explained she would be leaving the next morning for Hallerton, her childhood home.

'I would very much like you to accompany me, Rose, but I won't be entertaining a great deal, and I understand if you would prefer to seek another, more exciting post in London. I would, of course, pay you this quarter's salary in lieu of longer notice.'

'I'll come with you, Miss Lucinda, if you don't mind.'

'Why, thank you, Rose,' Lucy said. 'I shall enjoy Hallerton so much more in your company. I have a few errands to complete this morning, before we leave. Could you choose a cape for me to wear?'

Lucy left the house with an absent-minded nod for the footman, and a firm refusal of his offer to summon the carriage. She desperately needed to walk—and to be alone. For a split second, she wondered if she ought to have brought Rose with her, then dismissed the question as absurd. At this stage in her life, her reputation had passed well beyond the point when it could be redeemed by the presence of a maid. Solitude was a luxury she could now permit herself.

Her thoughts tumbled in hopeless, unsettling confusion for the twenty minutes it took her to walk to the bachelor quarters the Baron shared in his uncle's house. Beneath all her confusion lay the bitter ache of hurt feelings. She could understand, perhaps, why Lord Ridgeholm had chosen not to reveal his true identity during their dangerous escape from Afghanistan. She couldn't begin to understand why he had deliberately lied to her ever since her return to London. Was he afraid that she would make some ridiculous appeal to his sense of honour? Was he afraid that she would insist upon an offer of marriage simply because they had been forced to spend lonely nights together under the

stars? Could he possibly have understood her character
so little?

Lucy found number twenty-five St James's Street
without difficulty. As she raised the gleaming brass
knocker on the front door, it occurred to her that the
Baron might not be at home. He undoubtedly took his
duties at the foreign office more seriously than she had
once supposed.

'Can I help you, madam?' A stout, dignified butler
surged forward, the personification of disapproval. In
well-appointed bachelor households, unaccompanied
ladies didn't knock upon the front door.

'I would like to speak with Lord Ridgeholm,' she
said. 'Please give him my card and tell him that I plan
to leave town tomorrow. He will understand that the
matter is somewhat urgent.'

The butler showed her into a small, unheated drawing-room. 'I will see if his lordship is at home, madam.'

Lucy walked over to the window and eased herself
behind a high-backed chair, lifting the lace curtain so
that she could see out into the garden. In Kuwar most
of her life had been spent outdoors and, since her
return to England, she had sometimes found the over-
furnished rooms of London town houses claustropho-
bic. Looking out over a lush prospect of green grass
and leafy trees helped to lessen her feeling of
oppression.

'Uncle Harry, what the devil have you done with. . .?
Lucy!'

She whirled around at the sound of Edward's voice
and they stared at one another in taut silence.

'I'm sorry,' he said at last, gesturing to his clothes. 'I
had no idea you were in here.'

He wore narrowly striped formal morning trousers,
but he had not bothered to put in the studs needed to
fasten his shirt. It hung open, revealing his white linen
undershirt and several inches of darkly tanned skin.
Convention demanded that he should leave the room
immediately. Since he didn't leave, Lucy ought to have
kept her gaze averted from this blatant exposure of

masculine flesh. Instead, they continued to gaze at each other, both of them seemingly afflicted with an identical paralysis.

Lucy finally managed to swallow. 'How did you darken your skin?' she asked.

His gaze was fixed on her mouth, and he blinked before answering her question. 'With a tobacco dye,' he said. 'It's virtually impossible to wash off, except with a special lye soap that removes almost as much skin as it does brown dye.'

Why did you kiss me last night? Why did you leave without coming to see me? What do you feel when you look at me? Lucy stared down at her hands. 'Where did you learn to speak Pashto so fluently, my lord?'

'My grandfather took me out to India when I was sixteen and we discovered that I have a knack for picking up foreign languages.' He turned abruptly. 'I should not. . . I cannot stay here with you, Miss Larkin. I'm not dressed to receive visitors. I was looking for my uncle and had no idea you had called.'

Lucy suddenly regained the use of her legs. She hurried across the room, putting her hand on his arm to stop him leaving. 'Edward, please don't go! There is so much I must ask you.' She used his name unconsciously, not even aware that she had done so. 'Oh, Edward, why didn't you tell me the truth? Why did you deliberately set out to deceive me? In the park, when I asked if we had ever met before, why did you lie?'

Edward swung around, his eyes dark with remorse. 'Lucy, I didn't want to lie to you. I did what I thought would be best for *you*. Dear God, can you not see that it would be a thousand times better if you had never discovered the truth?'

'No. Why would it have been better?'

'Oh, God, Lucy, because I cannot speak to you as I wish. And because this is torture for us both.' He reached for her hand and clasped it between his. Somehow, without either of them taking a step, their bodies swayed closer together. Edward raised her hand to his mouth and kissed the tip of her fingers.

'Lucy, go now, and I will call on you this afternoon. If anybody saw you here with me like this, you would be lost. . .'

She felt bereft when Edward moved away from her.

'I'm sorry,' she said, refastening her cape. 'I should never have come here, my lord, but I leave for Hallerton tomorrow morning and I felt some things needed to be discussed between us. I realise now that you owe me no explanations.'

'On the contrary, I think I owe you several. Instead, I am merely going to ask for yet another favour. Would you please never reveal to anyone that I am the man who escorted you out of Kuwar? There are reasons why it will be better if nobody ever finds out that Baron Ridgeholm and Rashid the trader are one and the same person.'

'You have my promise.' She held out her hand. 'Goodbye, my lord. I wish you well in your future endeavours and thank you from the bottom of my heart for your role in my escape from the Khan of Kuwar.'

He stood stock-still in the corner and, for a moment, she was afraid that he would not shake her hand. Then he moved and gave her hand one brief, firm shake. 'Your thanks are unnecessary, Miss Larkin. If you recall, you saved me from drinking poisoned tea, so I am at least as much in your debt as you are in mine.'

'Perhaps, since our debts cancel each other out, we may consider ourselves friends.'

'Yes.' Edward drew in a deep breath. 'Yes, I dare say we could call ourselves friends.'

Lucy knew that she ought to leave before she said or did something disastrous, like throwing herself into Edward's arms and begging him to kiss her. But the strange paralysis gripped her again and she simply stood there, separated from him by no more than a few inches of space—and a heart overflowing with regret.

She had no idea how long they both stood there before a new disturbance in the doorway marked the sudden arrival of Lord Triss, Edward's uncle.

Lord Triss marched into the drawing-room and eyed

the silent couple sternly. 'This is a fine how-do-you-do,' he asserted gruffly. 'I am shocked and disappointed, Edward. And I must say, Miss Larkin, I would have credited you with more. . .discretion.'

As if shaking off a heavy mantle of uncertainty, Edward slowly drew himself up to his full height. The full power of his presence flowed into the room, dominating the setting. 'I think you have misunderstood the situation, Uncle. I am sure you will be delighted to know that Miss Larkin recently honoured me by agreeing to become my wife.'

Lucy paled, and Lord Triss shot one startled, questioning look towards his nephew. Edward's dark brows rose in an expression of faint, unmistakable hauteur. 'The wedding will make no difference to my commitments to you,' he said.

'Ah, I see.' Lord Triss did indeed seem to find the final remark enlightening. Lucy scarcely registered its possible significance. Lord Triss bowed over her hand with old-fashioned courtesy.

'Miss Larkin, it will be a pleasure to welcome you into our family, and I congratulate Edward on his excellent choice of a bride. Nevertheless, fiancée or not, you shouldn't be here, my dear. Allow me to offer you my escort home.'

Lucy felt her brain reel. Her glance swept Edward's face, but she could read nothing there of what had prompted him to make his shocking announcement.

'I will call upon you and your stepmother this evening,' he said courteously, but without meeting her gaze. 'Until then, Miss Larkin, I trust you will think kindly of me.'

'She is your fiancée,' Lord Triss interjected, a shade too heartily. 'My dear boy, I dare say she will think of you a deal more than kindly. Come, Miss Larkin. Your family will be wondering what has kept you so long. Fortunately, my carriage was summoned a quarter of an hour since. It should be waiting for us by now.'

'I am coming, my lord.' Lucy hesitated, then held out

her hand once again to Edward. 'Until this evening, my lord.'

He bowed, scarcely touching her hand. 'Until this evening.'

Lucy had spent the entire day listening to her step-mother and sister bewail the loss of the Baron's title, the Baron's money, the Baron's properties and the Baron's dazzling position in London society. The Baron himself did not seem to be very much missed.

By the time dinner was over, Lucy's nerves were stretched to breaking point. Her ears suddenly detected the rumble of an arriving carriage, the clatter of carriage steps being let down and footsteps climbing the marble entrance stairs. A crisp rat-tat-tat on the doorknocker, murmurs of greeting from the servants and feet walking purposefully along the hallway. A footman announcing the arrival of Lord Ridgeholm. Edward's voice. Her heart, beating so loudly that it drowned out all other sounds. Dear God, he was here!

'Good evening, Lady Margaret; thank you for agreeing to receive me at this late hour. Good evening, Miss Larkin.'

Lucy tried to smile and hold out her hand, but discovered to her chagrin that she couldn't move a single muscle. Her body seemed to have petrified on to the sofa.

Edward, as so often happened, sensed her problem. He came and stood before her, taking her hands and bowing over them just as if she weren't staring at him like a mesmerised rabbit cornered by a hungry stoat.

'Miss Larkin, you look even lovelier than usual this evening.'

She tried to say, 'Thank you, my lord.' Her throat muscles moved just enough to produce an odd croaking sound, like a rusty winch grinding inside a well.

Lady Margaret rose to her feet. 'Lord Ridgeholm, I understand from your uncle that you have something of *particular* importance you wish to discuss with me.'

'Indeed I have something special to say, my lady. I

have called here this evening because I wish to discuss the future of your stepdaughter. As my uncle, Lord Triss, mentioned earlier today, I would deem it a great honour if I might be permitted to pay my addresses to Miss Larkin.'

Lady Margaret gestured towards the sofa. 'You see her before you, my lord.'

Lord Ridgeholm did not seem perturbed by Lucy's gaucheness. Taking her hands, he pulled her gently to her feet and escorted her over to the bay window, where he drew back the draperies, unveiling a view of the dark London street and the shadows of a distant hackney cab. Lady Margaret remained in the drawing-room, but the position of the furniture and a large Chinese screen enabled them to maintain some illusion of privacy.

'Miss Larkin,' Edward said softly. 'May I have the great honour and privilege of asking you to become my wife?'

Lucy's stomach knotted with a sensation somewhere between excitement, reckless anticipation and fear. Despite hours of worrying about what she would say, now that the moment of decision was actually upon her she realised that she didn't know what her answer would be.

Did she want to marry a man who might be proposing out of a sense of duty? She had recognised days ago that she was fathoms deep in love — not with Rashid, not with the foolish Baron who was on public display here in London, but with the man she had seen tantalising glimpses of hiding behind both impersonations.

So much for the state of her own feelings, but what of Edward's? He had kissed her with passion on two occasions, which presumably meant that he found her attractive. But he had never given the smallest indication that any of his deeper emotions were involved. Lucy knew that men could feel passion for women they actively disliked. Would Edward propose marriage to a woman he disliked, even if he felt he had compromised her?

A rueful smile flickered briefly across Edward's mouth. 'You keep me in dreadful suspense, Miss Larkin. I had hoped you would not find the decision such a difficult one. Your acceptance of my suit would make me a very happy man.'

He looked as if he truly wanted her to say yes. Perhaps, even if he didn't love her, he would continue to lie so gracefully that she would never discover the truth about his feelings. Provided the bubble of her dreams never burst, would it matter if she lived in a fool's paradise? She wanted — desperately — to convince herself that she would be happy if she seized the chance to marry him. But she couldn't. Not without asking him how he really felt. Tightening her grip on his hands, she raised her eyes to his.

'Why do you want to marry me, my lord?'

There was a fatal moment of hesitation before he replied. 'Because I love you more than life,' he said at last.

His voice was flat and expressionless, and she didn't believe him for an instant. She knew already that he would lie when he felt it necessary, and for both their sakes he no doubt felt it necessary to lie.

Stiffening her resolve, Lucy sought for a polite way to express her refusal.

'Thank you, my lord,' she said, her voice firm although her body trembled. 'I am appreciative of the honour you do me, but. . .'

He lifted her gloved hands and brushed them very gently against his cheeks. Her words of refusal died away and she gazed into the dark, unfathomable depths of his eyes.

'Don't turn me down, Loo-sie,' he murmured. 'Please.'

She heard herself speak as if the words came from a great distance. 'I appreciate the honour you do me, my lord, and I would be. . .delighted to accept your offer.'

His breath exhaled in a sudden, sharp sigh. He turned her hands over and pressed a swift, hard kiss into the cup of her palms. Lucy recognised the dark, hot leap of desire in his eyes and felt a quick shudder of answering passion. At that moment, she didn't even care whether or not he loved her. To experience the mysteries of the marriage bed in his arms would be enough.

His voice was unexpectedly husky when he spoke. 'I will do everything in my power to make you happy, Lucy. You have my word on it.'

'I hope we may make each other happy, my lord.'

He circled his thumb lightly around her palm and she felt the movement throughout her body. 'This morning you called me Edward. I find the strangest need to hear you say my name again.'

She looked up at him, memories of another occasion vivid in her mind. 'Given names can be powerful weapons, my lord. I have been told that it is rarely wise to plunge headlong into such dangerous intimacy.'

He smiled, and murmured in Pashto, 'Ah, but Englishwoman, you Britishers are so free and easy with your use of personal names. Could you not bring yourself to humour me in this small matter?'

Her blood turned hot and thick in her veins at the sound of his teasing voice — Rashid's voice. The desire to feel his arms around her became so intense that it was a physical ache tingling beneath her skin. Looking away from him, she pressed her hands to her burning cheeks.

'Say my name, Loo-sie,' he murmured, still speaking Pashto. 'Tell me if you truly wish to marry me.'

She responded in the same language. Somehow it was easier to reveal the truth in an alien tongue. 'Yes, Edward, I wish to marry you.'

'Good,' he said, his voice rich with satisfaction. 'I think it must be very soon.'

The wedding date was set for the fifteenth of July, precisely three weeks and one day after Lucy had accepted Edward's proposal. Plans for the wedding ceremony positively flew ahead, thanks in large measure to the combined efforts of Lord Triss and Lady Margaret. The morning of the ceremony dawned overcast, but the rain held off and Lady Margaret declared this a good sign. At this stage of the game, she considered the wedding ceremony to be her show, and she was anxious for it to go off well, despite the dreadful handicap of having Lucy as the bride.

Ten o'clock approached and the family members assembled in the drawing-room waited with varying degrees of impatience and excitement for the bride to descend. At ten o'clock precisely, Lucy descended the staircase, escorted by the Bishop of Cirencester, who had offered to stand in stead of her father and give her away.

Lucy paused in the doorway for a few seconds, a slender vision in deep ivory satin. Her delicate lace-embroidered veil was held in place by a circlet of cream rosebuds entwined with ivy. The gown had no frills and no ruffles, but the seed-pearls stitched along the seams emphasised the femininity of her figure, and the grace-ful line of her body. Her hair, and the dark golden glow of her skin, shone through the concealing lace veils, transforming her into a vibrant, exotic presence in the grey morning light.

For a moment there was silence in the drawing-room, then Penelope exclaimed, 'Why, Lucy, you look truly lovely!'

Lucy hoped — very much — that her sister was right. She wanted to wipe out Edward's memories of a gaunt Afghani prisoner and replace them with the image of a desirable, fashionable woman. She didn't want their relationship to be based on pity.

She took her place in the carriage next to the bishop, feeling so tightly strung that she scarcely recognised the streets they drove through on the way to St Margaret's, Westminster.

The carriage drew to a halt in front of the church. For a moment, the sun came out from behind a cloud, lighting the age-darkened stone with a flash of warm colour. The bishop spoke as the footmen prepared to open the door and let down the steps.

'My dear, Edward needs a very special woman as his

wife, and I am confident you are that woman. I wish
you both a lifetime of joy and adventure together.'

Joy and adventure. The bishop's words rang in Lucy's
ears as she began the slow procession down the church
aisle. At the altar steps Edward waited for her,
resplendent in the dark grey trousers and lighter grey
tailcoat of his formal morning clothes. The church was
crowded, but as she drew closer to Edward Lucy was
aware only of him. When she finally stopped at his side,
he took her hand and greeted her with a smile so full of
warmth and admiration that her throat constricted with
sudden tears. During these past few weeks she had
learned to read behind the various façades Edward
mounted so skilfully, and his expression no longer
seem unfathomable. His eyes were dark not with
secrets, but with intense, controlled emotion. His voice
was deep and confident when he spoke his vows, but
his hands, normally so strong and competent, shook
slightly as he placed his ring on her finger. She was glad
to know that this ceremony inspired such intense feelings within him.

The Baron and his new bride arrived at Ridgeholm, his
country seat in Sussex, on the afternoon train. Ten
servants and two carriages waited at the station to
escort the newly-weds to Ridgeholm Hall. Thirty more
servants lined the marble-pillared entrance, curtsying
and bowing as their master and mistress entered the
ancestral Hall.

Lucy had progressed since the wedding ceremony
from a state of eager curiosity, through resignation, to
her present state of stupefied nervousness. Her conversation with Edward in the train had been a little stilted,
but not unmanageably so. Being married was a new
experience for both of them, and Lucy was sure they
would eventually relax with each other and move to a
new level of intimacy.

They had separated to change for dinner as soon as
they finished greeting the senior servants, and Lucy
looked forward to this separation as a time to rest and

recover her composure. She might be a total novice as
regarded what lay ahead, but Edward — somehow she
was quite certain of this — was an expert in the field.
Surely he would find a way to put her at ease?

She discovered, unfortunately, that her bedroom was
not conducive to rest and relaxation. It was the huge,
antique bed that finally reduced Lucy to ignominious
panic. Brooding over her from its gilded dais, the
carved, curtained monstrosity mocked her with its
threat of the night ahead. Lucy began to remember —
vividly — that few Afghani brides found their wedding
nights happy. She had seen several, in fact, who
emerged bloodied and tearful from the first encounter
with their new husbands.

All might still have been well if she and Edward had
been able to eat a light meal alone together. Unfortunately, the cook had prepared a banquet of five courses,
served by more footmen than Lucy could count.

Thankfully, once the horrible dinner was over,
Edward didn't linger at table. He declined brandy or
cigars, and guided Lucy into a small sitting-room made
cheerful by a blazing fire.

'I've asked Timms to serve tea early this evening,' he
said, sitting down in a chair across the fire from her.
'I'm sure you must be tired after such an eventful day.
You will probably want to go to bed early.'

If she said yes, would he think she was eager to
receive his attentions? Or would he take her reply at
face value and leave her to sleep alone? What did she
want to have happen? Did she want to postpone her
initiation into the mysteries of marriage?

Half laughing, half on the verge of tears, Lucy
thought that it had never been so difficult to answer
such a simple question.

Edward saved her from giving a reply. 'Oh, God,
Lucy, this is ridiculous!' he said, springing to his feet.
He paced restlessly for a few moments before kneeling
beside her chair and running his hand over the back of
his neck. 'Lucy, we are husband and wife, and I think
we can deal more honestly with each other than this. I

don't want to bring back harsh memories for you, but I know better than most people what you must have endured during your captivity, and I understand how you must be dreading the night ahead.' He raised her hands and kissed them gently. 'Lucy, promise me that you will remember always that I am not one of your captors, and I will never hurt you, or require you to perform any —— ' He broke off, springing to his feet in a single impatient movement.

'Yes, Timms, what is it?'

'Tea, my lord, for you and her ladyship.'

The butler left the room in less than a minute, but, to Lucy's intense frustration, her moment of intimacy with Edward seemed to have vanished. He retreated to the sofa and stared into the leaping flames of the fire.

'Will you pour?' he asked.

'Certainly.' A flash of inspiration seized Lucy as she lifted the heavy silver pot. Pouring a cup of fragrant China tea, she added lemon, then crossed the room and knelt in front of Edward. Bowing her head, she murmured in Pashto, 'Would my lord care to have sugar in his tea?'

Edward accepted the offering gravely, taking two or three sips before setting the cup on the table. 'Thank you, but I need no sugar,' he replied, also in Pashto. 'The tea is made sweet enough by your presence. Will you share some with me?'

'If it pleases you, my lord.'

She did not move from her position in front of him, so he took his cup, raising it slowly to her lips and tilting it for her to drink. When she had finished, he returned the cup to the table and leaned forward to clasp her hands.

'Light of my life,' he said softly. 'I care only that you should be happy. Are you happy, Loo-sie?'

'Very happy, my lord.'

'May it always be so, woman of my heart.'

'To be your wife brings me happiness,' Lucy said, thinking how miraculously easy it was to speak the truth when she took refuge in the lilting, flowery rhythms of

Pashto. Perhaps Edward felt the same, for he made no effort to switch their conversation back into English.

'My heart beats more swiftly when I see the beauty of my bride,' he said, caressing her cheeks. 'Most beautiful of women, I drown in the dark promise of your eyes.'

The seductive stroking of his fingers burned her skin and set a thousand pulses racing. Trembling with pleasure, Lucy tilted her head backwards, lifting her mouth to receive his kiss. She closed her eyes, overwhelmed by sensation when Edward traced the outline of her lips with a gentle fingertip.

'Look at me, most beautiful of women,' he commanded, his words a velvet caress. 'Keeper of my heart, look at me once more before I kiss you.'

Her eyelids felt almost too heavy to obey, but she slowly opened her eyes and stared into the mesmerising darkness of Edward's gaze. She could not guess what emotions he read in her face, but his expression changed from tenderness to desire, flooding his lean, bronzed features with all the sensuality normally concealed behind the mask of his disguise. She reached out to touch his cheek, and he took her hand, guiding it to his heart.

'Most beautiful of women, feel the power you exercise over me. In your presence my heart races and my body is feeble with desire.'

Shocked by her own daring, Lucy took his hand and placed it beneath the swell of her breast. 'Feel the power you exercise over me, my lord. In your presence my heart races and my body is feeble with longing for your possession.'

Edward held her gaze for a long, silent moment. Then he gave an odd, harsh sigh and his hands curved upward, cupping her breasts and brushing her nipples with his thumbs. They peaked to an aching hardness beneath his touch. He gave her no time to think about this strange new experience, or about the tension suddenly vibrating in the air between them. Drawing

her swiftly on to the sofa, he held her a willing captive
in his arms.

He looked down at her, his eyes slumberous. 'Light
of my life, your lips promise me the joys of paradise.
Let me taste them now.'

She offered no resistance as he bent his head to claim
possession of her mouth. The moment his lips touched
hers, she knew this kiss would be nothing like the
others they had shared. This time there was no reluctance on his part, no hesitancy, no holding back. He
took his time, testing her mouth with unhurried
pleasure, probing and nudging with his tongue until her
lips parted to receive him. Slowly, expertly, he explored
the warm honey of her mouth until she moved her lips
hungrily beneath his, seeking some more intimate form
of contact, although she had no idea precisely what.
His kiss deepened when he felt her response, increasing
its mastery until her body trembled in his arms and her
thoughts tumbled in a whirl of chaotic sensuality.

'Loo-sie, we cannot stay here.' His voice was a husky
murmur against her mouth, an unwanted intrusion into
the dark, heedless turmoil of her desire.

'Where must we go?' she asked, dazed by the fever
in her blood.

'To my room. To bed.' He stood up, lifting her easily
into his arms, and carried her across the room. Before
he could open the door, it swung open. A footman,
staring rigidly into space, spoke woodenly.

'Goodnight, my lord. Goodnight, my lady.'

'Goodnight, James.' Edward sounded almost
amused, but the cloud of Lucy's passion disappeared
the instant she saw the servant. Scarlet with embarrassment, she struggled to free herself from her husband's
arms.

'Edward, what will he think?' she whispered, morti-
fied. 'Please put me down. I can walk!'

His eyes gleamed with laughter. 'Are you sure, my
heart? If you can walk, then I cannot have kissed you
properly. I must try again as soon as we are upstairs.'

He reached the top of the grand staircase and strode

easily along the corridor. A smothered gasp indicated the presence of Lucy's maid.

'Goodnight, Rose.' Edward spoke smoothly. 'Thank you for waiting up, but your mistress won't need you tonight.'

'Very good, my lord. Sleep well. . . That is — er — goodnight, my lady.'

Lucy wondered if it was possible to die of embarrassment. At this moment, it seemed likely. 'Edward, for heaven's sake! Please, *please* put me down!'

'Certainly, my heart.'

He stepped into a bedroom and closed the door with his foot. He laid Lucy on the bed and immediately sat down beside her. Smoothing a loose curl away from her forehead, he leaned over and kissed the spot where the curl had rested.

'Dear God, Lucy,' he said, and there was no longer any hint of laughter in his voice, only stark, urgent desire. 'I have wanted to make love to you for so long. Kiss me, my heart. For God's sake, kiss me.'

CHAPTER SEVEN

THIS was going to be one hell of a long night, Edward reflected grimly, tearing himself away from his wife's tempting kisses. God in heaven, how was he going to hang on to sufficient will-power to control the urgency of his lovemaking?

He looked down at Lucy. She lay on his bed, her rumpled dress revealing an enticing few inches of slender ankle, and her hair already beginning to tumble from its pins. His body hardened with a hot, fierce rush of desire. His wife! God, how he wanted to make this woman his wife in fact as well as in name.

Edward grimaced ruefully. So much for all those fancy vows he'd taken, swearing to himself that he wouldn't make love to Lucy until after he returned from Afghanistan. In his heart, he'd always known he lied.

The guilt that had been gnawing at him all evening hooked its claws a little deeper into his gut. Lord knew, he had no right to marry Lucy when he was committed to a mission that might well cost him his life. But the temptation to allow himself a few weeks of happiness had proven too strong. Duty to his country had surrendered to desire for an extraordinary woman. And he hadn't even put up much of a fight.

He wondered when he had started on this slippery slope to involvement. Had it been when he'd seen Lucy bow before the Khan of Kuwar and known instinctively that she despised the fat slug from the depths of her being? Or had it been that night he'd kissed her under the stars? Or later, when he'd sent Abdullah to give her the diamond-eyed camel? Certainly when he'd seen her again in London it had been already too late to pretend he didn't care.

Lord Triss had been furious about his nephew's

146

involvement with Lucy. Edward was valuable to the British government, both in his role as a bumbling British diplomat and in his role as a Punjabi gun-runner. Lord Triss wasn't prepared to lose one of his most effective agents.

'You've agreed to undertake a mission that's important to your country,' he complained after Lady Margaret's ball. 'Stop mooning over Lucinda Larkin, Edward; it's dangerous. I've never seen you come so close to betraying your disguise. The pair of you were practically making love out there on the dance-floor. This isn't the moment to let your emotions overrule your common sense. For heaven's sake, you're the man who told me there are a million beautiful women in the world, so no man should settle for just one. Find yourself a pretty opera dancer, and get your mind out of your breeches. You have the Russians to worry about, and their plans for Afghanistan. Forget about Lucinda Larkin.'

Edward, unwilling to admit even to himself that he needed Lucy, not just any woman, tried to follow his uncle's advice. His lack of success had been spectacular. The talented, experienced women of the *demi-monde* suddenly had no appeal. Lucy, as courageous and witty as he remembered her — and three times as beautiful — haunted his dreams.

His uncle warned him to stop visiting the Larkin household, but Edward disobeyed, swearing that he wouldn't allow Lucy to penetrate his disguise. Even in that, he'd deceived himself. Surely he had always known Lucy was far too perceptive to be tricked by a change of clothing, a drawling accent and an oversized monocle? Hadn't he secretly hoped she would recognise the man behind the mask? Why else had he played his role of bumbling diplomat so poorly? For a man whose life had often been saved by skilful acting, Edward realised he had been remarkably inept at maintaining his disguise when Lucy was near.

So now, for good or ill, he and Lucy were married. Tonight, however, he wanted to forget about the long-term problems of their relationship. Right at this moment, a more immediate problem confronted him: he wanted to make love to his wife.

Edward never doubted that Lucy had been raped by her Kuwari captors. He guessed that the rapes had occurred frequently, and over a long period of time. Her attitude the first night they met had suggested that she expected him to demand sexual services. Edward didn't need to be a paragon of sensitivity to realise that sex for his wife was almost certainly associated with pain and humiliation.

He had been surprised and delighted by Lucy's eager response on the few occasions he had kissed her, but Edward didn't delude himself. He had detected the immediate stiffening of her body whenever he pushed the boundaries of their embrace beyond a simple kiss, and he anticipated that it would take weeks of nerve-racking patience before he managed to bring Lucy to the point where he could finally seek consummation. And their time together would be measured in days, not weeks.

Edward grimaced wryly. God in heaven, what a prospect! Not only to be celibate, but to be celibate in the face of such temptation! But the last thing he wanted was to add to Lucy's fears, and, at the moment, she looked very frightened.

Moving slowly so as not to startle her, Edward reached out and pulled two or three pins from her hair. Then he smiled casually, determined to lower the level of sexual tension between the pair of them.

'Shall I get your hairbrush while you take out the rest of these pins? Since I was the one to send Rose to bed, I will do my best to prove what a good lady's maid I can be.'

Lucy seemed preoccupied with pleating a series of folds into her silk skirt. 'Usually I get undressed before Rose does my hair for the night.'

She couldn't be offering to have him undress her— could she? Gritting his teeth, Edward pushed the tempting thought aside. He smiled again.

'Tonight let's reverse the order, shall we? Hair plaited first, and then we can see what further help you need.'

He got up and crossed to the door connecting Lucy's bedroom with his. He found her brush without difficulty on the dressing-table, and returned to his room, feigning a composure he definitely didn't feel.

Lucy sat propped against the headboard of his bed. During his absence, she had removed all the pins from her hair, and it now cascaded over her shoulders in a rich fall of dark, gleaming chestnut-brown. Her eyes sparkled, a faint blush stained her cheeks, and she looked altogether good enough to eat.

Edward muttered a trenchant curse beneath his breath. Resisting the impulse to stride across the room, rip off Lucy's clothes, and fling himself on top of her, he held out the hairbrush. He hoped his smile didn't look as strained as it felt.

'Success! Your maid has everything very well organised. Er—why don't you sit at my dressing-table?'

'You could sit here.' She patted the bed. 'It's more comfortable here.'

From Edward's point of view, that was debatable, but there seemed no gracious way to refuse. He sat beside her, breathing in her lavender perfume and trying to ignore the increasing ache in his loins. He ran the brush through her thick tresses, watching the candlelight ripple over her curls and wondering how in hell he was going to keep his hands off the rest of her body. He slipped the brush underneath the weight of her hair, pulling it through his fingers and lifting it away from the nape of her neck. When he felt as though he might explode from frustration if he didn't touch her, he bent his head and pressed a swift, open-mouthed kiss against the back of her neck.

She didn't jump away as he had feared. She turned slowly in his arms, reaching up to touch his face and finally to push his hair away from the bullet scar high on his forehead.

'How did you get it?' she asked softly.

He tried to focus his thoughts on the old wound, as opposed to the wandering caress of her fingers. 'By carelessness. By assuming my opponent was disarmed because I had taken away his rifle. Thank God he was a terrible shot, and I was still young enough to jump fast, or I would never have lived to benefit from my lesson: never assume you've disarmed your opponent until he's dead and you've searched his body.'

Lucy grazed her fingers lightly over the ridge of scar tissue. 'I'm glad you survived,' she whispered.

Her husky words served as a final spark to the glowing ember of his desire. For a few blazing moments, Edward didn't care if he was doing the right or the honourable thing. He swept Lucy into his arms and kissed her — hard. His lips moved urgently over her mouth and slender throat, then trailed, moist and seeking, to the upthrusting swell of her breasts above her satin evening gown.

Lost in the pleasure of his own passion, his kiss became more masterful with every second. His tongue thrust purposefully into Lucy's mouth, at the same time as his hand sought the fastening of her gown. Holding her tight with one arm, he undid the tiny concealed hooks with an impatient skill born of long practice.

Her bodice was hanging half off her shoulders before he registered the unpleasant fact that Lucy's yielding softness had changed to a rigid, doll-like stiffness, and that she was no longer returning his kisses, merely enduring them. With a shudder of self-disgust, Edward released her.

'I'm sorry,' Lucy said at once, dipping her head so that a curtain of hair fell forward, concealing her face. 'Edward, I'm so sorry.' She tugged at her gown in a pathetic attempt to restore some modesty and dignity to her appearance.

Edward cursed himself roundly. 'You have nothing to apologise for,' he said, his voice curt. 'It is I who should apologise. Would you like to return to your own room?'

Lucy glanced up, her cheeks scarlet behind the veil

of her hair. 'It's not that I don't want to be a good wife, Edward. It's just that I'm not sure what to do.' She looked away again, twisting her hands tightly together. 'Everybody assumes that I am. . . People think that during my captivity in Kuwar Village. . .' She drew in a deep breath, obviously seeking the courage to continue. 'The fact is, Edward——'

'The fact is, my dear, that you have nothing to explain,' he interrupted gently. 'What happened in Kuwar is past, and you must strive to put those experiences out of your mind.' He crooked his finger under her chin and urged her to look up. 'Lucy, can you believe me when I say that the physical union of a woman with a man is not always painful? That a man need not be cruel and thoughtless, and a woman need not be debased?'

Lucy gave her husband a wry smile. 'Certainly I will believe you, Edward. You see, I think you may have misunderstood my problem.'

Edward went cold. 'Are you—injured?' he asked.

Lucy swallowed a gasp of laughter. 'No, Edward, I'm not injured. The truth is, I am a virgin. Probably the oldest virgin ever to emerge from Afghanistan.' Speaking in a rush, before she could lose courage, she confessed the whole. 'Not only am I a virgin, but I'm rather an ignorant virgin. You see, Edward, I'm not terribly certain what I'm supposed to do when you—er—make advances to me. That is probably why you find my reactions so unsatisfactory.'

Edward regarded her in stunned silence. 'You are a *virgin*?' he said at last.

She laughed ruefully, aware of the total absurdity of the situation. A bride was not usually called upon to apologise for her innocence. 'I'm very sorry, Edward, but actually I am. I saw one or two babies being born in Kuwar when I was first taken prisoner, but that didn't help me to understand how the babies were conceived in the first place. My mother died when I was a child. My father naturally was entirely silent on the subject——'

'But what of the Kuwari tribesmen? They couldn't have ignored such a beautiful woman in their midst, particularly the daughter of one of their enemies. Lucy, my dear, *please* accept that there is no need to pretend with me. There is no shame in anything that may have happened while you were in Afghanistan. I met the Khan of Kuwar. I, of all people, understand that you had no choice——'

'Nothing happened to me when I was a prisoner in Kuwar,' Lucy said. 'At least, nothing of the sort everybody is so convinced must have happened. The Khan kept me locked up in his palace for the first two months of my captivity, and by the time I emerged the other Kuwari warriors all believed I was a *jinn*.'

'Because of the way Hashim Khan's brothers died?'

'Exactly. By the time you arrived, some of the villagers were beginning to wonder if they could have been mistaken about my magic powers, but the men were all sufficiently frightened to prevent them attempting any sexual advances. They believed I would rob them of their potency if they slept with me, and the women believed I would make them barren.' Her smile was only a little tremulous as she looked at Edward. 'So you see, everybody assumes I am a woman of vast experience, when the reality is that I'm almost as ignorant as the most naïve English schoolgirl.'

For a second, Edward stared at her in blank astonishment, then he burst out laughing. Taking her into his arms, he rested his cheek against her hair, nuzzling gently. 'Oh, Lucy, my poor sweet, what a tale of woe!'

'It is rather, isn't it?'

Edward grinned. 'What a relief to know that I have only to explain the mechanics of the procedure! Some might consider that a daunting task, but, in comparison to wiping out two years of bitter memories, it seems a mere nothing, I assure you.'

Lucy twisted the button on his jacket. 'And will you explain the. . .mechanics of the procedure?'

'It will be my pleasure,' Edward said huskily. He took her hands and held them against his face. 'Most beautiful of women, I believe this is a lesson best taught by practical demonstration. Are you ready for the first assignment, my heart?'

She nodded, a little frightened at what might lie ahead, even though her body already ached with the need for some fulfilment she couldn't quite visualise.

Edward was too experienced a lover to give her fear time to develop. He took her into his arms, his mouth seeking hers, his tongue trailing lightly into her mouth, teasing and enticing her into what had already become a familiar pleasure.

Encouraged by the new honesty between them, Lucy allowed herself to relax, to sink into the feelings aroused by Edward's kisses. Gradually the reality of her surroundings faded away. With every touch of his mouth, with every caress, something deep within her struggled to be free. Her body ached. Her skin burned. Her breasts tingled. The touch of his hands brought her the illusion of relief, but her inner yearning increased step by inevitable step.

She progressed so far and so swiftly along the path of arousal that she scarcely noticed when Edward drew off her bodice and camisole, tossing the offending garments to the floor along with his jacket and shirt.

'Lesson number two, my heart,' he whispered, propelling her back against the pillows, his knowing hands tracing the curve of her naked breasts.

Heat arrowed from her chest into the lower part of her body. Instinctively, she arched herself up to his mouth, giving a soft moan of incoherent pleasure. Passion vanquished her inhibitions even as it destroyed the remnants of her self-control. Through the haze of her desire she recalled the fact that ladies were not supposed to enjoy the bothersome masculine attentions of their husbands. The worry that she might be undesirably wanton vanished as soon as Edward cupped his hands around her breasts and closed his mouth over her nipple. If these strange, glorious sensations were the reward for becoming a woman of easy virtue, then Lucy had no wish to remain respectable.

Time and space lost all meaning. Lucy was aware of nothing save the masterful caress of her husband's fingers and the enticing pressure of his mouth against hers. His lips slid down her warm skin towards her waist, feeding her hunger, yet leaving her starved for something more.

The coolness of air struck her skin as he unhooked the waistband of her skirt and petticoats. Skilfully, he slid the heavy clothes over her hips, baring her lower body to his view. Lucy's breath caught in her throat as the flick of his tongue around her navel changed the night-time coolness into a sudden raging heat.

'You are truly the most beautiful of women,' he whispered, moving away from her for a moment to strip off the remainder of his clothes. His nakedness shocked Lucy, but the shock was exciting rather than frightening. He returned to the bed, and his lips moved quickly up her body, trailing kisses. When his mouth once again settled over hers, Lucy arched her hips, unconsciously inviting him to take more intimate possession of her body.

'Not yet, most beautiful of women, not quite yet.'

Her husband's words broke Lucy's intense self-absorption. His body was hot and hard and urgent against hers, but for the first time she became aware of the fact that when she moved he trembled in her arms. Not fully understanding the connection between her movements and his reaction, she twisted beneath him, wanting to see his face more clearly.

Edward made a sound deep in his throat, and caught her hips, forcing her to lie still. A rueful smile crossed his lips.

'My heart, if you wish me to remain sane during this course of instruction, I must beg you not to jump ahead to the final lesson.'

'I would like to be a. . .good pupil.'

'Light of my life, you are the best pupil any man could ever hope for. Much too good for my self-control.'

She didn't entirely understand what he meant, but

thankfully he didn't seem perturbed by her wanton behaviour, so she reached out to stroke the dark hair that angled down from his chest towards his flat stomach. When her hand hesitated in the region of his waist, Edward's eyes clouded with an emotion somewhere between despair and laughter.

'Dear heaven, Lucy, but you are a most talented student! Ah, no, my heart, don't stop.'

'Should I not?' Greatly daring, she allowed her hand to dip towards his groin. He groaned. Breathless, provocative, she peeped at him through half-closed lashes. 'I hope I am progressing in the right direction, master?'

He reached for her hand and dragged it against his arousal. 'Now you are,' he murmured, pulling her into his arms, trapping her hand between their two bodies. Against her breasts, she could feel the strong, steady beat of his heart. Against her thighs, she could feel the thrusting pressure of his hips. His hands moved over her body, impatient, ardent, arousing.

'I dreamed of holding you like this during those long nights under the stars.' Edward's voice was rough. 'Do you remember the last night of our journey when the jackal woke you?'

'Of course I remember. I remember also that you kissed me.'

'I wished our kiss might never end. When I went back to my own blanket, you reached out and took my hand. Our fingers barely touched, but in my dreams I tasted your kisses in my mouth and felt your thighs parting to receive me. Dear God, I have wanted you for so long, Lucy.'

Knowledge of her ability to arouse him became the ultimate aphrodisiac for Lucy. Blood raced through her veins and a sweet weakness seized her. The instinctive demands of her body had long since drowned out fear of Edward's possession. She watched his face, drawn taut with desire, and gloried in her power to overcome his awesome self-control. She guessed that few people ever succeeded as she had in stripping away the layers of his disguise, and she wanted to carry her discoveries to the ultimate limit.

'Love me, Edward,' she whispered.

He brought her to a state of white-hot readiness. Drowning in a sea of new sensations, she made no protest when his hand slid over her stomach, seeking admission to the dark, throbbing place between her thighs.

But when his fingers finally touched the core of her, Lucy gave a startled cry and pushed herself upright in the bed, startled out of her passion-induced stupor. Edward ceased his intimate probing, but he didn't move his hand, despite her confused efforts to free herself.

'Edward, no!' she protested.

'The final lesson, keeper of my heart,' he said softly. 'Don't close yourself against me, Lucy. There will be only one moment of pain, and then I swear I will bring you pleasure.'

Edward's words were tender, but his voice was harsh with the strain of controlling his desire. Lucy heard only the harshness. The horror stories of the Kuwari village women and the strictures of her Victorian upbringing finally caught up with her. Fearful, bewildered, shamed by her own tumultuous response, she tensed in shocked resistance.

Edward's body pulsed with a need that surpassed anything he had ever known. Somehow he managed to remain still, to wait for his wife to regain some measure of calm. Holding her captive beneath his straining body, he claimed her mouth again, waiting patiently until her little sigh and the parting of her lips told him what he wanted to know.

Ignoring his own aching need for release, he teased her sensitive nipples with his mouth until gradually her panic-stricken tension dissipated. Slowly, tenderly, he resumed his stroking.

Lucy didn't want to respond. Twenty-three years of social conditioning convinced her that she ought not to be feeling — could not be feeling — what she actually felt. In the end, though, Edward's masterful lovemaking conquered her most deeply rooted inhibitions. Her pulses throbbed to the erotic rhythm of his touch. Her hips arched against his hand, quickening to the pace he set. Her nails dug into the firm, tanned skin of his shoulders, and her teeth clenched together in an effort to contain her cries. And then, when she wondered how she could bear the painful pleasure for another second, her body convulsed in a spasm of unimaginable release.

Dazed by what had happened, she lay on the bed, staring up into Edward's dark, aristocratic features. Her body quivered in the aftermath and yet some deep inner need remained unfulfilled.

Edward brushed a damp curl away from her forehead. 'My heart,' he whispered. 'Let me show you how much more there can be.'

'There. . .is. . .more?' Lucy could barely speak.

'Much, much more.' Edward thought he had never seen anyone as beautiful as Lucy. She lay beneath him, panting slightly, her hair a wild tangle of brown velvet, her skin still warm with the flush of desire. He had never before felt such an intense need to give a woman satisfaction. Ironically, he had also never known such fear of causing pain.

When her fingers twined in his hair, pulling him down to her, the final vestige of Edward's control snapped. He parted her thighs and thrust into her, his penetration swift, deep and immediate. Lucy's sharp cry gave him pause, but only for a moment. As their bodies locked together, he drove deep into her softness, slipping his hands beneath her hips to press her body high and tight against his.

Lucy was astonished when a searing moment of pain disappeared in a wave of pleasure. As Edward's movements quickened, she responded, automatically lifting her hips to welcome his thrusts. Her mouth sought his, her hands dug into his skin, and she realised that her body was once again hot and feverish to his touch.

Edward sensed her desire rising to meet his. Surrendering to the demands of his body, he claimed possession of his wife with an urgent, climactic passion that demanded and received the reward of her ultimate response. Together they soared to the heights, lost in the febrile, glittering dance of ecstasy. Together they drifted down from the peak. Together they fell asleep, weary survivors of an experience whose devastating intensity neither of them was quite ready to acknowledge.

The chill of a pre-dawn breeze woke Edward from his sleep. He clasped his hands behind his neck and leaned back against the pillows. For a moment he stared straight ahead, deliberately not turning to look at the woman who lay curled innocently at the opposite side of the bed.

He was, Edward acknowledged, in one hell of a mess. How was he going to face Lucy over the breakfast-table and inform her that he would be leaving for India by the end of the month? And how the devil was he going to face months of separation from Lucy? The morning after the night before was bringing its inevitable problems and regrets.

But, whatever reason and honour might dictate, Edward couldn't be sorry for what had happened. During the past few years, he had slept with women in three different continents. Last night, for the first time in his life, he had made love.

Lucy. His wife. God in heaven, how loving and responsive she was! The memories crowded in, and Edward succumbed to temptation. He rolled on to his side, propping himself on one elbow so that he could look at Lucy.

She slept the deep, exhausted sleep of fulfilment, her waist-length hair tumbled over the pillow, her mouth swollen with the imprint of his kisses. The curve of her arm, the slope of her shoulder, the tiny mole at the nape of her neck — every part of her body brought back some vivid memory of pleasure. Desire, unwelcome but insistent, stirred within Edward as his gaze traced the mound of her breast and the slender, supple length of

her legs hidden beneath the linen sheet. In comparison
to other women, her entire body was taut with muscle.
Edward couldn't understand how he had once found
the typical plump, soft female body attractive.

She stirred, and the sheet slipped a little, to reveal
one firm breast and a pink nipple, erect and enticing in
the pale light of dawn. Edward resisted the urge to lean
over and take the tempting nipple into his mouth. Lucy
needed her sleep.

He lifted a strand of her rich chestnut hair, winding
it around his forefinger. When he had first met Lucy in
Kuwar, her hair had been so oiled and impregnated
with dirt that he had thought it was black. He lifted the
lock of hair and rubbed it softly against his cheek. What
would happen if he never came back from Afghanistan?

You know damn well what would happen. Lucy was
young and beautiful, and at his death she would become
rich beyond most men's dreams. Of course, she would
marry again. The primitive intensity of his jealousy
surprised him. He realised that he didn't want any other
man to experience the wonderful, sensuous richness of
Lucy's lovemaking. He was the man who had shown
her what passion between a man and a woman could be
like and, by God, he didn't want anyone else to benefit
from his lessons.

Edward cut off his maudlin train of thought. Besides,
he thought, managing a wry smile, there was always the
remote possibility that he might not die. After all, he'd
survived pretty handily for the past dozen years. The
trouble was that, when playing games with fate, it
helped if you didn't care over-much whether you lived
or died. The desire to return to Lucy had taken away
his crucial advantage. Now he cared.

Time to get up. Just one kiss wouldn't hurt, though.
A light one. Something she couldn't possibly feel since
she was sleeping so deeply.

He leaned over, breathing in the warm, drowsy smell
of her skin. He touched his mouth to her cheek in
a caress so delicate it was scarcely a kiss. She woke
at once.

'I'm sorry,' he said. 'I didn't mean to disturb you.'
Didn't he?

Her brown eyes were huge, dark with awareness of all that had passed between them. 'Since my time in Kuwar, I've slept very lightly.'

'Go back to sleep, Lucy. I'll take my clothes into the dressing-room so as not to disturb you.'

'Actually, I'm not very sleepy. Just — lonely.'

Edward's mind went blank. He stared at Lucy, aware only of the thick, pounding beat of his heart and the shy, husky appeal of his wife's words.

'Edward?'

'Yes?'

'The oddest thing.'

'What?'

'I think I may expire if you don't kiss me.'

His heart stopped. He turned to look at her, his throat tight with emotion. She smiled at him, a tiny, teasing smile that tore at his gut.

'I love you,' he whispered, gathering her into his arms. 'Wife of my heart, I love you more than life.'

For a week, Lucy lived cocooned in the paradise she and Edward had created for themselves. Each day, after a leisurely breakfast, they spent the long summer hours riding across the hills, talking about anything and everything that caught their attention. At night, as early as they could, they closed themselves into the privacy of their bedroom, where they explored the limitless boundaries of their passion.

Lucy's first warning of trouble came as she and Edward settled down after dinner on Saturday.

'The vicar will expect us to attend morning service tomorrow,' she said, smiling at Edward as she poured their nightly cup of tea. 'And I dare say by Monday we shall have to brace ourselves for a round of visits from the neighbours.'

'We are lucky they have kept away for an entire week.' Edward made the appropriate response, but he didn't really seem to be paying attention. He poured himself a second cup of tea and stirred it with excessive concentration. 'A message from my uncle was delivered today,' he said abruptly.

'From Lord Triss?' A warning danced with icy fingers along Lucy's spine. Trying to sound unconcerned, she asked, 'Does he need you to return to London?'

Edward set down his still full cup. 'Not to London,' he said. 'To India. He wants me to leave at the end of next week on the *Empress of India*, the new P and O steamer. I should not be away for. . .too long.'

Dear heaven, he was going back to India! 'This is very sudden, isn't it?' Lucy asked.

'Not entirely. I promised my uncle some time ago that I would return to the East. The *Empress* is so much faster than other ships that it seemed sensible to take advantage of her imminent departure.'

Lucy understood at once that she was not included in Edward's travel plans, but she feigned incomprehension. The prospect of being separated from her husband was so terrible that she could not — would not — face it. She forced a smile, hoping Edward wouldn't divine the grim determination hiding behind her cheerful expression.

'My dear, why do you sound so unhappy? A trip to India is no reason for us to be wretched. True, Lord Triss has given us rather short notice, but we have a house full of excellent servants. I dare say they will not find it impossible to pack our trunks in five days. We can travel via London and say goodbye to my stepmother and Penelope on our way to Southampton.'

Edward was not deceived. He knew she had understood. He turned away, unable to bear the hurt in her eyes. 'Lucy, you know I can't take you with me.'

'Why not? I am healthy and accustomed to travel. I know India, and the climate doesn't exhaust me as it does many people. Why should I not accompany you?' She placed her hand on his unyielding arm, her throat aching with unshed tears. 'Edward, I am your wife and my place is at your side. Do you not wish me to accompany you?'

If only she knew, Edward thought. God, if only she knew how badly he wanted to take her with him.

Unfortunately, there were a dozen compelling reasons why he could not. Once he made contact with Abdul Rahman Khan's supporters, his life might well depend on his powers of concentration and observation. In order to cross into Afghanistan unobserved, he would have to shed the trappings of an English nobleman and once again become Rashid. It was Edward's uncanny ability to immerse himself in the role of an illicit gun trader that had prevented his unmasking by the dozens of French and Russian spies working along the Indian-Afghan frontier.

For Lucy's own sake, he could not tell her the truth about his mission and condemn her to months of worry about his safety.

'Lord Triss doesn't expect me to be away for very long,' he said. 'Perhaps as little as five months. My uncle is sorry to interrupt our honeymoon, but he needs my special knowledge of Afghanistan.'

'Why does he need you at this precise moment? What is happening in Afghanistan that requires immediate attention?'

He gave her his approved cover story, which was true, as far as it went. 'Amir Sher Ali has agreed to send a delegation from Kabul to confer with a high-level British delegation in Peshawar. Lord Lytton himself will be conducting some of the negotiations.'

'The viceroy? Then these negotiations must be very important.'

Edward nodded. 'The Amir claims that he seeks a lasting settlement of all border disputes, and he wishes to accommodate our government's insistence on sending a British representative to Kabul. Lord Triss wants me on hand to offer advice to the British negotiators. Most of them, unfortunately, have little first-hand knowledge of conditions within Afghanistan.'

'Obviously your work will be crucial to the success of the talks, and I wouldn't dream of intruding upon it. Although, personally, I would be highly suspicious of the Amir's intentions. If he is proclaiming peace so loudly it probably means he needs a breathing space to improve his preparations for war.'

Edward laughed. 'I agree completely. Either that, or some faction within Afghanistan is about to launch a successful *coup d'état* and Sher Ali wants to pre-empt their attack.' He sobered, realising how easily he had allowed himself to be side-tracked.

'But that isn't the point, Lucy. This trip of mine is designed for speed rather than comfort. You will be much happier and more at ease if you remain in England.'

Lucy looked up at him, her eyes bright with tears. 'You may, if you wish, order me to stay in England, but do not, I beg of you, tell me that I shall be *happier* if I remain here. That is insulting to us both. I thought I deserved more honesty from you, Edward.'

Without waiting for him to reply, Lucy pivoted on her heel and walked blindly towards the door. She had taken no more than half a dozen steps when Edward caught up with her. He gripped her arms and swung her around to face him.

'All right,' he said harshly. 'You win this particular battle, Lucy. I am no match for your tears. Come to India with me if that is what you wish, but I pray we don't both regret this.'

She didn't like the feeling that she had torn the concession from him against his better judgement, but the relief of knowing they wouldn't be separated overcame all other emotions.

'It is very much what I wish,' she said softly. 'Oh, Edward, thank you for allowing me to come. You will not regret it, I promise you.'

She stared up at him, her eyes dark with love, her mouth full and soft, waiting for his kiss. Looking down at her, Edward realised he didn't even care if his decision was wise. He cared only that it had made her happy.

He took her into his arms, holding her tight against his chest. Only later, as he lay spent and exhausted on

the tangled sheets, did the worries crowd in again,
denying sleep. Edward stared into the shadowed cor-
ners of the room, feeling the warmth of Lucy's arm
across his ribs, and the icy chill of fear within his heart.

He would keep her safe, Edward swore silently. As
long as she never found out he was returning to
Afghanistan, there would be no danger for either of
them. As long as he lied through his teeth, all would be
well. One thing, above all else, was certain: Lucy must
never again see Rashid.

The sea voyage back to India was vastly different from
Lucy's homeward journey two months earlier. Lost in
love for her new husband, she laughed away the days
and made love all night. If she sometimes sensed a
frightening urgency in Edward's lovemaking, she
refused to acknowledge it. Their marriage was perfect,
and she would permit no cloud to hover on the horizon
of their happiness. Each day she allowed herself to
become a tiny bit more confident that Edward had
married her because he loved her. Each night she
blossomed a little more under the reassurance of that
love.

After a month of travel and several days in Calcutta
so that Edward could confer with the viceroy, they set
out on their long journey east to Peshawar. Another
woman might have been nervous at the prospect of
returning to a town where she had been so thoroughly
scorned, but Lucy knew Anglo-Indian society too well
to worry. Edward Beaumont, third Baron Ridgeholm,
would be a glittering star on Peshawar's limited social
scene. Lady Ridgeholm would be welcomed
accordingly.

Lucy's assessment proved entirely correct. Mr and
Mrs Rutherspoon hosted the official dinner party to
welcome the new arrivals. Mrs Rutherspoon, whose
imagination was not of a high order, seemed to have no
difficulty at all in disconnecting her memories of the
disreputable Miss Larkin from the present splendour of
Lady Ridgeholm, Baroness. While the men lingered

over brandy, she took her seat next to Lucy in the drawing-room, but seemed too overawed to speak. Lucy filled the gap.

'I do not see your daughter, Rosamund, Mrs Rutherspoon. I trust she is not indisposed?'

Once set off on the subject of her daughter, Mrs Rutherspoon chattered without stop until the arrival of the gentlemen set her off in pursuit of Lord Ridgeholm, her prize guest. Lucy remained seated and was joined by her host, who greeted her with what seemed genuine pleasure.

'Thank you for your letter, my lady. It arrived about a month ago, and I was delighted to hear that you had enjoyed a safe and comfortable journey home. The account of your ship's passage through the Suez Canal was most interesting.'

'The speed of the mail is one of the canal's greatest blessings,' Lucy remarked. 'Only four weeks for a letter to travel from London to Calcutta!'

'And at a cost of pennies,' Mr Rutherspoon agreed. 'Although sometimes I wonder if speed of communication is such a marvellous thing. In some instances, we would be better served if the messages coming out of London could all get lost at sea like they used to in the old days.'

'You are not an admirer of Mr Disraeli's policy in regard to India?'

Mr Rutherspoon cleared his throat. 'I'll be honest with you, my lady. I believe Mr Disraeli's forward policy will prove disastrous for the British Raj. We don't need to be aggressively seeking new boundaries for our empire. Half the world is already under our direct control. How can we govern more?'

'There seems to be no shortage of willing administrators.'

'Willing is not the same as competent. Here in India, for example, we should concentrate on improving the efficiency of our civil service, not chasing off in pursuit of some mythical Russian army that may or may not be threatening our northern frontier.'

He lowered his voice. 'My theory is that the Russian Emperor would forget about Afghanistan if we didn't keep declaring that the country lies exclusively within our sphere of interest. He never had any interest in marching in until we ordered him to keep out.'

'You believe the Russian Emperor is childish enough to go to war simply because our government has asked him not to?'

Mr Rutherspoon grunted. 'Why else would Tsar Alexander want to acquire a country that consists of impenetrable mountains and squabbling goatherds? The Tsar is using British interest in Afghanistan as a diversion. He has to find some way to keep his serfs too busy to notice that they're starving. What better way to occupy them than to conscript them into the army and send them off to fight the wicked British in Afghanistan?'

'Has he considered recruiting them to plant food, so that they would no longer be starving?'

'Hah! That is not the way of emperors, my lady. I'll admit it's a relief to know that your husband is here to advise our team of negotiators. This may be Great Britain's last chance to avoid a terrible mistake in Afghanistan. We need a few voices of cool reason to hold back Lord Lytton's crew of imperialist hotheads.'

'My husband has made no public statement concerning his instructions from the foreign secretary,' Lucy said.

'True, but I have known Lord Ridgeholm for some years. I've noticed that whenever he is involved in a treaty negotiation, or in some discussion with the natives, we end up with a sensible agreement that can actually be implemented. The trouble with the viceroy is that he's playing to the political gallery back home instead of considering the situation under his nose.'

Back home. Mr Rutherspoon had lived in India for over twenty years. He condemned the lack of understanding shown by British politicians legislating for India across thousands of miles of ocean and a universe of misunderstanding. And yet, like his wife, and like every other Anglo-Indian Lucy had ever met, he still referred to England as 'home'.

'You are looking amazingly pensive, my love.' Mr Rutherspoon had been called away by a guest, and Edward came to take his place at Lucy's side.

'Mr Rutherspoon gave me a great deal to think about.'

'I am alarmed. Experience has warned me to be wary of that particular expression of yours. I fear I am to be subjected to another of your lectures on the inalienable right of educated women to cast votes in public elections.'

She smiled. 'Not tonight.'

'I am amazingly relieved.'

'Prematurely, perhaps. Tonight you are to receive a special treat. I plan to lecture you on the need for Great Britain to avoid going to war over Afghanistan.'

'What a horrible prospect! Worse even than the rights of women. If I listen with due humbleness, what is my reward?'

'You become better informed.'

'Somehow, such a reward quite fails to tempt me. Could you not stretch your imagination a little?'

She pretended to give the matter serious consideration. 'Well, let me see. What sort of reward would you have in mind?'

He bent his head and murmured in her ear. 'Anything that involves your naked body in my bed would be acceptable.'

'My lord, I'm shocked by your lewdness!' She flipped open her fan. 'But since this is a *very* important subject you shall have your wish. One naked wife in exchange for your earnest attention to the subject of British war policy in Afghanistan.'

'One *willing* naked wife,' he amended, his eyes gleaming with laughter — and something more.

Lucy yawned, concealing the little coil of excitement already tightening inside her. 'My lord, you drive a monstrous hard bargain.'

He reached out solicitously to raise her to her feet.

'Others have commented on the same thing. If you are ready to leave, my dear, I believe we should be on our way. Let us find our host and hostess. Oh, look, how fortunate; they are coming in this direction.'

'Leaving already?' Mr Rutherspoon said.

'I'm afraid we must.' Lucy might be blushing, but Edward's voice was as smooth as cream. 'My wife has something she wishes to discuss with me, and I feel a most urgent need to become better informed.'

'Actually,' Lucy interjected, 'I am a little tired. The strains of the train journey must be catching up with me.'

As soon as Edward and Lucy were back in their own rented accommodation he dismissed the servants and propelled Lucy into their shared bedroom. He seated himself on a straight-backed chair of carved Indian mahogany and folded his arms.

'You see me before you, all dutiful attention,' he said, his eyes dancing. 'First, sweet wife, I listen to your lecture, and then you give me my reward. I am all eager anticipation.'

Lucy decided to ignore the dangerous, enticing gleam in her husband's eyes. 'It seems to me,' she said, clasping her hands primly in her lap, 'that Mr Disraeli errs in thinking he can find the perfect safe boundary for our empire. If we extend the boundary of northern India up into Afghanistan, where will the Prime Minister declare the borders of our next safety zone? Uzbek? Khiva? Edward, do not look at me so.'

'How so, my love?'

'As if. . .as if you will pounce upon me at any moment and tear off my clothes.'

'Why should I do that, my heart, when you have promised faithfully to perform the task yourself?'

'I promised no such thing!'

'How do you propose to end up naked and willing in my bed if you never undress?'

Lucy decided to ignore this question. 'I have not yet finished my lecture,' she said with considerable dignity. 'I have *lots* more to say.'

Edward inclined his head politely. 'You were, I believe, discussing where Mr Disraeli might draw the final boundaries of the empire, bearing in mind the strictures of his forward policy. Have I mentioned that your lips are quite the most kissable lips I have ever seen on a woman anywhere in the world?'

'Yes. I mean, no. Edward, will you please stop staring at me?'

'I don't wish to miss a single one of your wise words, my love. Do, pray, continue.'

Lucy drew in a laboured breath. 'In my opinion, Afghanistan should be established as a strong independent nation under an honest, efficient ruler who will dominate the warring tribes and factions. Its borders would then be guaranteed by a world——'

'A most admirable goal,' Edward said. 'My love, I am so grateful for your lecture. Please take off your gown.'

'Edward!'

'My love?'

'You are not keeping to the terms of our agreement. You said you would listen dutifully until I had finished. I have barely begun.'

'My heart, you have now learned the first and most important rule of diplomatic negotiation. Assume that your opponent will change the agreed terms of the treaty at his earliest opportunity. Please take off your gown.'

She could have refused, of course, but she had no real desire to postpone their lovemaking. Tonight, before she told him her incredible, wonderful news, she wanted to tantalise him just a little, to dazzle the worldly, jaded Baron Ridgeholm with the seductive powers of his wife.

'I can't take off my dress until somebody unfastens the buttons,' she murmured. 'Shall I summon a maid?'

'I think you know better,' Edward said huskily, rising to his feet.

He made short work of the tiny pearl buttons, and soon slipped the dress from her shoulders, along with her chemise. The dress fell in a pool at her feet, and she stepped out of it, pivoting slowly beneath his ardent gaze.

'You become more beautiful each day, I swear it,' he said. 'Ah, Lucy, how did I survive before I loved you?'

'By loving many other women?' she suggested teasingly.

'No. By walking through life only half alive.' Abandoning their game, he kissed her deeply, his tongue filling her mouth with the promise of ecstasy to come. Not halting their kiss, he guided her to the bed. Her knees connected with the cool, linen-covered mattress and she fell back on to it, unashamedly pulling him with her.

His hands stroked over her breasts, cupping each in turn, until her nipples sprang into revealing hardness beneath his touch. Trailing kisses along her collarbone and between her breasts, he finally took one of her swollen nipples into his mouth.

Instantly, he went still.

'What is it?' Lucy pushed herself up in the bed, struggling to free herself from the pleasant haze of rising passion. 'Edward, what is it?'

'I think you must know. Even I can feel the changes in your body.' Slowly, sensuously, Edward's hand traced an enquiring path over her stomach. Then his hands once again cupped the new, heavier fullness of her breasts.

'Lucy, my heart, can it be. . .are you with child?'

She laughed with the delight of confirming his guess. 'Yes, how did you know? I have been almost certain for nearly two weeks. I think our baby will be born in seven months, at the end of March or the beginning of April.'

'You must have conceived while we were still in England.' His normally austere expression softened with wonder. 'So soon! I never dreamed it would be so soon.' His hands circled her tiny waist. 'There doesn't seem to be much room inside here for a baby.'

A rueful smile curved her mouth. 'That problem will

soon be taken care of. Unfortunately, I am likely to expand in several inelegant directions.'

'And then you will be more beautiful than ever.' He kissed her deeply, one hand tangling in the mass of curls spread out over the pillow, the other stroking her flat stomach with an odd mixture of desire and reverence. 'I want to see your body swell as my son grows inside you. I wish I could already feel his legs and arms kicking against my hands.'

'You have played the role of a Punjabi trader for too long,' she said, stirring drowsily. 'You begin to think like a Muslim. How do you know I carry your son and not your daughter?'

He tickled her stomach with tender, teasing fingers. 'In my family we have a history of twins. Perhaps you are carrying both a son and a daughter.'

Speechless, her eyes wide with alarm, Lucy stared up at him. Laughing, Edward dropped a loving kiss on her nose. 'Never fear, my heart, I doubt if you need to worry. We don't have *that* many twins sprouting from my family tree!'

Once again, his hand travelled down her body, no longer searching for signs of her pregnancy, but simply seeking to bring her pleasure.

'I love you,' he whispered.

Despite the passionate intensity of their lovemaking, he rarely expressed his feelings in words, and Lucy's heart soared high with happiness. She sighed his name, arching her hips, kissing him in willing surrender.

They lay together for a long time, bodies entwined, throbbing with the aftermath of completion. Edward was the first to speak. 'Was I too rough?'

'No. . . It was wonderful.' Lucy touched him lightly on the cheek, already half asleep.

Edward smoothed the tangle of curls out of her face, but sleep claimed her totally before he could say anything more. Gently, he drew the thin linen sheet over her shoulders. Her body seemed so slender beneath the covers. Too fragile to give birth easily.

Against his will, Edward felt his hand drawn once again to her stomach.

Lucy was going to bear his child. What the hell was he going to do? Today the message had arrived from Abdul Rahman Khan, summoning him to the top-secret, all-important meeting in the heart of the Afridi stronghold. Next week Edward would leave for Afghanistan. The future of an entire nation might depend on what happened at that meeting, and there were a lot of people trying to make sure that Edward and Abdul Rahman never met.

He hoped to God he could outwit them.

He hoped to God he would live to see the birth of his child.

CHAPTER EIGHT

GOSSIP in Peshawar maintained that the talks between the Amir's emissaries and the British delegation were not going well. The approach of winter meant that the pass over the Hindu Kush into Afghanistan would soon be closed, and the pressure of lack of time was added to all the other pressures affecting the negotiators.

Lucy had good reason to believe the pessimistic rumours. Edward had been working twelve-hour days ever since his arrival in India, but recently his workload seemed never-ending. After sixteen hours around the negotiating table, he would return to their bungalow, apologise for his late return, then immediately closet himself in his study. Conversation between the two of them became limited to the exchange of brief, everyday courtesies. Lucy began to worry about the grey tinge of fatigue developing beneath Edward's tanned complexion.

'My dear, you need rest,' she said one night, entering his study with a cup of tea. 'I'm sure you didn't come to bed last night at all.'

'I can't.' He rose without looking at her and walked over to the window. 'I told you before we left England that I would be too busy to dance attendance on you. Please don't interrupt me any more, Lucy. I simply don't have time for playing husband at the moment.'

Lucy couldn't control the hurt that shadowed her eyes at his curt words. 'I'm sorry,' she said coolly. 'I didn't mean to intrude on your work. It won't happen again.' Back rigidly erect, she walked from the room.

Edward gripped the arm of the chair to stop himself running after her. 'It's for your own sake, Lucy, my heart,' he whispered. 'I don't want you to question me when I leave, and I shall be leaving very soon.'

* * *

Mr Carradin, senior aide to Lord Lytton, and leader of the British team of negotiators, was a seasoned diplomat. As such, he had long since learned the value of interspersing hard-hitting bargaining sessions with pleasanter diversions. On Saturday evening, a week after Edward's rebuff to Lucy, Mr Carradin decided the weather was cool enough to permit ending his dinner party with some informal dancing. Lucy did not share in the general anticipation of pleasure. Edward seemed positively buried in work and he had already announced that he would be unable to accompany his wife to Mr Carradin's party.

'But you should go, my dear,' he said. As was his habit over the past few days, he didn't look at her as he spoke. 'You certainly deserve a break from this tedious round of solitary meals and early bedtimes.'

Lucy wanted to remind him that she had endured two years in Afghanistan when sometimes weeks might pass without a single person speaking to her, other than to hurl abuse. Here in Peshawar, she had a household to control, neighbours to visit, baby clothes to sew and books to read. Boredom was the least of her problems.

But she said nothing, unable to breach the invisible boundary Edward seemed to have set between the two of them. She hoped Edward's withdrawal from her was caused by nothing more than pressure of work, but she feared that somehow it was caused by her pregnancy.

Without her husband at her side, Lucy didn't expect to find the dinner party particularly enjoyable. As she left, Edward appeared in the hallway, complimented her on her gown, and bade her farewell with his now habitual formality. Too hurt to be perceptive, Lucy quite failed to notice the agony of indecision in his gaze as he watched the pony-trap pull away from the doorway.

Mr Carradin was an excellent host, with a chef he had bribed away from the French ambassador. The unusually palatable food added to the lustre of a party that was a success right from the outset. Since the gentlemen outnumbered the ladies by a considerable margin, Lucy found herself seated among a group of high-ranking diplomats, including a dour Russian nobleman and a young Tuscan count from the newly united country of Italy. Discreet questioning on Lucy's part soon revealed that Count Guido had no idea why he was in an obscure Indian border town observing treaty negotiations that were entirely without interest to his country. He was, however, a charming flirt, and Lucy enjoyed listening to him compliment her in seductively accented English.

The dancing afterwards was less agreeable. Because of the shortage of female partners, Lucy felt obligated to dance as much as she could. She wasn't suffering from nausea, but she soon discovered that her stamina was sadly lacking. Instead of dancing light-footed until the early hours, by eleven she was forced to retreat to a cool corner of the makeshift ballroom, where she hoped to doze quietly till the dancing was over.

Her solitude lasted less than two minutes. Monsieur Armand, a French gentleman she had met briefly before dinner, came and stood beside her.

'If you do not dance, my lady, I shall take zis opportunity to converse wiz Mr Carradin's most beautiful guest.' He gestured to the chair. 'If I may be permitted?'

She fanned herself, smothering a sigh of regret for her lost isolation. Something about Monsieur Armand struck a false note, and she would have preferred to sit alone. Good manners, unfortunately, prevented her from replying honestly.

'Of course, *monsieur*, I should be delighted to have your company. Are you here to attend the treaty negotiations also?'

'Not at all, my lady. Alas, I am not ze diplomat. I am a merchant of furs.'

'Of fur?' she asked, wondering why in the world a fur trader would visit a hot country like India. 'Then you are in Peshawar on holiday, *monsieur*?'

He laughed heartily. 'Not at all, my lady. Peshawar is not ze ideal spa for a vacation, no? I seek a supply for sheepskins. For ze famous sheep from Afghanistan. It is called *garakul* by ze natives, but in France we say Persian lamb.'

'Oh, yes, of course.' Lucy immediately understood. 'I had heard that this particular wool is becoming fashionable in Paris, particularly for winter hats and as a trim for Berlin capes.'

He laughed again. 'You are right, my lady. We 'ave given zis wool a new name. We call it Persian lamb instead of *garakul*, and now fashionable ladies 'ave decided zey cannot live wizout it.'

'So do you plan a trip into Afghanistan, Monsieur Armand? That's rather a risky venture this late in the year. You must take care the passes are not closed by the time you and your guides are ready to come out.'

'Ah, no! I do not go into Afghanistan. I 'ave been told it is of all places most dangerous. Your so good 'usband 'ave give me zis warning 'imself. Ze tribesmen, you know, zey are always at war. I wait 'ere in Peshawar for my contact to arrive. He 'as promised me a mule-train loaded wiz sheepskins. I am in expectation of a most 'andsome profit when 'e finally arrives.'

Lucy hoped that Monsieur Armand would not wait in vain. From experience, she knew that Afghans and Europeans had quite different perceptions of time.

A flourish from the violinists announced the start of the final waltz. The young Tuscan count appeared at Lucy's side, claiming that she had promised him the final dance.

Lucy wasn't at all sure she had done any such thing, but she allowed herself to be led out on to the dance-floor anyway. The Tuscan, despite his outrageous compliments, was much more enjoyable company than the French merchant. He not only proved to be an expert dancer, he made her laugh with wry witticisms and harmless jokes. After they had said farewell to Mr Carradin, Count Guido requested permission to escort her home. 'So beautiful a *baronessa* should not ride through the streets alone.'

'Hardly alone, *signor conte*. I am surrounded by

servants, and the streets of Peshawar contain few dangers at this hour.'

'For so beautiful a woman is always danger,' the Count murmured, his eyes soulful. 'I will keep you entertained with amusing stories from my past life of wickedness. That is better than travelling alone, no?'

Lucy laughed and moved over in the pony-trap to accommodate him. She signalled the driver to begin the short drive home. She was laughing at his nonsense when the carriage drew up outside her bungalow. The Count quickly walked around to open her door. 'Alas, *baronessa*, I perceive you are as virtuous as you are desirable. An affair with you, *baronessa*, would have been delightful.'

She allowed her hand to tighten momentarily on his supporting arm. '*Signor conte*, no affair could ever be as delightful as marriage to someone you love.'

He escorted her to the shaded portico of the bungalow, then carried her fingers to his lips. The action was brief and respectful. His flirtatious manner returned almost at once and he swept her a deep, exaggerated bow. 'If you ever tire of trying to melt the reserve of your so cold English Baron, remember that I am the expert in frivolous affairs.'

She smiled, wondering why she wasn't offended by his boldness.

'Well, *signor conte*, you may live in hope if you wish. Let's say that if I ever decide to have an affair I will remember your unique skills.'

'An interesting promise, but one, I regret, you will have no occasion to act upon.' The voice that spoke from the darkened hallway was soft, cold and deadly. His face a mask of controlled fury, Edward strode towards the doorway, and nodded to the Count.

'My wife appreciates your escort service, *signor conte*. My driver will be pleased to take you to your destination.' He slammed the door without waiting for the Count's reply.

Lucy was appalled, almost as much by Edward's rudeness as by the obvious misinterpretation he had placed on her silly, teasing remarks. 'Edward, he is a mere boy,' she murmured.

'A mere boy who is three or four years older than you,' he said. 'And a reckless womaniser. What are you trying to do, Lucy? Punish me for neglecting you? Does it take so little to make you restless? A mere two weeks of hard work on my part, and already you are looking for a new man to warm your bed?'

If she had stopped for a split second she would have realised how out of character Edward's accusation sounded. If she had listened to the pain behind his words she would have realised that something must be troubling him greatly for him to speak with such harshness. But Lucy's emotions had been on a six-month merry-go-round, and she was in no condition to make subtle judgements about her husband's state of mind. Worse, she felt guilty because Edward was partly correct: she *had* flirted with the Count to ease the pain of her husband's rejection. And that guilt made her feel angry. By what right did Edward condemn her for flirting when he hadn't attempted to apologise for his own weeks of coldness and neglect?

'Why shouldn't I seek another man to entertain me?' she demanded hotly. 'You are certainly never available!'

Say that you will be there in the future she pleaded silently. Say that you love me and that you don't regret marrying me.

Edward's brows drew together in a black frown. 'You are my wife, and you carry my child. Is that not reason enough to expect absolute propriety in your behaviour?'

'I behaved with perfect propriety! You are deliberately misunderstanding a harmless remark.'

'To promise an affair strikes you as harmless?' Edward grabbed her hand and propelled her into the drawing-room. 'Or have I been a fool, sweet wife? Do you carry some other man's child that you wish to foist off on to me?'

Lucy felt the blow of his words as if he had punched

her in the stomach. She sank on to the sofa because her legs would no longer support her. Instinctively, she cradled her arms about her waist, protecting her child from the bitterness of its father's accusations. 'My God, Edward, how can you ask me such a question? You, of all people, should know the child I carry is yours. I was a virgin when we married!'

Edward had no idea where his angry taunts sprang from. He didn't question Lucy's chastity for an instant, nor was there any doubt in his mind that he was the father of her child. But the desperate need to prevent her questioning his departure had tormented him all week. The need to build a wall between them, at the same time as his heart and soul yearned to spend every moment locked in her arms, resulted in a total disconnection between the words his mouth spoke and the emotions his heart felt. 'I think we should continue this conversation some other time, Edward.' Her words sounded harsh as they squeezed out over the lump in her throat. 'I'm very tired and I would like to go to bed.'

'Not yet,' Edward said. 'If you are so hungry for a man's attentions, let me remind you that I am the man to answer your hunger.'

'I don't want. . .a man's attentions.' I want you. Oh, God, I want you.

He smiled without mirth. 'You lie, sweet wife. Your eyes tell me that you lie. You want to make love.' He took her into his arms, holding her with passion but without tenderness. His body was heavy over hers, his weight enforcing his will. His head bent purposefully towards hers.

'Don't!' she spat out. 'Edward, no!'

He ignored her protests, covering her mouth and kissing her with hard, hungry aggression. Soon there was no need for him to hold her captive. She lay quiescent beneath his mouth as he trailed his hands over her body, seeking her breasts and brushing his thumbs over her nipples until they sprang into hardness beneath his touch.

Lucy despised the response of her own body. Why was she allowing herself to melt into his arms? She and Edward ought to be talking, reasoning out their problems, not lying on the sofa, coupling like mindless animals.

The comparison was so humiliating and so apt that she renewed her struggles to escape. She strained and twisted, fighting her own body's weakness far more than her husband's strength.

Edward stopped kissing her long enough to frame her face between his hand. 'Lucy, don't fight what we both long for,' he murmured. 'Kiss me, my heart.'

With a soft moan, half of regret, half of yearning, she ceased her struggles and returned Edward's kiss. At the touch of her tongue, his kiss gentled, and the aggressive probing of his hands changed to a slow, delicate caress. Lucy writhed with pleasure. Tonight, as on every other night, Edward's touch was a match to the dry tinder of her passion. When he held her in his arms, when she felt his body tremble in her clasp, she wanted nothing more than to bring their lovemaking to its burning conclusion. She thought she heard him whisper her name, a murmur of regret and longing as he buried his face in her neck and spent himself within her.

As soon as their heartbeats slowed and their breathing resumed its normal pace, Edward picked her up and carried her into the bedroom. Without speaking, he laid her on the bed and took her into his arms, cradling her against his chest. He drew the muslin curtains, closing them into a world bounded by the gauzy limits of the draperies. Inside their tiny universe, silence reigned as he led her again and again to ecstasy. Each time, she thought her body must have passed beyond the point where response was possible, but each time he proved her wrong. He made love to her with a passionate, desperate urgency, as if seeking some means of imprinting the shape and texture of her body permanently on his mind. And all the while, no word was exchanged between them. It was nearly dawn when she finally fell into an exhausted sleep on the rumpled, sweat-soaked sheets. It was high noon when she awoke and discovered Edward had left the bungalow.

'What do you mean, the sahib left early this morning?' Lucy demanded, barely able to keep still while the maid fastened the buttons on her morning gown. 'Did he pack a suitcase? Where did he go?'

The ayah looked at her pityingly. 'Your lord told his servant that he leaves for Delhi this afternoon. I was instructed to give you your lord's letter when you awoke. That is all I know, memsahib. Does the sahib's letter tell you nothing more?'

Lucy had no need to look at her husband's note to recall exactly what it said, but she read it again anyway.

My dearest, I am summoned to consult with Lord Lytton on our current deadlock in negotiations. Events within Afghanistan are escalating out of control, and Amir Sher Ali must accept a resident British agent in his capital if he wishes to avoid war. Lord Lytton suspects that the Russian Emperor is using his armies massed at the northern border of Afghanistan to influence political decisions pending in Europe. I fear it may be some weeks before I am able to return to you. Take care of your health for the sake of our child, whom I long to see, but most especially take care of yourself. I love you. Edward.

Lucy closed her eyes, trying not to let frustration overwhelm her. She pulled a chair up to the dressing-table and allowed the ayah to start brushing her hair.

'If my husband doesn't leave for Delhi until this afternoon, did he tell you where he planned to spend this morning?' she asked, not really expecting the maid to give her an answer.

'Of course he told me where he was going this morning,' the ayah replied, as if she had made this perfectly plain several times already. 'He sees first the barbarians from across the mountains, then he meets with His Excellency the Prince Carradin for lunch.'

Lucy's heart gave a little jump of relief. Edward was

still in Peshawar! She still had a chance to see him. She glanced at the clock on her beside table. Almost one o'clock.

Less than twenty minutes later she was at Mr Carradin's lodgings, being shown into his private sitting-room.

'My dear Lady Ridgeholm.' The diplomat rose from his seat behind the desk, greeting her with a friendly smile. 'You look perturbed, my lady, and a little hot. Allow me to offer you some refreshment.'

'Thank you, but I have no time. I understood that I might find my husband here with you, Mr Carradin. Am I too late? Could you tell me where he has gone?'

'Lord Ridgeholm here? Alas, no, dear lady, I fear you have been misled. Your husband was anxious to catch the earliest possible train from Lahore. But I will be happy to see that a message is forwarded to him if that is of any help to you. I trust nothing is amiss at home?'

'No, nothing. We are. . .I am very well.' Her supply of energy seemed to drain away in a single, despondent gush. Lucy struggled to smile. 'I had hoped to see Edward once more before he left, but I suppose my messages can as easily be contained in a letter.'

'Good, good. I shall be delighted to include your letters in the diplomatic pouch travelling to Delhi each week. That way you'll be sure your news gets through swiftly and safely.'

'How very kind,' Lucy murmured. 'I must not keep you any longer, Mr Carradin.'

He walked with her to the front door. 'My dear Lady Ridgeholm, you have not delayed anything important. Don't worry, my dear, I'm sure you will hear from the Baron before the end of the week. I expect a courier from Delhi next Friday.'

'How kind,' she said again mechanically, allowing Mr Carradin to hand her up into the carriage.

Lucy had no idea what impulse caused her to turn around at the last moment before leaving the grounds, and even less what caused her to lean back, shielding her movement behind the polished cotton sun-canopy affixed to the open pony-trap. The brilliant light of the early afternoon sun was dimmed by the fringe of the canopy and the decorative tassels of her parasol, so that when she stared into the dark windows of Mr Carradin's lodgings the contrast was less intense than might have been expected. She could see the inside of Mr Carradin's library quite clearly. There were two men inside the library: Mr Carradin and her husband.

Lucy knew then why she had been so fearful ever since she awoke and found herself alone in bed. At some primitive, intuitive level, she had never believed Edward was going to Delhi, or she wouldn't have chased him so frantically. Her instincts warned her that there could be only one reason for his secretive departure — he was planning to return to Afghanistan.

Her carriage was just passing the Rutherspoons' bungalow. Quite calmly, Lucy leaned forward, tapped the driver on the shoulder with her parasol, and ordered him to stop. 'I have to visit Mrs Rutherspoon,' she informed the driver. 'I will return in her carriage, so you may go home now.'

Bowing respectfully, the driver opened the door of the trap and waited to see the memsahib safely inside the Rutherspoons' gate.

As soon as her carriage turned the corner, Lucy spoke to the Rutherspoons' gatekeeper. 'Oh, dear! I have forgotten something. Please open the gate; I must leave at once.'

The gatekeeper smiled kindly and swung open the gate. 'Certainly, memsahib. May Vishnu bless your footsteps.'

Mr Carradin had his lodgings in a large house built in the Indian style, with a separate *zenana* and a rambling collection of service buildings closed within the compound wall. As Lucy expected, the doors to the servants' quarters stood open at this hour of the day. She encountered many surprised glances but no opposition when she entered the rear courtyard and walked across the well-swept, beaten earth to the main house.

'Good afternoon,' she said, walking into the kitchen with a regal twirl of her parasol. 'I have remembered something important I must discuss with Mr Carradin. Please don't let me keep you from your duties.'

None of the servants attempted to stop her as she swept out of the kitchen and walked briskly towards Mr Carradin's library. Lifting her hand to knock, she hesitated then opened the door without knocking.

The two men in the library froze to their chairs.

'How nice to see you again, Mr Carradin,' Lucy said. 'And Edward, too. What a surprise!' She smiled sweetly. 'What brought you back from Delhi so soon?'

The men exchanged swift glances and Mr Carradin turned a most undiplomatic shade of red. Edward finally unfroze himself from the chair and came forward to take her hand. She clasped her parasol and pretended not to notice.

She knew he was aware of her rejection, but he took her elbow without comment and guided her towards the room's only armchair. 'Lucy,' he said quietly. 'You look hot and tired. Please sit while I send the boy to fetch something cool for you to drink.'

She sank into the chair, but stared up at him defiantly. 'No wonder I appear hot and tired. I've been chasing over town all day trying to find you.'

'I explained in my note that I have been summoned to Delhi.'

'And the ayah told me that you planned to lunch with Mr Carradin. Why wouldn't you speak with me when I called here an hour ago?'

Mr Carradin's brick-red complexion turned puce. He cleared his throat and sidled towards the door. 'I will go and rustle up the servants, Edward. I'm sure Lady Ridgeholm would enjoy a glass of fruit juice. I will be back directly, my lady.'

Lucy scarcely waited until the elderly diplomat had left the room. 'You are going to Afghanistan,' she said flatly.

Edward's gaze slid sideways. 'Afghanistan? Why in the world would you think such a thing?' He walked over to the desk and picked up a steel-nib pen, playing with it. 'Lucy, where is your carriage? I didn't hear it draw up. Did you send it home?'

'Yes.'

'You shouldn't be walking around in this heat, my dear. It isn't good for you, especially in your condition.'

'I am much stronger and healthier than I was when we escaped from Kuwar. A fifteen-minute walk isn't likely to overset me, Edward.'

'No, but at this time of day the sun could give you heat-stroke. My dear, let me escort you home as soon as you have taken some refreshment.'

'You haven't answered my question, Edward. Why are you going to Afghanistan?'

He flung the pen on to the desk. 'Lucy, I'm not going to Afghanistan. I've no idea where you would have acquired such a strange idea —'

'You left without saying goodbye.'

Edward turned slowly, and his voice was grim when he spoke. 'I thought, after what happened last night, that you might prefer to receive my apologies by letter.'

'I would never prefer our communication to be by letter. I have thought for the past week that we are in great need of honest conversation. Last night. . .last night made no difference to my opinion.'

He drew in a deep breath. 'Then I will apologise to you now, in person, for my conduct. Will you accept that my barbaric treatment of you sprang in part from the knowledge that I was about to leave Peshawar?'

'How long have you known you would have to go to — Delhi?'

'For some days. As I told you in my note, Lucy, Lord Lytton wishes to consult with me. I speak Pashto, a fact which nobody in the Afghan delegation realises. Because of that I have valuable insights to give the viceroy. For instance, we know that the Amir has formed an alliance with the Russians, but we have never understood his reasons for signing the treaty. I have learned in the past few days that the Amir cordially mistrusts the Russians and only maintains his alliance with them in order to protect himself from the rivalries of other tribal leaders within Afghanistan.'

'Could you not inform the viceroy of this in a written report?'

'Possibly. But Lord Lytton needs somebody close at hand to lead him through the maze of tribes and princelings all competing for British support. I am personally acquainted with many of the rival khans now seeking our assistance or threatening to do battle with us. Naturally, Lord Lytton would like to hear my opinions at first hand.'

It all sounded wonderfully plausible. Lucy stood up and approached the desk where he was standing, trying one last time to fathom the truth of Edward's plans. Her legs trembled, but not with fatigue. 'Why did Mr Carradin lie to me earlier on this afternoon?'

'He didn't lie, my dear. He told you I had left town, and, at the time, he believed he was telling the truth.'

'But you were here this morning and you're here now. Isn't it strange that I called during the only period you were *not* with Mr Carradin?'

'My dear, you find me here now simply because I unexpectedly obtained some important information which I decided should be shared with John Carradin at once. I therefore delayed my departure for a couple of hours and came back to speak with John. You must have been driving out of one gate as I entered by another.'

'Edward, swear to me that you are not returning to Afghanistan.'

His hands closed over hers, enfolding them in his firm, reassuring clasp. 'I swear it,' he said softly. He raised her hands to his lips and brushed loving, tender kisses over her knuckles. 'Lucy, my heart, I love you so much.'

A cough and the rattle of glasses on a brass tray alerted them to the fact that they were no longer alone.

Edward refused the offer of a drink. 'If you will

excuse me, sir, I am going to drive my wife home as
soon as she's finished her juice. Could I beg the use of
one of your carriages, do you suppose?'

'Certainly, my boy, certainly. Well, Edward, do we
have anything further to discuss before you leave for
Lahore?'

'I believe not, sir. I plan to set out this afternoon, as
we arranged. As soon as I have seen Lucy safely tucked
up in bed, that is. She must be exhausted after all this
activity.'

'Indeed she must.' Mr Carradin shook Edward firmly
by the hand. 'Never fear, my boy. We shall keep an eye
on her while you are gone.'

Edward laughed a touch ruefully. 'I fear you will
have your work cut out, sir.'

'Nonsense. I am an old hand at keeping the ladies
under control. Well, the best of luck in your endeavours, my boy. I shall eagerly await news of your success.
In the courier's bag from Delhi, of course.'

Lucy's throat closed up and, despite the heat of the
room, the blood turned to ice in her veins. During the
months of her captivity, she had learned to listen for
the tiny nuances that might mean the difference
between life and death. She could not fail to hear the
subtle undercurrent to Mr Carradin's words. In that
moment she knew beyond a shadow of a doubt that,
wherever Edward might be going, it was not to Delhi.

Once they were home, she didn't utter a word of
protest when he insisted on taking her to their bedroom
and summoning the ayah.

'Rest, my heart,' he murmured, sitting on the edge
of her bed and holding her hand lightly within his own.
He had already taken off her shoes and skirt, and
unfastened her bodice. Fortunately, he hadn't insisted
on undressing her any further. Which was useful, seeing
that she planned to follow him right out of the house.

'I have to leave soon, so when you wake up I shall
probably be gone. But I promise to write faithfully
from Delhi every day.'

She smiled, inwardly seething. 'Thank you, Edward,'

she whispered tremulously. 'I shall look forward to hearing from you.'

'Make sure your mistress sleeps,' Edward instructed the ayah. 'She has had an arduous day.'

That was certainly true. And she had an even more arduous time ahead of her. Lucy fluttered her eyelashes and faked a yawn. 'I am almost asleep,' she said drowsily. 'Have a good journey, Edward, dearest.'

He looked at her quickly and for a second her heart stopped beating. She opened her eyes and smiled sleepily. 'You are lucky I feel so tired, Edward, or I shouldn't allow you to leave without nagging to come with you. It must be the baby making me feel unusually compliant.'

He laughed, and rumpled her hair. 'That sounds more like my Lucy.' He kissed her forehead. 'Take care, my heart.' He strode quietly from the room.

As soon as the door closed, Lucy shot bolt upright in the bed. 'I'm hungry,' she announced to the startled ayah. 'Could you bring me some fruit? And perhaps some rice pudding?'

Nothing in the lord's instructions prohibited her from bringing the memsahib food, and the ayah departed willingly. When she returned, bearing a platter of sliced mango, dates and sweetened rice cooked in buffalo milk, she thought at first her mistress had fallen asleep wearing her hat. When she looked more closely, she saw that the bed was empty save for a bolster stuffed under a sheet and a discarded bonnet arranged on the remaining pillow. The memsahib was gone!

The ayah screamed, a heartfelt cry of desolation and panic. Unless her mistress returned soon, the ayah had nothing to look forward to except a whipping from the chief houseboy.

CHAPTER NINE

FROM her hiding-place behind a sack of rice in the pantry, Lucy listened as the ayah decreed that an urgent message must be sent to the lord sahib. This was exactly what she had hoped for. And, as she had expected, one of the servants knew precisely where Edward had gone. The lord sahib was, according to the groom, 'At his other house with the servant Abdullah.'

Edward's other house? Lucy's worries coalesced into sharp-edged fear. Emerging from the pantry into the kitchen, she informed the reluctant groom that she would go with him to find the sahib.

The door of Edward's dilapidated 'other house' fronted directly on to the street. Lucy was in the midst of pulling the bellrope when the door opened. Rashid stood framed in the darkened hallway.

She could find no words of greeting, and they stared at each other in tense, edgy silence. Eventually she blinked, trying to overcome her shock. After all these weeks of living with Edward, it was startling to find she still hadn't succeeded in melding the separate images she carried of the English aristocrat and the muslim gun-runner. Seeing her husband brown-skinned, turbanned, and clothed in the garb of a Punjabi trader, his English heritage faded and he once again became Rashid, a man who exerted a powerful attraction over her, but whom she scarcely knew.

Telling herself that this was Edward, her husband, the man who only one night earlier had made love to her until they both were nearly faint with exhaustion, she forced herself to speak. 'I. . . I n-needed to talk to you.'

Silently, Edward reached out and pulled Lucy into the garlic- and clove-scented hallway. He shut the door behind her before speaking in grim, angry Pashto. 'Why

189

are you here, Englishwoman? You put many lives at risk.'

She instinctively replied in the same language. 'I am not an "Englishwoman". I am Lucy, your wife. You lied to me, Rash — Edward. You swore to me you were not going to Afghanistan.'

'Perhaps because I wished to avoid precisely this sort of dangerous encounter. My safety lies in two things, Englishwoman: secrecy and total immersion in my role. I cannot allow myself to remember the weaknesses of Edward Beaumont when I conduct the business of Rashid.'

Lucy swallowed hard, uncertainty replacing anger. 'I have betrayed no secrets of yours, ever. I have never told a single soul that you are Rashid. Besides, to whom would I betray your secrets?'

'You alone have knowingly seen me both as Rashid and as Edward.'

'How can that be? Your identity as Rashid is no secret to your uncle——'

'Lord Triss knows that I assume a disguise in entering Afghanistan. That is the full extent of his knowledge.'

'What about Mr Carradin? He knows you are planning to return to Afghanistan; that much was clear to me this afternoon.'

'Mr Carradin knows that I plan to make contact with certain vital people at a meeting-place within Afghanistan, but he has no idea what role I will play in order to reach the agreed rendezvous. I repeat, nobody in the world except you has seen me in both my role as Rashid and as my true self. Even Abdullah, the young boy who takes care of this house, knows me only as a Punjabi trader. I send him away whenever I plan to make the change of roles, for the sake of his safety as much as for mine. What he doesn't know, he cannot reveal. But you, Englishwoman, can unfortunately reveal a very great deal.'

'Then take me with you,' she pleaded. 'Edward, you know I would be of help to you. Think how it was when we encountered those Russian soldiers! A man and his pregnant wife are much less likely to become objects of suspicion than a man travelling alone.'

For a moment his voice softened. 'Lucy, you cannot possibly journey with me. My meeting has been endlessly delayed, and winter already spreads its icy fingers into the mountains of the Hindu Kush. The travel would be too difficult for you.'

'It wasn't before, when we escaped from Kuwar.'

'Before you did not carry a child,' he said, his voice hardening once again. 'When we escaped from Kuwar, your body had been toughened by two years of forced labour. Now it is soft after weeks of pampered living. No words of yours will sway me, Lucy. I tell you again that you endanger my life and the lives of all I am hoping to meet if you linger here. It is past time for me to be gone. Abdullah already waits with my horse at our agreed meeting-place.'

She turned away, knowing he was unlikely to answer her but compelled to ask the questions anyway. 'Where are you going, Edward? How long will your meetings in Afghanistan take? Is there any hope that you can return before the passes are closed by winter snow?'

He hesitated and for an endless moment she was convinced he would not answer. 'I travel only as far as Qur'um,' he said finally. 'It is a small nomad winter settlement that lies less than two days north-east of the Khyber Pass. It lies within fifteen miles of the point where you and I encountered the Russian soldiers when we made our escape from Kuwar.'

'Then there is hope you will be back in Peshawar before winter closes the pass?'

'There is always hope.'

'Edward. . .' She turned back to face him, wanting to touch him, to kiss him farewell, but somehow afraid to initiate any intimacy with this man who was her husband—and yet was not. She tried to superimpose the image of Rashid over her images of Edward, but her eyes were blinded by tears and, perhaps for that reason, she could not get the picture straight in her mind.

'Edward,' she repeated helplessly. 'I am stronger than you think. Let me come with you.' She didn't add her unspoken fear: Or I am afraid I will never see you again.

'You cannot come with me, Lucy. Please don't ask again. Go home now. You are the wife of Baron Ridgeholm, and you carry his child. As such you owe him absolute obedience should he demand it. And he does, Lucy. On this occasion he demands that you return home and ask no more questions. He also asks that you reveal nothing to anybody of what you have learned here today.'

Lucy realised in that moment why she was having such difficulty in collapsing the two separate images of her husband into one: it was because Edward himself kept the identities separate. When he donned the clothes of Rashid, he did not so much play a role as enter into a totally different life. With regret, Lucy recognised that by pulling him out of character and forcing him to acknowledge her as his wife she achieved nothing save putting his life at risk. The greatest service she could do him would be to leave — and quickly.

The tears she had been holding back spilled on to her cheeks as she reached for the latch of the front door, pulling it open with stiff, jerky movements. She couldn't bear to look at him, and she spoke more to the roadway than to him. 'Goodbye, Edward. Have a safe journey and come back as soon as you may. I will be waiting anxiously for your return.'

He didn't reply and she stepped out into the dirt-packed path, fumbling in her reticule for a handkerchief. The door closed behind her with a soft click. Blinded by the sun and her tears, she didn't at first recognise Count Guido, who stood talking to her groom.

Lucy pushed her wet handkerchief back into her reticule and forced a smile. 'Good afternoon, *signor conte*. How are you today?'

'Less well for seeing you so troubled.'

'I am concerned over a sick servant who had delivered a stillborn child,' she said. 'In this part of the world, child-bed fever is so often fatal.' Dear God, had the Count seen Rashid? Had he overheard her fare-wells? A sinking feeling in the pit of her stomach warned her that she had called Edward by name after the street door was opened.

'You are good to express such concern over a servant you can scarcely know, *signora baronessa*.' The Count politely handed her into the pony-trap.

'I have known her for several years. She once served my father. May I offer you a ride, *signore conte*?'

The Count climbed into the carriage and Lucy instructed the driver to return home.

'I have a small matter of business to discuss with Baron Ridgeholm. In connection with the treaty nego-tiations, you understand. Would it be convenient for me to call upon him now, do you suppose?'

'I'm afraid that my husband has left for Delhi, *signor conte*. But I'm sure Mr Carradin would be able to answer any questions you may have.'

'Of course. It is of no matter.' The Count pulled out a large gold pocket watch. 'But it is four o'clock, *signora baronessa*, the hour of the English tea. If your husband is not at home awaiting you, why do you not join me on my veranda? I have the new tin of English digestive biscuits, which I will be delighted to open in your honour. They are not yet soaked by the humidity and remain crisp as the day they left Birmingham.'

Whether it was the appeal of the biscuits, the lack of desire to return to a bungalow without Edward, or sheer inertia, Lucy accepted the Count's invitation. She leaned back against the hot leather seat cushions, conducting a polite but desultory conversation with less than one tenth of her attention.

She was greatly relieved that the Count seemed to have heard nothing of her final exchange with Edward. Peshawar was thick with spies of every stripe and description. It would be all too easy for the Count to let drop some careless remark in the wrong circles that would identify Rashid as Baron Ridgeholm, an agent of the British government.

And how the Russians and their informers would love to get hold of that little titbit! Lucy decided she wouldn't be in the least surprised to discover that several of the people she had met at recent social events were actually spies. Monsieur Armand, for example. She would wager that the French sheepskin merchant traded as frequently in information as he did in *garakul* wool. Lucy thanked her lucky stars it hadn't been Monsieur Armand waiting outside the door when she'd said goodbye to Edward.

Her lucky stars were obviously in the mood to be capricious. Lucy's suspicions about Monsieur Armand had scarcely formed when her groom drove into the small grounds attached to the Count's bungalow. And there, seated on the veranda, sipping tea, was Monsieur Armand, together with another man whose name Lucy couldn't remember.

'Alas, it seems I have unexpected visitors.' The Count pulled one of his endearing, comical faces. 'I am desolate, *signora baronessa*. I thought at last we would be alone, you and I. Sometimes I fear our love-affair is destined never to start.'

'Then perhaps we should simply resign ourselves to becoming friends,' Lucy replied with a laugh, allowing the Count to assist her from the pony-trap. 'Have I not made that suggestion before, *signor conte*?'

Lucy was hungry and thirsty enough to be quite relieved that tea was already served. A blessed late afternoon breeze stirred the hot air as Lucy acknowledged Monsieur Armand's greeting and sank into a comfortable basketweave chair. Monsieur Armand made haste to introduce his friend, Monsieur Bruno, a partner in the sheepskin trade who had only just arrived in Peshawar.

Lucy scrutinised Monsieur Bruno as he apologised in French for the fact that he spoke almost no English. Odd that she should have thought she recognised him, particularly since his features seemed unfamiliar now that she saw them more closely. She shrugged off a slight feeling of unease. Really, she would have an intolerable few months if she allowed her worries about Edward's safety to taint every chance acquaintance with the suspicion that he was not quite what he seemed.

Lucy did her best to contribute her share of both English and French platitudes to the ensuing conversation, in between sipping excellent tea, eating sandwiches, and munching on digestive biscuits. If she allowed her attention to wander, her mind immediately blazed with frightening images of the danger that lay ahead for her husband. She knew all too well that in a country like Afghanistan, teetering on the edge of chaos, not even the most consummate survival skills could guarantee Edward's safe return. Lucy finished her tea and rose gracefully. 'I have been absent from my home long enough to cause concern, and I should never have stopped for tea. The Count tempted me with his offer of biscuits newly arrived from England, which were as delicious as he promised.'

The Count sprang to his feet. 'But of a certainty, *signora baronessa*, I must escort you home.'

'Of a certainty, *signor conte*, there is no need whatsoever for you to leave your other guests. My bungalow is no more than a few minutes' drive from here.'

After another ten minutes of polite argument, the Count agreed to summon the carriage and allowed Lucy to depart without any accompaniment other than her driver. All three men stood guard and waved as the little carriage pulled out of the driveway. Monsieur Bruno cast one longing look over his shoulder towards the shaded veranda, but then resumed his gallant waving.

Lucy returned the waves measure for measure, but her hand suddenly trembled. She swallowed, trying in vain to moisten her throat, which was parchment-dry. Dear God, she finally remembered where she had seen 'Monsieur Bruno' before! His glance towards the veranda had triggered the key to her memory. The last time she had seen 'Monsieur Bruno' look over his shoulder in that precise fashion, she had been wearing a sack of food strapped to her abdomen to imitate pregnancy, and he had been wearing the uniform of a Russian Cossack soldier.

Hard on the heels of this realisation came one that was far more frightening. If the Count ever mentioned to Monsieur Bruno that he had seen Lady Ridgeholm bidding a tearful farewell to a Muslim trader, Edward's life would be in twice as much danger as before. And — worst of all — she was the person responsible for Edward's increased danger. The short journey back to the bungalow seemed interminable. Clearly, this was no longer a situation she could handle alone. Should she call on Mr Carradin personally, or send a note explaining the situation? Was she over-reacting in thinking something needed to be done right away? After all, there was no reason to suppose that the Count had any intention of telling his visitors that he'd seen Lucy in the market-place. Such a trivial incident surely couldn't have been of much interest to him.

Like a red-hot poker blazing a path through the thicket of her mind, Lucy suddenly recognised a dreadful truth: she had no reason whatever to suppose that the Count could be trusted, no reason whatever to suppose that his presence in the market-place this afternoon had been accidental. Just because he was charming and made her laugh didn't preclude the possibility that he was a spy. On the contrary, charming spies were probably far more successful.

With the all too clear vision of hindsight, Lucy realised that the Count's behaviour had been a touch off-key. Given that he must have seen Rashid quite plainly, had he not accepted her tale of a sick maidservant a little too easily? Why hadn't he asked more questions about the supposed maidservant, and what she was doing living in a house owned by a Punjabi merchant? Add these doubts to the fact that the Count had been talking to the groom while waiting for Lucy to put in an appearance, and his behaviour became even more strange. Surely he must have asked the groom why Lady Ridgeholm's carriage was standing in this shabby part of town? And the groom must surely have replied that the memsahib was visiting her husband.

Lucy shivered despite the heat. If the Count was a spy, then it followed as certainly as night after day that the presence of Monsieur Armand and the Cossack captain on his veranda was not mere coincidence. The three men must be working together, and the Count would already have passed on the news that Edward had left town in the guise of a Punjabi trader. She had to warn Mr Carradin, so that the three spies could be arrested before their information about Edward could spread any further. What was more, she must get to Mr Carradin's house without being spotted by any of the three men.

The ayah entered the bedroom and salaamed. Lucy looked at her thoughtfully. They were much of a size, and two Indian women could move around the streets of Peshawar far less conspicuously than the Baroness Ridgeholm and her maid.

'Please bring me a spare set of your clothes,' Lucy said.

The ayah scurried away, returning less than five minutes later carrying a bundle of freshly laundered clothes. Lucy changed quickly and the ayah followed her out of the bungalow and on to the main dirt road, which connected virtually all of the diplomats' various lodgings and bungalows. In their simple saris, their faces veiled, Lucy and Dira aroused little interest. The streets were busy with people taking advantage of the remaining light, while the evening breezes blew away the worst of the day's heat and made walking tolerable. Lucy's spirits gradually lightened as she and the maid walked toward Mr Carradin's lodgings, jostling good-naturedly with the crowds on the pavement. Goodness, but she had blown a small molehill into a very large mountain. What, after all, could the Russian captain, alias Monsieur Bruno, do even if he discovered Edward was entering Afghanistan in the guise of a Punjabi merchant? There were no telegraph offices in Afghanistan, no border police, no efficient systems of communication. Edward would be over the pass and lost in the trackless wastes of the arid high country long before the Russians could mount an effective pursuit. This, after all, was the same captain who hadn't been able to find his way from Qandahar to Kuwar without getting lost.

Lucy quickened her pace, eager now to reach Mr Carradin. After today's experiences, she was going to become the most virtuous, stay-at-home wife Edward could possibly want. She would ask Mr Carradin to place all three conspirators under arrest, and that would be the end of the matter as far as she was concerned.

This was certainly the day for fate to play games with her, Lucy reflected. As she passed by Count Guido's driveway, Monsieur Armand and the Russian captain walked out of the gate and entered the flow of pedestrians. Like Lucy and her maid, the two men seemed to be progressing in the direction of Mr Carradin's lodgings.

For one heart-stopping moment, panic overwhelmed her, then courage returned in full measure. This was an opportunity not to be missed. She drew her veil higher over her face and grabbed her maid's hand, indicating by gesture that the maid was to remain silent and follow Lucy. Cautiously, feet making no sound in the dirt, the two women edged closer to the two men.

They were only a few hundred yards from the entrance to Mr Carradin's lodgings, and so far the men had said nothing that could not equally as well have applied to sheepskin merchants as to spies. Lucy recognised that any serious investigation should be left to Mr Carradin, and she allowed the distance between herself and the two men to increase slightly.

It was a street urchin who betrayed Lucy's presence to the two men. A small boy, still inexpert in his thievery, jostled against Monsieur Armand, presumably hoping to snatch a pocket watch or some other valuable trinket.

'Oh, no, you don't, my lad!' Bruno exclaimed in French. Then he lunged after the terrified boy, who somehow managed to squirm between the two men and leap into the roadway, almost knocking Lucy off her feet in the process.

'Let him go,' Armand said, as the boy dodged bullock carts and donkeys, and disappeared into a narrow alley. 'He didn't get anything, after all.'

He turned to walk on, when his attention was suddenly attracted by the ayah, who was muttering reassurances in English and trying to reaffix Lucy's veil, which the street urchin had ripped off. Lucy turned away, indicating with frantic hand gestures that the maid should be silent, but the maid couldn't see what threat was posed by two harmless European gentlemen. She was much more worried about the pearl pin that had somehow become lost in the dirt.

Monsieur Armand gave a small exclamation before reaching out to grip Lucy's arm, thrusting her hard against the wall and clamping his hand over her mouth before she could scream. When the ayah emitted a shriek of outrage, Armand simply ordered Bruno to take care of her.

Bruno obeyed, screening the maid from any passers-by with his body, and knocking her unconscious. He then swung her up into his arms, presenting a perfect picture of a considerate master carrying home his fainting servant.

Monsieur Armand looked at Lucy, his expression openly mocking. 'My dear Baroness, zis is a most big surprise. My colleague and I, we are most 'appy to be of service to you at zis moment. You have ze choice. I will remove my hand and you will accompany me quietly. Or you may try to scream just once, and your fate will be as your servant's. Shall I remove my hand, *madame*?'

Lucy nodded, then tried to smile, hoping against hope that a bluff might work. 'Monsieur Armand, I would be very grateful if you would let me and my maid return home at once. It would be most embarrassing if

word got out in the British community that I had
ventured forth into the streets dressed in native costume. I hope I can rely on your instincts as a gentleman
to forget this little incident.'

'Indeed, Lady Ridgeholm, I am all concern for your
problems. But alas, I also have problems. Imagine if
word got out in ze British community zat Monsieur
Armand is not a merchant of furs, but a seeker of
informations. I zink my embarrassment would be
greater than yours.'

'I don't understand.'

'Do you not, my lady? Oh, I zink you do. Walk,
please. My lodgings are very private and quite close to
here. We will discuss zis most interesting situation
where we are alone.'

'I can't come to your lodgings, *monsieur*. It would
not be proper.'

He laughed. '*Madame*, please. Do not insult your
intelligence and mine wiz zis feeble pretence. I am
curious only for one zing. Why do you follow me and
my colleague? What do you hope to learn?'

'I wasn't following you. I need to see Mr Carradin.'

'And for zis you dress up in native costume and roam
ze streets?'

Her laughter had a bitter tinge. 'At the time, it
seemed like a good idea. A way to remain
inconspicuous.'

'Forgive me, Baroness, if I tell you zat I find your
story difficult to believe.'

'Eventually, Monsieur Armand, you will have to let
us go.'

'My dear Baroness, I can zink of no reason at all why
zat should be so. It is one of ze advantages of India zat
it is so easy to dispose of an unwanted body. Ze police
here, zey have not ze skills of your English policemen.
The so sad end of the so beautiful Lady Ridgeholm will
be mourned by all.'

It was clear that she had absolutely nothing to lose
by running. And Mr Carradin's house was fairly near.
Monsieur Armand was so confident of his superiority

that he had loosened his grip on her arm to the point where it offered almost no restraint. Lucy would have liked to dash straight forward, towards Mr Carradin's house. Unfortunately, Bruno blocked her way. To dodge backwards around Monsieur Armand was almost impossible, so she had no choice other than to wait for a side-alley, where she could break away and run all in one movement. A narrow alley came up soon enough, and she jerked her arm free, tearing down the road and screaming for help.

The element of surprise worked in her favour, and she might have succeeded in her ploy if luck had been on her side. But the alley ended in a high, barred gate, and she had no time to reach up and tug at the bellrope before Armand caught up with her.

He seized her shoulders in a vicious grip. 'You should not have run.' he said, his voice cold with fury. 'You definitely shouldn't have run.'

His fist landed squarely beneath her chin, and a scarlet starburst of pain ended abruptly in cool blackness.

When Lucy regained consciousness, she was lying on a comfortable sofa in somebody's study. Her jaw felt as if it had been pulverised, and her head ached abominably. Otherwise she seemed in amazingly good shape.

Her brief surge of relief vanished as soon as she became alert enough to take better stock of her surroundings. She wasn't alone. Messieurs Armand and Bruno were seated in the same room, discussing — in calm, polite French — where and by what method to kill her.

Bruno favoured a quick slash of the knife. Armand, on the other hand, favoured devising some convincing form of accidental death. His personal favourites for the 'accident' were either death by bullock cart wheels or death by drowning.

Lucy wasn't anxious to die in any fashion, and considered both these methods particularly horrid. Bruno merely considered them inconvenient.

'Why do we need such elaborate preparations?' he asked impatiently. 'I slit the woman's throat, or her belly, and then we toss her body into a ditch and the maid along with her. If the authorities find them before the jackals, they will assume the women were robbed. The Baroness's servants will confirm that she insisted on walking out with only her ayah for protection. If we are lucky and the dogs get there first. . .then, my friend, there will be no need for explanations, because there will be no identifiable body.'

'Hmm, perhaps you are right. Although the Indians don't go much for knifing, you know. Strangling is more their style. The legacy of the *thuggees*, and all that.'

'So we strangle her.' Bruno shrugged. 'Let's have done with talking, my friend, and get on with the action. I must leave for Afghanistan at dawn if I am to have any hope of staying reasonably close to Lord Ridgeholm. There's little enough chance of picking up his trail, but knowing what disguise he uses makes things easier for me. At least we know that his meeting with Abdul Rahman Khan must be scheduled to take place soon. But God damn it! Still nobody can tell me where they will meet!'

'That is one of the reasons the Khan of Kuwar is sending a band of his men to join you,' Armand reminded him. 'The Khan swears that his men will be able to lead you to the place of meeting. Holy Mother of God, Abdul Rahman is living on Russian territory! How is it possible that none of your spies and none of the Amir's spies and none of the Khan's spies can tell us precisely where this meeting with Baron Ridgeholm will take place?'

'If only we dared risk killing Abdul Rahman while he is still on Russian soil!'

'We would face an outcry from every nation looking for an excuse to complain about Russian intervention in Asia.'

'Perhaps the woman knows something about the meeting,' Bruno said, not sounding too hopeful. 'The

Count insists her husband is crazily in love with her. He may have been indiscreet.'

'If the British have chosen Lord Ridgeholm for this mission, you can be sure he is too professional to be indiscreet,' Armand said.

Bruno shrugged. 'What have we got to lose by asking?'

'Before we kill her?'

'Before we kill her. Whatever she says can make no difference to that decision.'

Lucy decided it was time to make her wakefulness known. Stirring noisily on the sofa, she groaned as if just regaining consciousness. In fact, groaning wasn't difficult since the act of moving her head caused a grinding sensation of pain similar to little men with hammers pounding nails into her teeth and jawbone.

The men eyed her with disfavour as she struggled to sit up. 'Water,' she murmured. 'Please give me water.'

'Zere is no water,' Monsieur Armand said. 'Here, drink zis.'

'This' was brandy, and Bruno's expression suggested that it was an appalling waste of good liquor to bestow it on a woman destined to die so soon. Lucy sipped the strong spirit cautiously, wanting to swallow enough to ease her throat and conquer her nausea without taking enough to blur her mental faculties.

'Where is Dira?' she asked, setting the glass aside.

'Dira?'

'My maid.'

'She is in ze kitchen,' Armand said smoothly. Too smoothly. 'Never fear, *madame*, she is quite well.'

Which probably meant that Dira was dead, or would be shortly. Despair and guilt threatened to overwhelm Lucy, but she fought them back. Despair could all to easily overcome the will to survive, and Lucy had no intention of dying. The child she carried was reason enough to fight for life, even if it hadn't been imperative to reach Edward.

'Why have you brought me here?' she demanded,

aware that her voice contained an annoying tremble, despite the fortifying brandy.

Monsieur Armand's reply was brisk. 'Come, *madame*, you know quite well why you are here. You have ze power and ze knowledge to unmask me, as well as my colleague, Monsieur Bruno, and our ally ze Count.'

Bruno spoke to Lucy for the first time, switching the conversation to French. Perhaps he really didn't speak or understand much English. 'The Count tells us your husband has left town, *madame*. Where is he going?'

Lucy picked up the brandy glass and took another slow sip. 'He has gone to Delhi for consultations with the viceroy,' she said.

Bruno scowled. 'You will not waste our time with such answers, *madame*. We know that Lord Ridgeholm goes to Afghanistan for a meeting with Abdul Rahman Khan. If their meeting is satisfactory, your government will throw its support behind Abdul Rahman, who is the only person strong enough to unite the warring tribes of Afghanistan. Your husband is the leader of a faction within the British government that wishes to see Afghanistan established as a strong, independent nation. A very inconvenient leader, whom we Russians intend to see does not succeed. Afghanistan is a natural part of our great motherland and we don't wish to see it become independent.' His eyes lit with an inner fire. 'You Britishers will be forced to acknowledge the truth before this century reaches its end. India may be the playground of your Queen Victoria, but Afghanistan is part of the imperial destiny of Mother Russia. In generations to come, the Tsar and his people will make Afghanistan great.'

Lucy ignored the impassioned rhetoric. 'If you know all this, *monsieur*, why do you ask me where my husband has gone?'

Bruno hesitated. 'Because we would like confirmation of the exact meeting-place.'

Lucy drew in a deep breath. This was her one and only hope for escape and she must grab it with both hands, despite the risk. 'No, *monsieur*,' she said steadily. 'You do not want confirmation of the meeting-place. You and your fellow spies have no idea where the meeting between my husband and Abdul Rahman Khan is to take place.'

'But you know?' Monsieur Armand interjected, unable to conceal his excitement. 'Your husband has told you?'

'If I did know, *monsieur*, I would be a fool to share my knowledge with you. To speak would be to sign my death warrant.'

'Nonsense. We promise you safe passage back——'

'*Monsieur*, you have asked me not to be foolish. Now I ask you the same. Why should you allow me to live once you know where the meeting is to take place?'

'I don't believe you know anything about the meeting-place,' Bruno said. 'This is nothing more than a play for time, and, as far as I'm concerned, it isn't working.'

Lucy forced herself to look at him without fear. 'I know a great deal more than you imagine, Captain, both about you and about this important meeting-place.'

Monsieur Armand gasped at Lucy's use of the title 'Captain', but Bruno refused to appear impressed. 'One of your husband's informers told you of my rank,' he said aggressively.

'Not at all.' Lucy allowed herself to smile. 'We have met before, you and I, although I don't believe I shall tell you where. I know that you are the commander of a troop of Cossack soldiers recently operating within the borders of Afghanistan. I know that you were sent on an urgent mission from Qandahar to Kuwar and lost your way, causing great danger to your men when you passed first near the Khyber Pass and then near the town of Jalalabad.'

'*Sacre Dieu*!' Bruno and Armand exchanged worried glances, obviously wondering how many other people shared this incriminating information. Lucy could almost see them thinking that perhaps it would not be

wise to kill this interfering Englishwoman until they
discovered exactly how much she knew. It was Monsieur Armand, all propitiating smiles, who spoke.

'*Chère madame*, your information is most intriguing.
I suspect you have some proposition you wish to make
to us?'

'Yes. A very simple proposition. I myself will lead
Captain Bruno to the meeting-place between my husband and Abdul Rahman, on condition that my husband and I are allowed to go free as soon as I have led
the captain there.'

Once again, Bruno and Armand exchanged glances,
lightning-swift and full of satisfaction. Monsieur
Armand stroked his moustache. 'That seems a very fair
bargain,' he said. 'Quite satisfactory.'

Of course it seemed satisfactory, Lucy reflected. In
fact, it probably seemed outstanding from Monsieur
Armand's point of view since he had not the slightest
intention of keeping it.

'We will need to travel fast and hard,' Bruno commented hastily. Perhaps he realised that his colleague's
acquiescence had been too easy. 'I doubt if you will be
able to keep up with the pace I set, *madame*.'

'I have probably travelled harder and faster within
Afghanistan than you, Captain. Have no fear. I shall
meet whatever pace you set.'

The Russian captain still seemed dissatisfied,
although he had little to lose. If Lucy was lying and
didn't know the meeting-place, he would be no worse
off. In fact, in some ways he would be better off, since
she would be much easier to murder on a mountain in
Afghanistan than in the British-controlled town of
Peshawar. Nevertheless, he tried to probe the precise
extent of her knowledge.

'Who else knows about my past activities in
Afghanistan?' he asked.

'Captain,' she chided gently, 'we have already agreed
that I am not a fool. You may not trust me, Captain,
and I certainly don't trust you, but at this moment we
are more or less equals. You need me. And as long as

you need me, I have some hope of living. Don't expect me to impart information that is going to change the balance of power between us.'

'Since we are being so frank, you will understand when I say that you must at least give us some indication of where the meeting-place is to be. We cannot afford to set out on a wild-goose chase. Time is too short.'

'The meeting-place is not more than thirty miles north-east of the Khyber Pass, Captain, and that is all I plan to reveal to you. Budget your supplies accordingly.'

She could tell from the expressions of the two men that she had given them information that coincided with whatever knowledge they already possessed. She drank the final swallow of brandy, more to disguise her shaking hands than because her throat was still dry. Dear heaven, but she had committed herself to a dangerous course of action! She would have to lead Bruno close enough to Edward's appointed place of rendezvous that she could slip away from camp and complete the journey on foot. Not only was her own life at stake, but the lives of people crucial to the future peace of Afghanistan and northern India. From what she had heard, it seemed obvious that Bruno had orders to kill Abdul Rahman Khan before he could rally the dissident tribesmen and unify Afghanistan. And Edward had undoubtedly been included in Bruno's assassination orders.

'We leave from the other side of town at dawn tomorrow morning,' Bruno said. 'You will come with me now to the house where I plan to spend the night. Armand, you will see about the carriage?'

'At once.' Monsieur Armand departed to summon the carriage, which arrived promptly. A shabby, hooded affair, drawn by a mule, it was unlikely to attract attention on the Peshawar streets even at this late hour. Bruno filled the minutes of waiting for the carriage by binding Lucy's wrists in front of her with a length of narrow cotton cloth, and tying an efficient gag over her mouth. He then rearranged her veil so that his handiwork was invisible at first glance.

He took out a small dagger concealed beneath his jacket and showed it to Lucy. 'To discourage you from any dramatic action such as attempting to throw yourself from the carriage as we pass Mr Carradin's lodgings, you should know that I shall hold this knife against your side, *madame*, and that I shall not hesitate to use it.'

The journey across town was completed with the tip of the knife pressed against Lucy's side. The pressure Bruno exerted was sufficient that when the carriage jolted over a couple of extra deep ruts Lucy felt the nick of the knife-point in her flesh. Bruno conducted her to a small, windowless room in what was clearly the *zenana* section of the tiny house. 'I will bring you the supplies you need for the journey,' he said, untying the gag and the binding on her wrists. 'A guard will be posted at your door. He is one of my men, and utterly loyal. For the ride out of town you will wear the clothes you have on now.'

'I have eaten almost nothing all day, and I am very thirsty. May I have some food and drink?' She asked the question as much to gauge Bruno's character as to assuage her hunger. Somewhat to her surprise, he agreed without hesitation. 'We have bread and cheese and goat's milk, or water if you prefer.'

'Water, please.'

He saw her considering look and smiled coldly. 'You wonder why I am so considerate of my prisoner, *madame*? The explanation is simple. At this moment you offer me the best chance of reaching my goal. I need you alert and healthy. It does not suit me that you should faint with hunger on the first stretch of the journey.'

Only a few minutes passed before a silent man brought in a tin plate bearing two varieties of cheese and a serving of flat, Indian-style bread. Lucy tucked in with a hearty appetite. For a woman who two hours ago had teetered on the brink of being murdered, she decided she wasn't faring too badly.

The first day of travel passed more in minor discomfort than in actual hardship. Bruno had provided Lucy with adequate supplies, including a donkey to ride on, blankets to sleep in, thick felt boots with leather soles and a heavily padded cotton jacket. At this early stage of the journey, most of this equipment was rolled and stored at the back of her saddle, since, until they started the climb to the Pass, heat and flies were far more of a problem than cold. Lucy had no trouble identifying the half-dozen men in his entourage as out-of-uniform military volunteers. She thought she recognised some of their faces as members of the Cossack troop she and Edward had encountered months before in the mountains. Lucy wasn't sure whether to be amused or worried sick by their inadequacy as actors. The Afridi tribesmen guarding the Pass were capricious in their activities, and such an obvious troop of soldiers ran a grave risk of being wiped out by Afridi warriors before they had ventured five miles into Afghani territory.

Bruno had made some effort to equip himself like a merchant trying to trade European luxuries for Afghan sheepskins. He had brought along four pack mules, loaded with hunting rifles, tea and tins of English biscuits. These latter, strangely enough, were known to be popular among Afghan warriors of every tribe. They would munch with gusto while waiting in ambush for unsuspecting enemies to pass within gun sight.

Fortunately, they were still in British-controlled territory by the time Bruno gave the order to set up camp for the night, so Lucy's fears about the Afridi weren't immediately put to the test. She offered to help prepare the evening meal, partly because she wanted to appear co-operative, but mainly so that she might have a better opportunity to steal extra food. Her gamble paid off. The soldiers assigned to cooking duty were only too delighted to pass off the burden of turning uninspiring supplies into edible meals. She was careful to stash away only the amount she would need to survive for two days in cold, high country, but, nevertheless, she was surprised at the captain's carelessness in failing to keep a closer watch on her.

The captain did not strike her as a careless man, nor was he slow-witted, but by the third day of their journey Lucy had concluded that his vision was so narrow as to severely limit his abilities as an undercover commander. Every step of their journey made a confrontation with Afridi tribesmen more likely, but Bruno showed no concern even when a small band of marauding warriors swooped down on the Russians just before dusk.

Lucy shuddered with anticipation of the worst. Stolidly, without a hint of subtlety or finesse, Bruno fell into his role as a merchant. One of the soldiers who spoke a smattering of Pashto was summoned to act as interpreter.

'We are merchants,' the soldier said to the fierce-looking Afghani fighters. 'We look for *garakul* sheepskins that have been promised us by the Ghilzai.'

Amazingly, the Afghani warrior seemed to sense nothing strange in the soldier's manner, or in the timing of this supposed trading venture. Perhaps he, along with his countrymen, considered all Europeans so crazy that travelling at the start of winter seemed no crazier than anything else the *ferenghi* might do.

'We tax all voyagers on this pass,' the warrior replied. 'You must pay the agreed toll.' Tax and tolls were a new concept for the Afridi, and they rather enjoyed the legal overtones it added to their age-old practice of extortion.

'We are willing to pay the tax,' the soldier replied.

The bargaining continued only briefly. The Afridi departed, six rifles and four tins of biscuits the richer, and Bruno simply gestured for his men to continue riding. The thought that the Afridi were quite likely to shoot him in the back didn't seem to cross his mind and — perversely — not another sign was seen of the fierce tribesmen.

That night, as she prepared the meal, Lucy observed

Bruno more closely than ever. He was a Russian military officer to the core of his being, she concluded, with all the faults and all the virtues of that calling. He shared a reasonable rapport with his men, but it was the rapport of a by-the-book officer for a troop of seasoned combat soldiers. His instruction that the men should not salute before they spoke seemed his only concession to the secret nature of their assignment, and his conduct towards his men scarcely deviated otherwise from what might have been expected of an officer in uniform leading a troop of soldiers into battle.

And that, Lucy felt sure, was exactly how Bruno viewed his current assignment as far as he was concerned, his mission to murder Edward and Abdul Rahman Khan was a battlefield operation. She concluded that Bruno must view her own role as something like that of a field scout, recruited from the native population to lead the army over rough or dangerous territory. Tolerated and necessary, but not altogether trusted. And eminently expendable once the operation was complete.

The mildness of her treatment never deluded Lucy into thinking she was safe. She never doubted that Bruno would kill her as soon as she had served her purpose of leading him to Edward and Abdul Rahman Khan. In the meantime, he had obviously decided there was no reason to worry about trouble from a mere woman surrounded by a troop of veteran Russian soldiers. She hoped this feeling of calm superiority on Bruno's part would be sufficient to get her out of the camp once she was close enough to Edward to make her escape.

Lucy's feeling of relative security was abruptly shattered at dawn on the fourth day of their journey when Bruno demanded concise directions to their destination.

'We must continue to proceed in a north-easterly direction,' Lucy said, anxious to keep her revelations to a minimum — not least the revelation that she herself was relying heavily on memories of her previous journey in order to determine which trail the men should follow.

'I want the name of our destination,' Bruno said grimly. 'And an estimate of how many days' march it will take to reach it.'

'Less than five days, unless we encounter real opposition from the Afridi.'

'I need a name, *madame*. It is time for you to give me name of the meeting-place.'

'Why should I give you such information?' she parried. 'We agreed to a bargain: my safety, and my husband's safety, in exchange for my services as a guide.'

'You will give me the information,' he said softly, 'because if you do not I shall beat you. A bargain, *madame*, requires the power to enforce it. You have no power.'

'And you,' she said, trembling, 'have no information.'

For answer, he reached out and grabbed her, calling two of his men to hold her immobilised as he ripped off her padded jacket. Then he unfurled his horsewhip and brought the lash stinging down on her back in a single economical movement. The men didn't attempt to hold her up, and she fell to the ground with the force of the blow.

Bruno looked at her dispassionately, a man executing his duty, without joy, but equally without sorrow. 'Resistance is not possible, *madame*. Do not prolong this unpleasantness. The name of the meeting-place, if you please.'

Would he kill her if she gave him a name? Surely not without checking first to see if the name was accurate? Besides, he must realise that in this desolate countryside a name would be of little value without a guide to follow up the name with directions. Perhaps she could safely give him a name?

The whip descended again, this time from the opposite direction. The cuts crossed with artistic accuracy in the middle of her back, and she felt a sudden searing pain in her womb.

Fear for her unborn child eliminated all thought of further defiance. 'All right,' she gasped. 'All right, I will give you a name.' She gagged with the effort of speaking, and he handed her his flask of brandy. She sipped gratefully, hating herself for her gratitude. How swiftly a prisoner descends to the point of being thankful to her captors for any spark of humanity, she thought bitterly.

'Abdul Rahman Khan will meet my husband in a village called Qim Koh.' She named a village that she guessed was about fifteen miles north-west of Qur'um. That fifteen miles of error would, she hoped, be a sufficient margin of safety for her to make her escape and reach Edward unobserved.

'Qim Koh. I know of this village.' Bruno narrowed his eyes reflectively. 'It is possible, I suppose. And now, *madame*, I would like an accurate estimate of how far we are from this village of Qim Koh.'

'Not more than three days, if we ride swiftly.' She estimated that Qur'um was about two days' hard march to the east, but she didn't want the captain to know their destination was quite that near. He might guard her more closely as they neared their destination.

'Three days,' he said meditatively. 'I think the timing should be about right.'

'But you cannot expect just to ride openly up to the village, Captain!' Lucy was genuinely horrified. 'This meeting takes place under the protection of the Afridi tribesmen who control this part of Afghanistan. Your men. . .our whole party. . .would be slaughtered before we could come within half a day's ride of the village boundaries. In fact, our progress is probably already being watched.'

'I shall take care of that situation,' he said. 'You may ask the sergeant for a dressing for your wounds.'

'Thank you,' she said.

Her irony totally escaped him. 'You are welcome, *madame*.'

* * *

Acting on Bruno's orders, two men broke off from the main troop that afternoon and rode away in a westerly direction towards Koh-I-Baba. Lucy guessed that they had been sent to make contact with the Khan of Kuwar's band of warriors. If she was correct, it probably meant that the Russian captain planned to set up ambushes at all the access routes into the village where Abdul Rahman and Edward intended to meet. Even Bruno, she thought, could not be hoping to launch a full-scale frontal attack on the village itself. He must realise that his men would be slaughtered.

It was clear that the time had come to make good her escape. Quite apart from the fact that Bruno would likely beat her to death when he discovered that she had lied about Qim Koh, she estimated that after today's travel Qur'um now lay less than two days' walk to the north. She certainly wanted to be well away from Bruno before any of her old enemies from Kuwar joined the Russian officer's band of merry men.

She had long ago discarded any hope of sneaking away while her captors slept. Within the first day of leaving Peshawar, she had realised that the hour immediately following the evening meal provided her only realistic chance of escape.

Once the men had eaten, they settled down for a smoke and a cup of tea, which they poured strong and boiling into their tin cups and laced with cheap brandy until it was cool enough to drink. Bruno didn't allow even mild drunkeness in his men, but they were more relaxed at this point of the day than at any other.

Lucy had taken advantage of this nightly period of relaxation to heat water for washing, and then to walk out of sight of the men to bathe and take care of her other personal needs. Each night, she had gradually extended the period of her absence, noting with relief that her absence never raised any alarm from Bruno or his troops. The previous night she had been gone for twenty minutes and her return had scarcely caused so much as a turned head from the men still gathered warm and comfortable around the camp-fire.

Despite this seeming laxity, she didn't hope for much of a head start. She guessed that Bruno had a seasoned military man's sense of impending danger, and that, while he might be unconcerned for twenty minutes, when twenty-five minutes passed without a glimpse of her some inner alarm signal would automatically trigger. It might, if she was lucky, take another five minutes to organise a quick search of the campsite surrounds. Thirty minutes in total before Bruno would realise that she had run away.

Thirty minutes. Her only other protection would come from the darkness, and the fact that mules or horses at night were more unwieldy than humans, so the men would need to pursue her on foot.

When she handed out the bowls of onion-flavoured rice that night, she wished she had some magic potion to sprinkle over the food that would send all the men deep into slumber. Barring such magic, she could do no more than make the portions a little more generous than usual, her garnish of dried peas and pepper a little tastier. Fortunately, the chill mountain air added zest to the men's appetites, and they ate with relish.

'How is your back?' Bruno asked as she gathered up his dish for cleaning.

'The sergeant gave me some salve,' she said neutrally. 'He cleansed the wounds with alcohol and he believes there will be no infection.'

'Good, good.' Bruno seemed genuinely pleased that the prognosis was favourable. Perhaps he preferred his victims healthy when he killed them. 'The food was well prepared, *madame*. Armand was correct in saying that you are not in the least like other English women.'

She made short work of the dishes, then had to slow down her pace. Tonight she mustn't suddenly be quicker than she had been every other night. Heart pounding, knees knocking, Lucy walked over the rough sage grass to return the clean bowls and cutlery to the soldiers. It seemed incredibly difficult to do something she had done easily on each of the preceding nights. Everyone seated around the fire must surely hear the throbbing drumbeat of her heart. How could they avoid scenting her fear? How could they avoid realising that tonight was different, that tonight she planned to run away? But nobody seemed to sense her nervousness. The men murmured drowsy thanks as she handed back their utensils, and one jumped up to unhitch the pot containing her washing water from over the fire. She murmured her thanks in French. At this moment it was a blessing that she shared no common language with the soldiers, so no one expected her to speak.

She had chosen her escape route as efficiently as she could. Perforce, she had decided to run back over the terrain she and the Russians had covered earlier in the day, otherwise she would be running blind into unknown countryside. Late that afternoon she had spotted a narrow trail, too rugged for horses, that stretched east and then seemed to circle back north. If she could manage to find it again in the darkness, she hoped it would eventually connect her with the main trail to Qur'um. Visually, the odds looked good, but trails could be deceptive once you started walking on them. Lucy prayed she had chosen well. Sometimes there was nothing left to do except pray.

She set the pot of water down behind a large boulder. At this distance from the camp-fire, only the silver light of the moon and the stars illuminated her actions. Please God, how about a cloud? she pleaded. Even a small one will do.

As if on cue, the moon's face was momentarily obscured by a thick veil of stormcloud. Drawing in a deep breath, Lucy ran into the welcoming darkness.

CHAPTER TEN

LUCY ran until her labouring heart threatened to burst. Then she walked until her lungs seared from the pain of her breathing and the stitch in her side stretched from her knees to her shoulders. Finally, she stopped to rest, leaning against a boulder and closing her eyes as the shuddering gasps of her breath gradually slowed.

She was frighteningly aware that she hadn't travelled very far — no more than five miles — and that her fatigue was out of proportion to the effort she had expended. She refused to think about the dull ache in the small of her back that had never quite gone away since she'd fallen to the ground after Bruno's beating.

No longer deafened by the pounding of her own heartbeat, she strained to detect the sounds of pursuit. She heard a man's voice call out in the far distance, but, however hard she listened, she could discern no tell-tale rattle of pebbles, nor see any beam of approaching lantern light. With only four men at his disposal, Bruno was having as hard a time as she had hoped in setting up efficient search-parties. At least she had done something right!

She couldn't afford the luxury of a longer rest. She set off again, drawing her veil across her nose and mouth to lessen the impact of the cutting night wind. Her pace was slowed by the need to walk to the side of the main trail, where the going was less sure, but where rockfalls and occasional stunted milk vetch bushes offered some hope of concealment. She also didn't want to risk leaving footprints in the sandy stretches of the main path, in case Bruno attempted to track her.

She had no idea how much time Bruno would waste in pursuit, but she suspected that if she could remain free for another couple of hours he would abandon any attempt to catch her. To that extent, Bruno's practical

217

nature worked to her advantage. She didn't think he would waste time on vengeance, or wreaking his anger, when he still had a mission to accomplish. Assassinating Abdul Rahman Khan and Lord Ridgeholm would strike him as much more important than killing a woman who was probably going to die of exposure in the mountains without any help from him.

Fate finally seemed to be on Lucy's side. After about an hour's walking, still without any hint of pursuit, the persistent cloud cover cleared. In the brilliant silver moonlight, the path she had been seeking stood revealed, stretching to her left in sandy, enticing clarity.

The surge of elation didn't help her fatigue as much as it should have done. The ache in her back had intensified as she walked, stretching out tentacles that settled into her upper thighs and lower abdomen. Gritting her teeth, she pushed her hair out of her eyes and tied the veil back in place as a protection from the continuing bitter cold of the wind. Oddly enough, although she felt chilled to the marrow of her bones, beads of sweat kept dripping off her forehead and into her eyes.

At first Lucy used a corner of her veil to wipe the sweat away. Soon, she ignored the sweat, as she ignored the cold and the grinding ache in her abdomen. With dogged determination, she put one foot in front of the other, reduced to a machine that permitted her no choice in the endless lift and fall of her steps.

When she finally stopped, it was not from choice but because the exhaustion of her body overcame her will-power. Her steps slowed to a stagger. Her dazed, exhausted brain functioned just clearly enough to warn her to pull herself to the side of the path and pillow her head on a boulder, before unconsciousness claimed her.

Her sleep was restless with fear and pain, and she awoke to the unpleasant sensation of being watched. She opened her eyes and saw the sun glint with menacing dazzle off the barrels of the three rifles pointed straight at her head, heart and stomach. She had time for only a moment of terror before a voice spoke to her in Pashto. 'Who are you?' a gruff voice demanded. 'Where is your husband and tribe?'

Lucy blinked, disengaging her eyes from the hypnotic glint of the rifles long enough to register that the weapons were held by Afghanis, not Russians. Her immediate feeling of relief was quickly tempered by the realisation that waking up to find oneself surrounded by Afridi warriors was scarcely a cause for celebration. Afridis were known for the speed with which they could wield their curved knives to gut their victims.

'I was taken prisoner,' she replied truthfully. 'I seek my husband, to warn him that enemies pursue him.'

'Who is your husband?'

She was too weary to lie, and anyway, she seemed to have nothing to lose by telling the truth. 'Rashid, the trader from the Punjab, is my husband,' she said.

The men's faces betrayed no reaction to her news, but they knew they couldn't be operating this close to the village of Qur'um without being aware of the fact that an important meeting was scheduled to take place there shortly between Rashid and Abdul Rahman Khan.

'We will take you to your husband,' the leader of the trio said. He gestured with his rifle. 'Come, wife of Rashid. We must walk quickly if we are to arrive in Qur'um while it is still light.'

She stood, relieved that the heavy ache in her abdomen seemed to have lessened while she slept. The men slung their rifles across their shoulder and set off at what for them was no doubt an easy lope. For Lucy, the pace demanded a stamina she just didn't seem to have.

When the sky started to dance around her head, Lucy had no choice but to ask the tribesmen if they would stop for a few minutes. 'Honoured sirs, could we please rest here and drink?' she asked when they came to a small widening in the trail marked by a thorn bush and the thin trickle of an autumn-dry stream.

The three men stopped, examining her with the unblinking gaze she had learned to expect during her captivity in Kuwar. 'We will rest here,' the leader announced. 'You may sit, wife of Rashid.'

She sank on to the sandy ground, too grateful for the rest to question the warrior's generosity. Only when one of the men silently handed her a cup of water he had collected from the stream did she try to pull herself to her feet. Something was wrong, terribly wrong, if these proud fighting men were allowing her — a worthless woman, not of their tribe — to loll around resting while they made preparations to refresh themselves.

'Sit, wife of Rashid.' The warrior who had brought her the water gently pushed her back on to the ground.

'I have food to share,' she said faintly, reaching into her pockets to find her supply of cheese, raisins and balls of rice.

'Thank you,' the warrior said gravely, accepting a piece of cheese and passing her grubby offering to each of his companions. When all three of them had eaten sparingly, they returned the remnants of the meal to her, together with their own offering of *bolani*, a bread baked with leeks at the centre.

She couldn't refuse without giving mortal offence. Lucy took the tiniest possible piece of bread, feeling her stomach rise up in protest. The men watched her without expression, until the leader finally asked her, 'Are you in pain, Daughter?'

Their faces might reveal little, but Lucy recognised the sympathy inherent in their decision to address her as 'Daughter'. She closed her eyes, rejecting the implications of their sympathy. She would not think of the grinding pain that had returned to settle in her womb. If she didn't acknowledge the agony, then perhaps the miscarriage she dreaded wouldn't happen.

She hadn't intended to let the word miscarriage slip into her mind. She swallowed the last of her water and sprang to her feet. 'No, no, thank you, I'm not in pain. I am very well, I'll come with you now, honoured sirs, if you are ready to leave.'

'With your permission, Daughter.' The tribesman did not stop to receive the permission he requested. He simply stepped forward, hitched his rifle out of the way, and swung her into his arms. He then resumed his march forward at the same half-running lope he had used all morning, her extra weight seeming of no consequence to his easy progress.

She dozed, or perhaps she was unconscious for a while. A shock of jarring pain jolted her awake. She felt the hot trickle of blood between her thighs and for a minute she thought she must have been shot. When she realised what was happening, she gave a cry of such bitter regret that the warrior who carried her actually deigned to stop and look down at her.

'We are nearly at the house where your husband stays, wife of Rashid. In ten minutes you will see our village of Qur'um.'

'Thank you,' she whispered through the haze of her pain. Oh, God, she thought. What shall I say to Edward? How shall I explain to him that I am losing his child? Even the need to warn her husband of Bruno's plans no longer seemed so important. If only she had stayed at home as a wife was supposed to do, their child would still be growing safely in her womb.

'We are here, wife of Rashid,' her escort murmured quietly. 'We have arrived in the village of Qur'um.'

The tribesman saluted the guards posted at the entrance to the village. 'I bring the wife of Rashid to safety.'

'Here is the house where your husband stays, wife of Rashid.' The tribesman who carried her stopped in the courtyard of a typical Afghani hut. Walls of sun-dried brick, covered with mud and straw plaster, supported a flat roof of rammed earth, interlaced with twigs. A woven mat, tied to four poles, sheltered the entrance way, and beneath this mat a group of women sat spinning wool.

One of the women jumped up as soon as she saw the tribesman and his burden. 'What do you bring us, Khushal?'

'Greetings, Homaira, honoured first wife of Yakub.

I bring one who claims to be the wife of Rashid. I fear she loses the son she carried for her husband.'

'No!' Lucy cried out. 'No, I'm not losing my baby!'

'Bring her inside to her husband. Allah have mercy, but her babbles make no sense. The fever must have taken her already.'

With her last remaining strength, Lucy disciplined her brain so that she would not speak English, would not betray Edward by using his English name. Khushal carried her inside the dark hut, and in the corner she saw her husband. Her heart leaped with joy, and then contracted with bitter sorrow, because she had failed him. She was losing their baby.

'Rashid,' she muttered through parched, cracked lips, trying to marshal her flying thoughts into coherent Pashto. 'Rashid, Monsieur Armand is a spy and so is Count Guido.'

He sprang to his feet, knocking over his stool. '*Lucy!* God in heaven, what have they done to you? My heart, what's happened?'

'Monsieur Bruno, the man who pretended to be Monsieur Armand's colleague, he is really the Russian captain we saw on the pass. And he has orders to kill you, along with Abdul Rahman Khan. The Count saw us when I came to your other house to say goodbye, so it's all my fault you are being followed. They took me prisoner, or I would have stayed at home like you said, truly I would. And I think Bruno has sent his men to join forces with the Khan of Kuwar. The Khan must have patched up his quarrel with the Amir. Or maybe Bruno is paying him to fight.'

Edward took her into his arms and brushed his cheek against hers. 'Lucy, my dearest, thank you for bringing me this information, but now you must rest.'

'You don't understand! You must send warriors to the trail that leads to Qim Koh. They'll find Bruno and the Russian soldiers and maybe the Khan's men, too. Bruno must be stopped. He plans to ambush Abdul Rahman, I'm sure of it.'

'Lucy, don't worry, my heart. Abdul Rahman Khan

is safely on his way back to Tashkent. Everything is under control.'

A burning contraction of her womb robbed Lucy of breath. She bit her lip to keep in the cry of anguish, and felt the uncontrollable gush of blood spurt between her thighs, seeping through her skirts, leaving the cloth clammy and wet. Dear God, her poor baby! 'I'm sorry,' she whispered. 'I'm so sorry.'

'Get me water!' Edward yelled. He sounded unbearably angry, and yet his arms around her seemed gentle enough. 'Homaira, for pity's sake, we need boiling water, salt and clean rags!'

'Right away, master, they come.'

Rashid looked down at Lucy, his eyes dark with emotion. 'You will be all right, my heart. I swear that you will be all right.'

The pain ripped at her again, but this time she scarcely felt it. She touched her fingers to the tears that ran wet and cold against the hotness of her cheeks. 'I thought I could be strong enough,' she said.

'Lucy, no one could have been stronger. Now rest, please, my love.'

Edward pushed aside the tattered leather curtain that separated the sleeping-room from the living quarters, and placed Lucy carefully on the rope-and-wood bed with its thin cotton mattress. Her face was white, her cheeks sunken, and her lips blue from loss of blood. Looking at her, he experienced fear such as he had never before known, not even in the fiercest battle.

Yakub, village chieftain and owner of the hut, took one look at the unconscious woman in Rashid's arms and tactfully prepared to leave. The approach of death could be watched in solitude. The community support would come later, after the woman was dead.

'I will dispatch some of my warriors to Qim Koh,' he said. 'The time has come, I think.'

'Yes. Bruno serves no useful purpose now that we know the names of his fellow conspirators in Peshawar.'

'Your wife has brought us valuable information,'

Yakub said. He patted Edward on the arm. 'Remember, my friend, Allah is merciful.'

He walked quietly from the room and a few moments later his senior wife, Homaira, bustled in carrying the requested hot water. Much more important to her way of thinking, she also carried the good-luck charm of honey, sesame seed and ground toadskin that might possibly scare away the evil *jinns* waiting to steal the soul of Rashid's wife along with the soul of the baby they had already claimed.

Seeing the snow-white face of the woman, and the pool of bright scarlet blood in which she lay, Homaira didn't have much hope, but she dutifully tied the charm around the woman's head. She then bent and whispered, 'Allah is great,' four times into each ear, hopefully terrifying the *jinns* with the mystical power of the incantation.

Glancing up from her efforts, she was alarmed to see Rashid dipping his hands into almost boiling water, then rubbing salt all over them and dipping them again into the same jug.

'You may leave us now, master.' Homaira spoke kindly, containing her irritation at the waste of heated water that could have made perfectly good tea. At this time of year, cooking fuel was scarce. 'I will give your wife every attention.'

'No, I can't leave her!' Rashid spoke sharply, and seemed to recover his composure with difficulty. His smile was strained when he spoke.

'Thank you, Homaira. I am grateful for your care and your kind offer to help, but I must stay with my wife and tend to her myself.'

'Master, with all humility, I tell you that this is woman's work. The sights that follow upon the loss of a babe are not suitable for a man to cast his gaze upon.'

Rashid took a clean rag, dipped it in the hot water, then leaned over and wiped away the sweat and dirt from his wife's face and hands. 'Homaira, what I need more than anything in the world is clean cloth, preferably white cloth, and more boiling water.'

'But master, you have an entire jug full of hot water at your elbow.'

'I know, but it's dirty now.'

'Very well, master,' she replied indulgently. 'I will bring you hot water.'

'Boiling,' he said, not looking at her. 'It must be boiling. And a bridal sheet, one that has never been used.'

Homaira had always considered Rashid a man of amazing good sense, but this suggestion was too much for her. 'A bridal sheet!' she exclaimed. 'What in the world do you want with that?'

He didn't explain, merely turned back to his wife and began to remove her layers of filthy, blood-soaked clothing, thus giving the *jinns* all the access they needed to her fragile body. 'Homaira, I beg of you. The water and the clean bridal sheet.'

Homaira couldn't bear to stay and watch the *jinns* take possession of the poor woman's body. She made hasty tracks towards the door.

'I will return with the water and the sheet soon, master.'

'Lucy, my love, my darling, you must not die. Life wouldn't be worth living without you to tease me, without the sight of your smile. Most beautiful of women, find the strength to fight for your life, I beg of you.'

Homaira returned in time to hear Rashid's murmured incantation. She couldn't understand what he was saying, but she was relieved that he had stopped doing dangerous things like exposing his wife to overheated water and fresh air and had started doing something useful like whispering spells. The fact that he spoke words in a tongue she couldn't understand seemed especially promising. *Jinns* were notorious for their inability to understand straight speaking, and it was very wise of Rashid to try all the languages he knew in order to scare them away.

'Here is the boiling water, master, and the bridal sheet.'

'Thank you. Could you bring them here? I want to keep my wife's hips elevated. It seems to help in controlling the bleeding.'

These were not promising remarks, and Homaira's optimism suffered a further blow when she approached the bed and saw that Rashid had taken off all his wife's clothes and washed off the entire protective layer of dried blood. Homaira watched, horrified, as he soaked a cloth in the fresh pot of boiling water, waved it a few times in the air to cool it off, then gently wiped away the little bit of blood still encrusted between his wife's thighs. Homaira felt obliged to offer a protest.

'Master, everybody knows that at the time of her flux hot water is dangerous to a woman, and, since your wife has just lost a babe, the danger to her is increased tenfold.'

Rashid turned to Homaira, his eyes unseeing. Then he blinked as if dragging himself back to the reality of his surroundings. 'Homaira, don't worry,' he said finally. 'The spells I use are very powerful, but to make them work properly I need boiling water.'

'I've never heard of any such spells, master.'

'These are spells given me by a powerful *khwajah* from across the ocean. He—er—lives on an island surrounded by sea, which is why his spells need water. He is so powerful that he was called in to help deliver the babes of the Queen-Empress Victoria.'

Homaira was impressed, and agreed to help Rashid lift up his wife and place the large bridal sheet beneath her limp body. Rashid brought the ends of the sheet up over his wife, so that she was neatly packaged in white cotton, every inch of her vulnerable skin covered, except for her face and neck.

'I will bring you tea, master,' she said kindly. It was obvious this would be a death-bed vigil, and Homaira wanted to ease Rashid's suffering as much as she could.

'Thank you, Homaira. I'm grateful for all you've done.' For a moment, Rashid actually smiled. 'Don't worry, Homaira,' he said softly. 'My wife is going to get better, you know.'

She hid her pity as best she could. 'Yes, master, I'm sure she is. I'll bring you that tea right away.'

To the astonishment of the entire village at dawn the next morning Yakub's youngest concubine reported the amazing news that the wife of Rashid the trader still lived. Edward waited with some anxiety for his wife to regain consciousness. His vigil was not solitary. Neither Yakub nor Yakub's wives nor any of Yakub's sons and daughters saw any reason to leave the room. Lucy had been brought back from the brink of death, and Yakub's family crowded forward, eager to hear the first exchange of words between the reunited couple.

Lucy finally stirred, her head shifting restlessly on the pillow. Edward's throat constricted when her eyes opened. They looked too big for her white, thin face, their size underlined by smudges of fatigue and their brown depths shadowed with pain. He wanted to take her into his arms and kiss away the shadows, kiss away the hurt. Instead, he could do nothing save smile encouragingly.

'Welcome back, my heart,' he said in Pashto.

Even after all she had endured, she realised she should not speak in English. 'Rashid?' she whispered, looking at the throng of faces surrounding her bed. 'Is everything all right?'

'Everything is very well now that you are feeling better.' He took her hand, wondering what in God's name he was supposed to say to the woman he loved so much and had caused to suffer so badly. He noticed her cracked and bleeding lips and said the first thing that came into his head.

'Would you like a cup of tea? Homaira has prepared some specially for you.' Wonderful, he cursed himself silently. That was a truly meaningful remark to make to a woman who has almost killed herself in her effort to save your life.

'Some tea would be welcome. My throat feels like the sand of the desert.' Her voice rasped with the effort of speaking, but at least she hadn't told him to go away and never come back. He helped her into a sitting position, then took the prized china bowl from Homaira and held it to Lucy's lips.

She sipped the steaming brew gratefully, obviously feeling better as the hot liquid seeped into her veins, bringing a trace of colour to her cheeks. Then, much too soon, Edward saw that she remembered. Her hands pressed against her stomach, and the flush of colour left her face.

'The baby,' she said, her voice grating. 'I've lost the baby.'

Yakub and his family drew in a collective breath, and turned expectantly towards Rashid. Men had been known to divorce their wives for the crime of losing a first-born son, although Rashid seemed too besotted with his wife to consider such a drastic step.

At that moment Edward would have ransomed his entire fortune to be able to take Lucy into his arms and pour out his confused, tumultuous feelings of sorrow and guilt and love. Instead, for the sake of the documents that burned in his inner pocket, he was forced to maintain his role as Rashid and abide by the customs of the Afridi. Even the fact that he was holding his wife's hand in public was stretching the boundaries of Afridi tolerance to the absolute limit.

'My dear,' he said softly, trying to tell her with the pressure of his fingers all that he could not say in words, 'our son is lost, but there will be other sons for us, I'm sure. And daughters, too. We have long years ahead of us to know the joy of having children.'

Yakub and his family murmured their approval, but Edward could feel the waves of Lucy's resistance. He knew exactly what she was thinking. The fact that there might be other children was no reason to dismiss the loss of this particular baby. In her physically exhausted state, it was useless to expect her to remember that Edward would lose stature before the Afridi if he entered into the feminine ritual of mourning for a miscarriage. Edward couldn't afford to appear a weakling in Yakub's eyes.

Gently, trying to convey by gesture all the apologies he couldn't make, and the words of love he couldn't speak, Edward stroked the hair out of Lucy's eyes.

'You need to regain your strength, my dear, and then we will have time alone to talk of many difficult matters. Homaira, first wife of Yakub, the chief of this village, has prepared some mutton broth for you. Will you please drink it?'

To his relief, she didn't refuse and he spooned bread soaked in mutton broth into her mouth until she murmured, 'No more, please.'

'Now it is time for your wife to sleep, master.' Homaira obviously felt that her position of authority in the sick-room had been usurped long enough. Bowing low to Yakub, she spoke with unmistakable firmness. 'You and your sons will wish to leave us, honoured husband. I know how many matters of urgent business await your wise attention.'

Yakub had been married long enough to know when he was being told to get out of his wife's way. Gathering his sons and sons-in-law about him, he nodded with great dignity towards Edward. 'You, Master Rashid, will wish to join us in waiting for the return of our warriors from Qim Koh. The women will take good care of your wife.'

Edward knew he had no choice. With a final frustrated squeeze of Lucy's hand, he followed the chieftain from the room.

Lucy awoke late in the afternoon to the sound of drums, whistles and hoarse cheers of laughter. The noise, she realised, came from outside the hut where a celebration was obviously going on.

'Harumph, so you are awake. Just in time for my *kichri*. Shiri, get the wife of Rashid a bowl of *kichri*.'

Shiri, a young girl of about thirteen, departed obediently and Homaira shook her head. 'I'm never going to get that one trained. She hasn't the brains of a stillborn camel.'

'She is your daughter?' Lucy enquired politely. 'She is very pretty.'

'Daughter! She is the latest concubine of my husband.' Homaira snorted her disgust, then leaned towards the bed, one married woman confiding in another. 'My husband has all the pleasure and I have all the training. Anybody who knows Shiri's mother would realise the girl hasn't a bit of sense, nor domestic knowledge. But men, you know how they are, and we women have to put up with them. At least your husband is still crazy about you. Is he planning to take another wife, do you know?'

Lucy cleared her throat. 'Not as far as I know.'

'Hurry up and give your husband his son, that's my advice. You may be feeling weak now and not want more babies, but that's a woman's lot, isn't it? Give him a son, wife of Rashid, and you will have his respect for ever.'

Lucy had a lowering suspicion that simply presenting Edward with a substitute heir would not make all right with their relationship. She sighed. Afghan marriages, despite the number of wives involved, seemed a great deal more straightforward than their European counterparts.

An especially loud cheer coincided with the return of Shiri, carrying the bowl of mushed rice and shredded lamb. 'What is happening out there?' Lucy asked, accepting her meal with a smile of thanks.

'They are bringing home the dead bodies of the murderers,' Homaira explained before Shiri could speak.

'Which particular murderers are these?' Lucy enquired. Any wayfarer killed by the Afridi was immediately transformed by popular acclaim into a 'murderer' or 'slaughterer of the innocent'.

'Russian murderers,' Homaira reported laconically.

'Russians!'

'Yes. My husband explained that these Russians are very wicked. They planned to murder Abdul Rahman Khan, and Yakub says that years of fighting would follow upon Abdul Rahman's death. Personally, I can't see what difference it makes whether Abdul Rahman lives or dies, since the men fight all the time anyway. What matter if they fight the Kohistani, or the Kirghiz, or the British, or some other foreigners?'

With masterly inconsistency, she took Lucy's empty bowl and smiled. 'But, there, a woman never understands these things, does she? Would you like me to help you walk across to the porch door, so that you can see the dead bodies? The warriors have them tied to their saddles.'

Lucy managed to conceal her shudder. 'Thank you very much, but I don't think I'm quite in the mood for viewing dead bodies.'

'That's understandable.' Homaira nodded. 'Besides, better that you wait until tomorrow to get dressed.'

A sudden thought struck Lucy. 'I'm sure I must be sleeping in your husband's bed. Shouldn't I come with you to the women's quarters?'

Homaira appeared gratified that Lucy realised the enormity of the privilege that had been accorded her. 'Yes, it's true that you spent the past hours in my husband's bed. If you can walk, wife of Rashid, it would be better if you sleep tonight with the other women.' She broke off irritably. 'Shiri, what in the world are you doing, darting about all over the place like that?'

Shiri reluctantly abandoned the clink in the mud-brick walls that had been her peep-hole to the outside world. 'They have another prisoner,' she said. 'A live one, and he is not a Russian. He wears very fine clothes.'

'Humph, wrap yourself in the bridal sheet and one of those blankets. Here, Shiri, take the other arm of the trader's wife, and help her into the living-room.'

Lucy was soon ensconced on a stool next to the window. From the position behind the tiny, screened window, she could at first discern nothing through the milling throng of strutting small boys, giggling girls and black-veiled women. Finally, the random movement of the crowd permitted her to view a row of tethered horses bearing horrible, limp burdens. She turned her gaze quickly in the opposite direction and saw a somewhat ramshackle palisade, some ten feet square, within which was confined no less astonishing a personage than the Khan of Kuwar

Lucy gasped. 'Hashim Khan!' she exclaimed. 'What in the world is he doing here?'

'He was taken prisoner,' Shiri said. 'A lot of Hashim Khan's warriors were killed, and the rest fled into the mountains, but the Khan wasn't killed because Yakub has decided to ransom him back to his people.'

Homaira cuffed the girl lightly on the ear. 'You refer to the master of this household as "my lord"', she said. 'Do you have no manners? How many times do I need to tell you the same thing?'

'I don't know,' Shiri replied saucily. 'Whatever I call him, "his lordship" seems quite content with what I do when I am in his bed.'

'Go and prepare a sleeping-mat for the wife of Rashid, and get her something to wear,' Homaira ordered sharply. 'And remember your place in this family!'

Shiri left the room, her mouth fixed in a sullen pout. Homaira's shoulders drooped as she watched the girl's departure. 'Sometimes I worry that I am getting too old,' she said. 'Shiri causes so much trouble with the other wives, and we were such a merry household before she came.'

'She'll probably settle down once she gets pregnant,' Lucy said encouragingly, wondering if perhaps Afghani marriages were not quite as simple as she had blithely assumed. Perhaps, when you loved someone, no system was easy.

'But can you imagine what sort of children she'll have, that one?' Homaira turned away from the window where the Afridi warriors were now engaged in the game of extending a leather bottle of *sharbat* to the Khan of Kuwar on the end of a long pole, and then snatching it away before he could drink any of the contents.

'Children,' she sniffed disgustedly. 'Men are nothing but overgrown children. Enjoy your life now, wife of Rashid, while you are still the only woman in his *zenana*.'

Lucy rewrapped herself in the blanket and walked towards the women's quarters at the back of the hut. 'That sounds like excellent advice, Homaira. I shall do my best to follow it.'

For five frustrating days, Lucy was confined to the women's quarters of Yakub's hut, and Edward saw her only once each day when she emerged, surrounded by Yakub's wives and daughters, to breathe in fresh air on the porch, and to help with the spinning.

From these brief glimpses, Edward was able to conclude that her physical health was no longer cause for worry. She had, by some miracle, avoided puerperal fever, and her terrible loss of blood didn't seem to have weakened her unduly. He watched with relief as the frightening fragility of her appearance faded and adequate rest filled in the hollows of her cheeks.

Unfortunately, Lucy's mental state didn't seem to show similar improvement. Edward worried about the listlessness of her manner and the heavy shadows that continued to bruise her eyes. An aura of weariness clung to her and, surrounded by listeners as they always were, it was impossible to broach any of the subjects that cried out for discussion between the two of them.

Only on the sixth day did they speak together at any length, and then it was the practicalities of their situation that were discussed. Still, as far as Edward was concerned, even this was a giant stride forward over the courteous nothings which they had exchanged for the past five days.

'My dear, do you feel you might soon be strong enough to face the journey back across the Pass to India?'

'We would have to walk?' she asked.

'No. Yakub is more than willing to sell me a horse, if you feel able to control one, or a donkey if you cannot.'

'I think the horse might be more comfortable, and certainly a lot swifter. When do you want to leave?'

'You must tell me that. Whenever you feel fit enough.'

'You've been waiting for me?'

A bellow of rage came from the palisade where the Khan of Kuwar remained confined. He was not proving a courageous prisoner, and the Afridi children had turned him into a favourite source of entertainment. Lucy winced as she heard the patter of falling stones and realised that the village boys were pelting him with pebbles. 'I never thought I would actually feel sorry for Hashim Khan,' she murmured.

'Don't waste your sympathy. His ransom will arrive soon and he will return home and avenge himself for this humiliation by beating all his wives. Not to mention his slaves and dancing boys.'

She actually smiled. Almost the first smile he had seen since she'd realised she had lost the baby. 'I'm sure you're right. In some ways, I'm surprised the Kuwari elders are willing to send the ransom price.'

'They will do it because they feel the honour of the Kuwari tribe is at stake, not because they want the return of Hashim Khan. In fact, I suspect when he reaches Kuwar he will find one of his sons firmly entrenched as the new Khan, with the village elders acting as regents.'

'Is it very ignoble of me to say that I can't help being rather glad that he has spent the past few days living in a palisade?'

'Certainly it's ignoble. However, it's also quite understandable. Would you like me to walk by and demand that he kiss my toe?'

This time she laughed out loud. 'You needn't bother. I think the small boys are punishment enough to satisfy my thirst for vengeance.'

'Hmm. I think I might just ask him how his Enfield rifles are working. I lack your essential kindness. In the meantime, Lucy, could you tell me when you might be able to travel, remembering that the journey over the Pass is not easy at this time of year?'

'Is it urgent for you to return to India?'

'I won't lie to you, Lucy. I should leave as soon as I can. I have documents and reports signed by Abdul Rahman Khan that should be seen at once by the British authorities. But your health is far more important to me than anything else.'

'Do we travel alone?' Lucy glanced self-consciously at the group of women gathered around them. 'Is there no danger that the documents you carry might be—stolen?'

'We are to be honoured with an escort of Yakub's most experienced warriors,' Edward replied, understanding at once her unspoken question. 'Yakub is a staunch supporter of Abdul Rahman Khan. They are cousins both on the paternal and maternal side of their family tree, and they consider themselves blood brothers. The men of this village have been monitoring every party that crosses the Khyber Pass ever since Abdul Rahman Khan set out from his temporary home in Tashkent.'

'You mean that Bruno and his soldiers were under observation all the time? I wondered why we encountered so little opposition.'

'You were very much under observation. The party that actually stopped Bruno reported back at once to Yakub. They brought word that a woman travelled with the group, but your disguise was too good and they assumed you were—ahem. . .'

'A camp follower?' she enquired politely.

'Something of the sort.' For a moment he allowed his amusement to show. 'I should have been smart enough to realise who you were the moment I heard there was a woman with Bruno's band of assassins. Lord knows, there aren't many camp followers prepared to pursue their profession across the Khyber Pass at the start of winter.'

'I didn't wilfully disobey you, Edw. . .Rashid,' she murmured. 'I didn't intend to follow you here.'

'We will talk of it later,' he said, touching her warningly on the hand. 'But you still haven't answered me, my dear. Can you give me a day when you might be ready to travel? Next week? In five days?'

'Tomorrow?' she said. 'Do you think we could leave tomorrow?'

In so far as any journey across a treacherous mountain pass at the start of winter could be considered tedious, that was how Lucy found the return to Peshawar. Accompanied by a troop of Afridi warriors some twenty strong, Edward and Yakub set a fast pace. A scout rode out a couple of hours ahead of the main party as a precaution, but since this territory was all controlled by Yakub's kinsmen the danger was almost non-existent.

From Lucy's point of view she really had nothing to do save sit on her horse and, at night, collapse on to her blanket and wait for Edward to bring her food and hot tea. Even this undemanding regime left her more fatigued than she wanted to acknowledge, partly because she found it difficult to sleep at night in the bitter cold.

She wished Edward would share his blanket with her. Each night she visualised lying in his arms, being curled against his warm body and feeling protected from the bite of the winter winds. Each night Edward politely bade her goodnight and spread out his blanket next to Yakub. In the village, when she'd slept with the women, she had hoped his avoidance of any personal discussion might be a reflection of their lack of privacy. Now she began to fear that he couldn't forgive her for the loss of their baby.

Yakub and his warriors, in a break with their normal custom of never crossing into British territory, accompanied Lucy and Edward to within five miles of the city of Peshawar. Their entire journey home had been completed in less than six days, record time for this season of the year and for the distance they had travelled.

The parting between Yakub and Rashid was emotional. 'Go with Allah, my friend.' Yakub kissed Edward on both cheeks, and embraced him in a bearhug. Public physical contact between the sexes was considered scandalous by all Afghans, but passionate embraces between those of the same sex were perfectly acceptable. 'Your work means much for the people of my tribe, and of my country. My cousin, Abdul Rahman, is a strong and a wise man. With his guidance, perhaps my countrymen will learn to think of themselves as members of the Afghan nation, as well as members of their own individual tribe.'

'That is what I work for, with Abdul Rahman Khan's help,' Edward said. 'Word will be sent to you as soon as I have spoken with the officers of the British government.'

Yakub bestowed a final smacking kiss. 'May the Prophet, peace be upon him, guide your steps home to safety.' Very much as an afterthought, he nodded his head towards Lucy and added, 'Blessings rain upon you and your future sons, wife of Rashid.'

She bowed suitably low. 'May Allah, in his wisdom, reward you for the kindnesses shown to me, Lord Yakub.'

After another ten minutes or so of exchanging courtesies, duty was done and the Afridi tribesmen cantered back towards the Pass. Lucy and Edward were alone together for the first time since their parting in the market-place nearly three weeks earlier.

The sudden isolation didn't cause any softening in Edward's manner. If anything, the tension vibrating between the pair of them increased noticeably.

'Lucy, I will have to leave for Mr Carradin's lodgings as soon as I have seen you safely returned to our bungalow. I apologise, but the documents I carry from Abdul Rahman Khan cannot wait for delivery.'

'I understand, Edward. Will you be able to order the arrest of Count Guido and Monsieur Armand?'

'I certainly hope so.' He turned to her, his face a mask that even months of marriage didn't permit her to penetrate. 'Lucy, why did you risk your life following me into Afghanistan?'

It was as she feared. His coldness wasn't imagined; it was a direct consequence of her disobedience. 'I'm sorry,' she said. 'But I had no choice. I wanted to speak to Mr Carradin, to give him the information that Monsieur Armand and Monsieur Bruno were both spies, and possibly the Count as well. I had only just realised, you see, that Bruno was not a sheepskin trader, as he claimed to be, but the Russian captain we had encountered during our escape from Kuwar. I wanted my visit to Mr Carradin to remain unobserved, so I made the mistake of dressing in some of my ayah's clothes, and going to his house on foot with only my maid for escort. By sheer mischance, Bruno and Armand discovered us and murdered poor Dira. The only way I could think of to bargain for my life and to warn you that your mission was in jeopardy was to persuade Bruno that I could guide him to your meeting-place with Abdul Rahman Khan.'

'Crossing a mountain pass in central Asia, with winter biting at your heels, would not strike most women as a bargain likely to save anybody's life.'

'I know,' she said humbly, 'and I am very sorry, Edward. I promise that in future I will be a better, more obedient wife.'

She wasn't looking at him, so she failed to see the rueful, crooked smile that stole across his mouth. 'That, my heart, seems a promise you are most unlikely to keep.'

CHAPTER ELEVEN

THE servants greeted Edward's and Lucy's return with storms of joyous weeping. A young girl, who tearfully announced herself to be the sister of the dead Dira, supervised the preparation of a warm bath for Lucy. The houseboy dispatched messengers to the Rutherspoons, the vicar and Mr Carradin, and the cook departed to his kitchen to begin preparations for a feast worthy of the momentous occasion.

Edward, still wearing the clothing and skin-stain of his disguise, appeared at their bedroom door just as Lucy was preparing to step into the steaming, amber-gris-scented tub. Oddly enough, despite the clothes, he no longer looked like Rashid, although Lucy couldn't define the subtle change that she observed in his appearance.

He crossed the room and took her hands into his. Recently, that was as close as they had come to intimacy. 'My dear, please rest and take great care of yourself while I am away. You do understand why I must leave at once?'

'Yes, of course. You have a mission to complete that is of great significance. I wish you every possible success, Edward.'

'Thank you.' He carried her hands to his lips, kissing the knuckles gently. 'We will have time to talk when I return, Lucy.'

'Yes.' She managed to produce a laugh that sounded almost natural. 'It's amazing how little time alone together a married couple sometimes has.'

'We will make time when I return,' he promised. 'Lucy, I must go. I have an obligation to get these documents into safe keeping and to inform Mr Carradin of how matters stand in Afghanistan.'

'I understand the urgency, Edward, but shouldn't

239

you change your clothes? Doesn't it matter that our servants must have realised that Rashid and Lord Ridgeholm are one and the same person?'

'No, it doesn't matter in the least,' he said. 'Rashid the trader has just completed his final assignment.'

She realised then what the subtle difference was in her husband's appearance. Before, when wearing the clothes of Rashid, he had always *been* Rashid. Now he was merely Edward playing a role. During their recent exchange, he hadn't even bothered to speak in Pashto. His walk, the carriage of his head, the very way in which he held his body was entirely different. Her heart gave a little lurch as she accepted that Rashid was gone for ever.

'Wait!' she exclaimed, hurrying to the door. He swung around to confront her and she reached up to stroke her fingers across his wind-hardened cheeks. His eyes gleamed dark in the candlelight and his teeth seemed extra white against the mahogany-brown of his skin. She brushed her thumb over his mouth.

'I would like to say goodbye to Rashid,' she said softly, deliberately switching from English to Pashto. 'I shall miss him. He taught me many important things.'

Edward caught her hand, stilling the questing movement of her thumb, but he replied in Pashto, 'He could teach only what you were ready to learn, Englishwoman.'

'Then I must have been ready to learn a most important lesson. Rashid taught me how to love — not like an English lady, but like a woman. I am most grateful to my teacher.'

For a split second she thought she saw passion blaze in the darkness of Edward's eyes. He opened her hand and pressed a hot, hard kiss against the palm of her hand. She swayed towards him, but he held her away and the momentary passion vanished from his gaze as if it had never been.

'My duty awaits, Englishwoman. There is no acceptable excuse for delay when so many crucial decisions hang upon my presence.' Without looking at her again, he pushed her gently back into the bedroom and closed the door. Seconds later, she heard him stride down the hallway, calling for his horse.

She had never felt so alone.

When she awoke the next morning, a letter from Edward waited by her bedside. She ripped open the thick cream envelope with trembling fingers, needing to read the message twice before she absorbed the simple contents.

> My dear Lucy, Mr Carradin has persuaded me that I must speak to Lord Lytton in person, since only the viceroy has the power and authority to put the information I have gleaned from Abdul Rahman Khan to its maximum use. I swear to you that I am indeed comfortably *en route* for Delhi by train, and not for any other more obscure or more dangerous point of the globe. My manservant has brought me a supply of respectable British suits and ties. I therefore travel to Delhi as Edward Beaumont, a dull Englishman who hopes that he, as well as Rashid, has played some small part in showing you what it can mean to be a woman. I love you, Lucy. Your devoted husband, Edward.

However many times she re-read this missive, Lucy could not find any hidden message of reproach for her disobedient behaviour in pursuing Rashid into Afghanistan. The mystery therefore remained to plague her. If Edward loved her, why had he avoided sleeping next to her on the journey home from Qur'um? Why had he never mentioned the loss of their baby? Why had he never taken her into his arms and kissed away her aching sense of loss? Why did she feel this worrisome sense of estrangement? True, for much of the time since her miscarriage they had been surrounded by members of Yakub's family, but Edward was a man who routinely achieved the impossible. Surely he could have found five minutes when he could have been alone with his wife?

Lucy would have liked to loll in bed brooding over the state of her marriage. Unfortunately, the residents of Peshawar were not prepared to co-operate with her wish. By ten o'clock, Mrs Rutherspoon had rushed to the bungalow to assure herself that dear Lady Ridgeholm was indeed safely returned to Peshawar. Lucy, who hadn't thought to discuss with Edward what she should say about her adventures, simply told her palpitating visitor that she had been abducted, but that Edward and his colleagues had rescued her.

'Oh, my dear Lady Ridgeholm! Abducted *again*! Some people really do seem prone to get themselves into the most awkward situations, do they not?'

'I was thinking much the same thing myself,' Lucy agreed wryly.

'Who would believe that such villainous abductors are free to roam the streets here in Peshawar? When we heard that your ayah had been found horribly murdered, her throat sl——'

'Yes,' Lucy interrupted hastily. 'Fortunately, I know who my abductors were and I expect arrests will be made shortly. They may even already have been made.'

'Perhaps the natives will learn their lesson at last——'

'But I wasn't abducted by natives, Mrs Rutherspoon. I was abducted by respected members of the European community.'

'Impossible!' Mrs Rutherspoon breathed, her eyes gleaming with delight. 'My dear, *dear* Lady Ridgeholm, you simply must tell me the names of these. . .these monsters!'

'I think perhaps I had better wait for Mr Carradin to announce the arrests. Would you care for some more tea, Mrs Rutherspoon?'

Mrs Rutherspoon weighed the possible advantage of staying to glean further details against the definite advantage of being the first to carry forth the news that the Baroness had returned safely from her latest abduction. The glory of acting as town crier won out. She rose to her feet, and delivered her most gushing smile.

'Thank you, Lady Ridgeholm, but I wouldn't dream of keeping you. After all the turmoil of the past few days, you must be sorely in need of rest. I will leave now, but I shall certainly call again tomorrow to see how you go on!'

Lucy's smile stretched to match Mrs Rutherspoon's. 'What a treat for me to look forward to!'

Mrs Rutherspoon was merely the first in an endless stream of callers, which culminated shortly before dinner in a visit from Mr Carradin himself.

He greeted Lucy with a warm handshake and a searching scrutiny. 'Well, my dear, Edward told me of the sad loss you suffered during your time in Afghanistan. You have my deepest sympathy, although I am glad to see you looking so well recovered.'

'My stepmother always tells me that I have the constitution of an ox,' Lucy replied, trying to make light of her grief.

'Perhaps so. I suspect, however, that it is your spirit which is so unquenchably strong rather than your physical constitution. When I heard that Edward had married, I confess I was troubled, but now I am convinced he has found his soulmate at last.'

Lucy's smile was a touch rueful. 'Let us hope, dear sir, that my husband reaches the same conclusion. I fear that he is very angry with me at the moment, and rightly so. Any normal wife would have stayed at home to wait quietly for her husband, instead of bounding off on some hare-brained scheme and getting herself abducted.'

'I'm sure you mistake your husband's feelings, Lady Ridgeholm.'

'I wish you were right, but you didn't see Edward's expression when I arrived in Qur'um. I can assure you he was not pleased to glance up from his crucial international negotiations to find his wife swaying on the doorstep, surrounded by Afridi warriors.'

'Think of the scene from his point of view! Can you imagine the panic he must have felt? The guilt that his work and his activities had dragged you into a position of such danger?'

Lucy had never considered the possibility that Edward might feel guilty. Mr Carradin's words opened up a whole new perspective on her husband's behaviour over the past few days. 'When do you think Edward may return from Delhi?' she asked thoughtfully.

'I'm afraid he's likely to be gone for at least a week, probably longer. Lord Lytton feels we should take care of the situation in Afghanistan by sending in sufficient troops to conquer the country and annex it to British India. Edward hopes at the very least to convey to the viceroy the message that Afghanistan is unconquerable by a traditional invading army. Our troops would win any pitched battle, of course, but the Afghanis are never going to stand and fight a pitched battle. As our soldiers advance, so the Afghani enemy will disappear into the mountains. They will simply wait until we're far enough from our supply lines to be in trouble. Then they will massacre us.'

'It is tragic that our imperial policy so often seems to be formed by men who have no idea what is actually going on in the territories they play with on their maps.'

Mr Carradin snorted. 'Sometimes I wonder if they can *read* a map. Otherwise they would surely realise that an area which consists mainly of mountains and deserts — liberally sprinkled with tribesmen who are brought up to fight to the death as a way of life — is not an ideal country for launching picturesque cavalry attacks!'

Lucy visualised a battalion of scarlet-coated British troops marching in set formation into Kuwar valley. She visualised the Afghani warriors, perched in their mountain eyries, raining down bullets on the British soldiers with absolute impunity. She shivered. If Edward could prevent such a massacre, his work and his efforts would certainly have been worth while.

Mr Carradin reached out and patted her hand. 'Edward is a persuasive man, my dear, and the documents he has succeeded in obtaining from Abdul

Rahman Khan should convince the most determined of sceptics. Anyway, enough of this grumbling about politics. I came, my dear, to bring you good news. Count Andrei de Karpovich from the Russian city of St Petersburg, otherwise known as Monsieur Armand, sheepskin trader, has been arrested on charges of murdering your maid, Dira, of complicity in your abduction, and of conducting espionage against the British Empire.'

'Oh, you caught him! I'm so glad he wasn't warned in time to escape.'

'He had no suspicion that all was not well with his schemes. His informers were recruited mostly from among the Kuwari tribesmen, and I understand from Edward that many of the Kuwari warriors were killed by Yakub and his men, which may explain why "Monsieur Armand" had no warning.'

'I'm glad he is to stand trial. Poor Dira! I feel such a great responsibility for her death.'

'Your sentiments do you honour, my dear, but sometimes it is better if we acquire a little of the eastern fatalism. What happens is meant to be. Such a philosophy can help to make the intolerable more bearable.' He hurried on before she could speak. 'I also have news for you about Count Guido.'

'Oh, the Count! You were able to arrest him, too?'

'We arrested him, but have decided to lay no charges, because his complicity might have been difficult to prove. He has been ordered to leave the country under military escort.'

'Is he also Russian?'

'No. He truly is Count Guido of Tuscany, but we have discovered that his mother is an impoverished member of the Russian nobility, which may explain the Count's willingness to throw in his lot with the Russian cause. I gather that he suffered a bitter personal rejection recently, and took himself off to India in some misguided fit of romanticism. I think this brush with the unpleasant realities of espionage has tempered his enthusiasm for the life of a spy. He didn't anticipate that you would end up being abducted, and he was horrified at the fate of your maid. He had never considered the possibility that innocent bystanders might get hurt in the course of his adventures.'

'I confess to being rather glad that some of what the Count told me was the truth. He is an engaging scoundrel.'

'He is indeed. A great success with the ladies.' Mr Carradin rose to his feet, smiling. 'Well, my dear, I will bid you good evening. But please, if by any chance you should acquire startling information which you feel I must share immediately, please do *not* attempt to deliver it in person. Send one of the servants to me with a note, and I will come running. Edward has left me with strict instructions to see that you do not vanish back into Afghanistan while he is gone.' Mr Carradin laughed. 'Although how he expects me to tame you when he has so signally failed in the task, I have not the slightest idea.'

The elderly diplomat did not intend to criticise, Lucy realised, as she mulled over their conversation during the next few days. However, it was obvious that she had been a most unsatisfactory wife, and she resolved that when Edward returned from Delhi he would find a reformed creature waiting to greet him. She would use the period of his absence to transform herself into a perfect English wife.

Since she had spent her formative years trailing around outlandish parts of the globe in the wake of her father, she had only a nebulous idea of how proper English wives conducted themselves. From her observations, she could deduce that aristocratic wives spent a great deal of time doing nothing in particular. They also gave explicit orders each morning to the cook, embroidered slippers for their menfolk, and nurtured the moral welfare of their households.

Lucy was optimistic that she could train herself to be quite as good at these tasks as any other lady, despite the fact that she abhorred doing nothing, that the cook cooked wonderfully without any instructions from her, and that Edward never wore slippers.

These trivial obstacles were not allowed to deter her. Lucy braved the wrath of the cook and entered the kitchen each morning to enquire into his plans for the day. She was wise enough to make no attempt to change his menus, and the cook nobly refrained from handing in his notice. The problem of the slippers was less easy to resolve, but necessity was the mother of invention. Lucy paid an afternoon call on Mrs Rutherspoon and returned triumphant, clutching a splendid pattern for a rose-decorated satin tea-cosy.

A visit to the vicar's wife produced a book of the Reverend Mr Jowett's collected sermons. Judging from the extreme tediousness of the sermons, Lucy could only assume they were exceptionally uplifting. She intended to improve her mind and the moral tone of the servants by reading Mr Jowett's strictures aloud during dinner, but since she was invited out almost every night this aspect of her wifely improvement programme didn't progress very far. The servants, at least, were grateful for their narrow escape.

Work on the tea-cosy fared better. Bullied by her maid into retiring for a nap every afternoon, Lucy whiled away the boring hours by stitching at the hideous pink cabbage blossoms. Lucy couldn't imagine covering one of her exquisite china teapots with something so ugly, but she supposed that wifely virtue was acquired more in the execution of the task than in the usefulness of the object produced.

By the happiest of coincidences, she was seated in the drawing-room industriously stabbing at a virulent green leaf when Edward finally returned to Peshawar after a ten-day absence. She heard his carriage pull upon the gravel driveway, then the swift stride of his footsteps in the hallway. With superhuman control, she refrained from hurtling out of the door and throwing herself into his arms. Her programme of self-improvement was already paying dividends.

'Lucy!' Edward strode into the drawing-room. He

slammed the door behind him and pulled her to her feet, crushing the pink-cabbage evidence of her reformed character as he swept her into his arms.

'You look wonderful, my heart.' He crooked his finger under her chin and tipped her face gently upwards. 'The colour has come back to your cheeks, thank God. You must have been resting and taking proper care of yourself for once.'

'Yes, Edward,' she said meekly. 'I have done exactly as you instructed. I have not been abducted, I have rested every afternoon, and I am making a tea-cosy.'

Edward looked puzzled. 'A tea-cosy? How—er—domestic.'

'I have also been reading Mr Jowett's collected sermons. They are most. . . They are very. . .'

'Boring?' Edward suggested politely.

'Oh, yes, terminally so! That is to say, they are no doubt very improving.'

'So are cold baths and hair shirts, but I have always tried to avoid both. Lucy, why the blazes are we discussing Mr Jowett's sermons?'

'It's Sunday,' Lucy suggested. 'A very proper day for us to turn our thoughts to consideration of higher. . . Edward, what in the world are you doing?'

'My heart, something seems to have seriously addled your wits since I left here last week. Isn't it obvious that I am undoing the buttons of your gown?'

'But Edward, we are in the drawing-room!'

He looked around, feigning astonishment. 'Good heavens, so we are! How splendid that I can rely upon you to keep me informed of such vital matters.' He resumed undoing her buttons and nibbling at her skin.

Lucy ignored the insidious heat rioting through her veins. 'Edward, the servants——'

'Are far too well trained to interrupt.'

'I hope your trip to Delhi was successful,' she said primly, pretending not to notice that her dress was now gaping open all the way to her waist, and that her knees were in the process of turning to water.

'A qualified success at best. Lord Lytton listened

with half an ear. I spoke with a few colonels who seemed to grasp the concept that marching cavalry regiments in line formation into a mountain valley wasn't likely to produce very desirable results. At least the people in Delhi finally recognise the name of Abdul Rahman Khan. I told them that one day soon he will be Amir of Afghanistan.'

Lucy's dress and camisole were now sliding gently to the floor and her knees had completed the process of dissolution. She collapsed against her husband's chest. 'Edward,' she said, searching desperately for a few remnants of ladylike virtue, 'I have turned over a new leaf while you were gone. I have learned to be a proper wife, just like Mrs Rutherspoon.'

'God forbid! Besides, I was rather fond of the old leaf myself.' Edward bent his head towards her breast. 'Mmm, indeed, you taste as wonderful as ever. Entirely proper for a wife.'

His tongue licked teasingly between her breasts and she gasped. 'Dear Heaven, Edward!'

'Heaven, my heart, is exactly where I plan to take us. The sofa, I think, is the first step on the way.'

He picked her up before she could protest — not that she had the faintest desire to object — and deposited her tenderly against the cushions. 'How convenient that you are wearing so few petticoats,' he murmured. 'I'm not sure that I would have lasted through more than three layers of enticement.'

Lucy abandoned the useless struggle for virtue. 'I've missed you so much, Edward,' she whispered. 'After I lost the baby I thought you would never feel able to forgive me.'

'Forgive *you*?' Edward's teasing smile faded. 'How could you dream that I would blame you for something that was entirely my fault? It was my activities as Rashid that led you into danger. It was my selfishness in bringing you back to India that placed you at risk. I should have insisted that you stay in England where you were safe, but I needed you too much. I wanted you by my side, and I brought you to India, knowing the dangers.'

'I'm glad I came. I'm afraid I shall never be a good wife who remains contentedly in the drawing-room while her husband departs for exotic foreign places. I make simply terrible tea-cosies.'

Edward raised himself on one elbow and looked at her in astonishment. 'My love, what is this sudden obsession with tea-cosies?'

'Well, wives are supposed to embroider slippers for their husbands, but you don't wear slippers, so Mrs Rutherspoon suggested——'

'Ah-ha! At last we reach the root of the problem! My heart, Mrs Rutherspoon may satisfy her husband by sewing tea-cosies. I, on the other hand, have very different methods of achieving satisfaction. Like this, for example.'

He bent his head swiftly and covered her mouth in a deep, endless kiss. Lucy sighed with the pleasure of joy rediscovered. Her hands crept up to twine luxuriously in Edward's hair while his hands brushed over her body, reacquainting himself with the curves and hollows he already knew so intimately. Then, with the assurance of a man confident his lovemaking is wanted, he wrapped her legs around his hips and locked her ankles behind his back.

'I love you, Edward,' she murmured, feeling her entire body flood with pleasure as he slowly entered her.

'Then kiss me again, my heart, my love.'

She felt him tremble beneath her kiss, felt the heat of his breath in her mouth, and understood suddenly that for this man she would never need to disguise her true personality, or pretend to be a woman she was not. Edward loved *her*, the woman she was. For him, she was already the perfect wife.

'I *hate* tea-cosies,' she declared, as their kiss momentarily ended. 'I shall never make one again.'

For a stunned moment, Edward stopped his passionate caresses, then he looked down at his wife and laughed softly. 'My love, for the sake of my masculine pride, not to mention my intense state of masculine arousal, do you think we could refrain from discussing tea-cosies for the next half-hour or so?'

Lucy framed his face with her hands, pulling his mouth down to meet hers. 'We could certainly try,' she whispered.

Success was theirs.

EPILOGUE

ON NOVEMBER the twenty-first, 1878, a combined army of British and Indian troops crossed into Afghanistan in a three-pronged attack against the faltering rule of Amir Sher Ali. The ostensible reason for the British attack was the Amir's failure to respond satisfactorily to a diplomatic note submitted by the British government in India. The real reason for the invasion was to prevent the Amir entering into an alliance with Imperial Russia, whose representatives were conferring at that very moment with the Amir in Kabul.

Thanks to the wonderful British-built telegraph system, news of this attack reached England promptly. Lord and Lady Ridgeholm, at home in Ridgeholm Hall, greeted the news with surprising indifference, possibly due to the fact that the Baroness had chosen that very day to go into labour.

Her twins were born at dawn the next morning after what the doctor termed an easy first labour. Lady Ridgeholm snorted and told him that, if he had spent the past twelve hours enduring what she had endured, words like 'easy' would not escape his lips.

The doctor patted her indulgently on the arm, told her that both babies weighed more than six pounds, and asked what she planned to name them.

'Our son is to be called Peter,' Edward said. 'After my wife's late father. Peter Edward Gervaise Beaumont.'

Lucy smiled at him, love and gratitude in her eyes. 'And our daughter is to be called Miryam, which is how the people of Afghanistan say Mary. Miryam Lucinda Elizabeth Beaumont.'

'A very fine choice of names.' The doctor snapped the locks on his black leather bag and took a final glance into the cradles where the Honourable Peter and the Honourable Miryam lay sleeping peacefully. 'Amazingly healthy babies, my lady. It's rare to deliver twins who are so sturdy. Congratulations to all of you.'

Lucy and Edward beamed with besotted parental pride. 'They are beautiful, aren't they?' Lucy said.

The doctor was old enough to understand the merit of addressing spiritual truth rather than physical reality. He ignored his vivid inner picture of two red-faced, bald-headed, wrinkled and pugnacious-looking babies. 'They're very beautiful,' he said. 'Indeed they are.'

Over the next twenty-four hours, the telegraph system not only buzzed with news of Amir Sher Ali's desperate attempts to raise a Russian army to fight the British invaders, it also buzzed with telegrams informing various members of Lucy's and Edward's family of the double happy event.

Lady Margaret, surprisingly mellowed, telegraphed a message of congratulation and added that she would deliver the traditional gift of silver christening mugs in person over the Christmas holidays. She was pleased to hear that the Bishop of Cirencester planned to be on hand for the baptismal ceremony.

Penelope, not to be outdone, sent an express letter from her home in Paris, announcing that she was immediately freighting her own gift: two paintings by her beloved husband Peregrine, one for each lucky baby. Her dearest Peregrine, her letter went on to say, was *much* influenced by the new Impressionist style, although the jealous French critics had quite failed so far to recognise his genius.

On a snowy day in January, Fletcher came to the drawing-room door and announced, in his most sepulchral tones, that a carrier had arrived with two wooden crates. 'Large wooden crates, my lady. Sent from France.'

'Peregrine's pictures for the babies!' Lucy exclaimed. 'Have somebody uncrate them and then carry them up to the nursery, will you, Fletcher?'

'Certainly, my lady.'

The two paintings were carried in state to the day

nursery. Peter and Miryam, awoken for the momentous occasion, stared with interest at the bright splotches of primary colour unveiled before their somewhat unfocused eyes. The remainder of the assembled group stared in mingled dismay and incredulity.

Edward was the first to break the stunned silence. 'Do you think Peregrine has been helpful enough to provide arrows to indicate which way is up?'

Lucy examined the pictures with care. 'No arrows,' she said. 'And the hanging cord is exactly across the middle.'

Edward, ever a man of initiative, positioned a painting randomly on a wall. 'How about this?' he asked.

'Coo,' said the Honourable Peter. It was the first time he had ever made any sound other than a bellow of rage when a supply of milk was not instantly forthcoming.

'He likes it!' Lucy exclaimed, her maternal powers of translation brought instantly into play. 'Peter likes his uncle Peregrine's painting!'

Edward grinned. 'My heart, don't despair. Our son has several more years in which to acquire some discrimination.'

The footman held up the second painting, a vivid portrayal either of a dubiously coloured fried egg, or possibly a sunset.

'Coo,' said the Honourable Miryam. 'Coo, coo.'

In February 1880, Abdul Rahman Khan, supported by a small army of about one hundred followers, crossed the Amu Dar'ya from Russia into Afghanistan. Joined by most of the northern tribes, he marched toward Kabul. On July the twentieth, 1880, at the town of Charikar, some twenty miles north of the capital city, he proclaimed himself Amir.

The history of an independent, unified Afghanistan had begun.

The other exciting

MASQUERADE
Historical

available this month is:

THE PRICE OF HONOUR
Mary Nichols

Olivia Pledger, through her own wilfulness, found
herself stranded in Portugal in the middle of the
Peninsular War! A resourceful lady, she was determined
to work her way back to the British lines and so get
herself home to England. But in foraging a deserted
mansion, she was discovered by Robert Lynmount, who
had been cashiered in disgrace from Wellington's army.
Although intent on scouting unofficially for Wellington
until he could clear his name, now Robert felt
responsible for Olivia's safety. In such circumstances,
falling in love was crazy, and personal feelings couldn't
be allowed to count . . .